LILLIAN LEANED ENTICINGLY CLOSE AS SHE PARTED THE CURTAINS . . .

Longarm caught the faint whiff of an indescribably delicate fragrance that drew him almost hypnotically closer to her.

The kiss was full, warm, passionate—her tongue an instrument of the devil as it probed deeply. She exercised a skill that was beyond craft.

She looked at him, her green eyes glowing softly. "You saved my life. Perhaps that small token of gratitude will suffice for now."

She smiled and rapped on the door. It was pulled open instantly. As Longarm stepped past the curtains through the open doorway, he looked back. But Lillian M'Ling was gone . . .

LONGARM

AND THE HATCHET MEN

TABOR EVANS

A JOVE BOOK

Printed in the United States of America

Library of Congress Catalog Card Number: 78-71576

First Jove edition published June 1979

10   9   8   7   6   5   4

Jove books are published by Jove Publications, Inc.,
200 Madison Avenue, New York, NY 10016

Chapter 1

Outside the Windsor Hotel—Denver's largest—Longarm paused in the act of lighting his cheroot. The dark night was suddenly filling with the clamor of fire bells. Other guests crowded out of the hotel to stand beside him on the sidewalk. Someone pointed to a ruddy glow building with alarming speed in the night sky. The fire could not have been more than five or six blocks away.

A short fellow beside Longarm cried, "Chinatown! They're burning out them damn heathen!"

A shout of approval went up from those around Longarm as this good news took hold. At the same time, two hook-and-ladder wagons thundered past, the eight powerful horses straining mightily. The glow in the sky was red now. Still other fire wagons streamed by, filling the night with the shrill clangor of their passage.

The crowd surged across the street, carrying Longarm with it, and headed down Walker Street toward the Chinese quarter. Longarm had expected something like this after news of the murder that same day of the Chinese merchant, Lo Hui, became generally known. It had given courage to others and become the

5

trigger for this madness—a madness building as the election campaign gathered momentum. The solution to the Chinese Question, as the politicians called it, was on everyone's lips—*The Chinese Must Go!*

Colfax led on to Rail Street. The crowd—growing rapidly into an aroused, swarming mob—surged onto it, crossed the tracks, and caught a glimpse of the flames leaping skyward. Black coils of smoke pumped into the night. Running figures were outlined against the flames. On some, Longarm could see the cowled hats of firemen, and on many more, the flying pigtails and conical hats of the milling, hapless Chinese.

Someone shouted a warning behind them. The crowd scrambled for the sidewalk. Longarm took this opportunity to pull free of the mob as two towering pump wagons swept past. He caught a glimpse of the horses' flaring nostrils, of their great, dark eyes starting out of their heads, of the drivers leaning far out over the backs of their plunging horses while their bell men yanked furiously on the bell ropes. The clamor was so intense that Longarm grabbed the brim of his hat and winced away from the sound.

The crowd swarmed after the fire engines as Longarm made an effort to hang back. Soon the crowd found itself blocked by fire wagons. Firemen were hastily playing out hoses. Moving close in behind the crowd, Longarm felt the heat growing more intense with each passing second. Abruptly, a building not half a block away literally exploded into flames, sending a shower of sparks and embers pulsing into the night. And then, from around the fire trucks and through the lines of firemen, poured a crowd of panic-stricken Chinese—only to find themselves in quick and ugly conflict with the crowd that had come to watch Chinatown burn down.

Shouts filled the air. Longarm heard screams, cries of pain. Men around him began to curse violently as they let their blood boil at this instance of Chinese

6

arrogance. They had no right, it seemed, to attempt to escape their hellfire. They should have turned back at the sight of white men, and plunged without qualm into the flames.

Only they were doing no such thing. With a violence born of desperation, they were clawing their way through the crowd. Muffled shots rang out. Screams and protestations uttered in a high sing-song grew closer to Longarm as the Chinese fought their way through the crowd toward him. Longarm saw heads bobbing, weaving—shiny, polished faces, eyes wild— some disappearing, never to reappear, others growing closer. Abruptly, one Chinaman burst through the crowd, with two others on his heels.

This fellow—a young man with a sleek, high-cheekboned face—was exhausted. He was bareheaded, and one arm hung limp at his side, yet he managed to stay on his feet as he stumbled toward Longarm. The crowd would not have this, however. A swarm of men fell back now to prevent the three of them from escaping their wrath. The two that had followed the first one out of the crowd were pulled down, then hurled back bodily into the surging mass of infuriated white men. Longarm caught a glimpse of two terrified faces as they were flung from one man to another, to be buried at last in the seething crowd.

As the young Chinaman continued his frightened scramble toward Longarm, with four or five men close behind, the tall lawman pulled out his .44-40 and pumped two quick shots into the night. The men chasing the Chinaman pulled up hastily—as did the young fellow they were after, his eyes wild with fear. Longarm reached out, grabbed the Chinaman's good arm, and hustled the fellow around behind him, then backed slowly against the brick wall of a warehouse, his Colt level now, its muzzle moving back and forth as it covered the suddenly wary members of the crowd

7

who were still anxious to get their hands on the China-man.

"Stay out of this, mister!" someone in back yelled. "We got to show these heathen who's boss around here!"

"They ain't even citizens!"

"Scabs! That's what they are!"

Encouraged by the sound of their own catch-phrases, they began to surge toward Longarm again. He fired, this time aiming lower. A few men just in front of him must have heard the slug whisper over their heads. They flung themselves about in a sudden panic and broke through those behind them. Their fear was contagious, and the rest took flight with them. Longarm watched them for a moment, then dropped his Colt back into the cross-draw rig he wore under his brown tweed frock coat, and turned to the Chinaman. He had sagged wearily against the warehouse wall and was holding his left arm, just above the elbow. It was bare and beginning to swell. In the dancing light of the flames, Longarm could see that the arm was already discoloring.

"You need a doctor," Longarm said. "Let's see if we can scare one up."

Astonished, but stoic, his eyes showing only wonderment at this treatment at the hands of a Caucasian, the Chinaman pushed himself away from the wall and accompanied Longarm back down the street and away from the fire. Men, and now some women, were still pouring along the street to get a closer look at the fire, many of them dumbfounded at the sight of Longarm with a Chinaman, others not even noticing as they hurried to get closer to the flames.

At last they were far enough away from the fire to have escaped the thrill-seekers. The streets were empty of people. Longarm turned to his companion.

"My name's Longarm, mister. What's yours?"

"I am Lee Shan."

8

"Okay, Lee. Right pleased to meet you. Sorry it couldn't have been under more pleasant circumstances." Longarm wasn't sure the fellow would understand what he meant. He was just trying to ease the tension.

"Indeed, it would have been fortunate for me to meet such a man as yourself under any circumstances, Longarm."

Startled at the fellow's command of English, Longarm laughed. "Looks like we'll get along, Lee. But we've got to find you a doctor. That arm looks plumb ugly."

"It feels ugly."

Turning a corner and heading toward Colfax, Longarm said, "There's a few doctors' offices down here. I've been noticing their shingles lately on my way by."

And then he saw a fashionable brick apartment building set well back from the sidewalk, a neat lawn and shrubs in front of it, the downstairs apartment displaying a doctor's sign in one of the bay windows: *CAPTAIN F. J. THOMPSON, MD.* Longarm was pleased. If the man was an ex-army doctor, they were in luck. Otherwise, they might have to deal with a sawbones who'd bought his diploma at the same time as he'd purchased his medicine bag and cures from Sears, Roebuck. The West was filling up with such quacks.

Longarm led the way into the building, found the door with the doctor's name lettered on it, and knocked. The doctor himself, in shirtsleeves, pulled open the door. He was a tall, cadaverous fellow with a full head of snow-white hair, who peered at them intelligently through steel-rimmed glasses. He glanced from Longarm to Lee, saw at once what was wrong, and stepped quickly back, pulling the door open wider.

"Come in! Come in!" he boomed, in a voice that was surprisingly deep for such a skeletal figure.

9

As the doctor closed the door behind them, his alert eyes were already studying Lee's swollen arm.

"That's a very bad break," the doctor commented to Longarm. "If I didn't know better, I'd say he got it falling off a horse."

Without waiting for Longarm's response, the doctor escorted Lee into his inner office and closed the door. Longarm took out a fresh cheroot and went to the bay window to look out. People were still hurrying along the sidewalk toward the fire, and what carriages he saw passing under the street lamps were also heading in that direction. Longarm shook his head. The hysteria, the bone-deep meanness he had had to confront this evening, made him a little sick that he was a member of the human race.

What was it old Wilson had told him that fellow Mark Twain said? *Man is the only animal that blushes —or needs to.*

He took short puffs on his cheroot until a small cloud of angry smoke floated about his head. *Mark Twain sure put his finger on it. Yes, sir!* He stood there by the window, simmering, watching the people hurrying to the fire. He was a big man, better than six feet tall, who appeared to loom giantlike in the dimly lit room. He was still at the moment; but when he moved, his friends were likely to josh him about a man his size being able to spook livestock and make people thoughtful. On the comfortable side of forty, Longarm's lean, lantern-jawed face bore the marks of one who has not turned away too often from the raw sun and cutting winds he'd had to ride through entirely too many times since coming West as a boy from West-by-God-Virginia. The results were raw-boned features cured as saddle-brown as an Indian's. If it were not for the gunmetal blue of his wide-set eyes, and the tobacco-leaf color of his close-cropped hair peeking out from under the brim of his hat, he could have been mistaken for an unusually tall Indian as he stood there before the bay window, peering gloomily out.

His gloom began to lift somewhat. He saw more than a few Chinese hurrying now along the streets, moving away from the fire, with uniformed roundsmen of the Denver Police Department escorting many of them. From the look of things, the roundsmen were doing what they could to help. A few even helped the women along, while others were carrying a few of the burnt-out refugees' belongings. A lamp. A statuette. Little Chinese men passed, bowed almost double under huge trunks. They trotted slowly, steadily, without apparent fatigue. It was a dreary, wretched sight. The only comfort Longarm got from it was the knowledge that some, at least, of the Chinese had escaped the flames and the mob.

He thought he heard something—a cry, perhaps— from the doctor's office, and turned about to face the closed door. But there was no further sound. Longarm left the window and settled in a soft armchair. His large frame sank well into it. He took off his hat and placed it on the small table beside the chair. By the light of the lamp on the mantel beside him, he took out his Colt to clean and reload it. He packed a deadly double-action Colt Model T .44-40. The weapon had a five-inch barrel for a faster draw and close-in work. Longarm had filed the front sight off.

He swung out the gate and shook the remaining couple of rounds into his palm, dropped them into the side pocket of his frock coat, and examined the firing pin critically. Black powder left a very gummy deposit after only a few rounds. He got up, walked over to the kerosene lamp on the mantel, lifted off the chimney, and blew out the flame. Another lamp on the far side of the room gave off enough light for him to see by, as he dipped the tip of his handkerchief into the bowl of kerosene under the wick, and cleaned out the gun. Then he replaced the chimney, relit the lamp, and sat back down to reload. He kept only five rounds in his weapon at a time, the hammer resting on an empty chamber for safety's sake. He had seen too many sports get their toes blown off drawing a fully loaded gun.

He was replacing the Colt in his cross-draw holster when the doctor pulled open the door. Lee stepped out, looking a little green around the gills, with a massive cast on his arm, which the doctor had enclosed in a sling.

"Took a little time to set the bone. Broken in two places, it was," the doctor said, smiling with pleasure at the memory. "But I think we got it. This Chinaman only cried out once. Brave young man."

"You know what happened, I suppose," Longarm said.

"Yes. I heard the fire bells and stepped out into the street and saw the crowds rushing to enjoy the spectacle. I heard what they were saying. Yes, I can imagine what it must have been like. I expect there will be other casualties before the night's over. Perhaps I should present myself to one of the police department's station houses. I might be needed."

"You will be, doctor. I'm sure of it."

Longarm turned to Lee. "Your place is gone, Lee. You're burnt out, I reckon."

Lee nodded.

"Lee will stay here, sir," said the doctor, "where I can keep an eye on him. I have a spare bed in the back room." The tall man looked down with great deference at the Chinaman. "Would that be suitable, Lee?"

"Lee Shan thanks you," Lee said with impressive dignity.

"And your name, sir?" the doctor asked, turning to Longarm.

"Custis Long, deputy U.S. marshal. My friends call me Longarm."

12

"Longarm it is, then." The man held out a bony hand.

Longarm shook it and was surprised at its strength, then turned to say goodbye to Lee. Before he could say anything, Lee Shan took from his pants pocket a small, glittering object, and handed it to Longarm. "You must take this," Lee Shan said.

"Hell, I don't want any payment for helping you!" Longarm was a little upset at the idea—until he looked closer into Lee Shan's eyes and got the impression he should accept the gift, that it would be an insult to reject it.

Examining the gift in the lamp's light, he found it to be a small, exquisitely crafted medallion, showing a white elephant raised on its hind legs, its trunk lifted. It appeared to be trumpeting, or whatever it was an elephant did when it wanted to make a noise. The lamplight winked back at Longarm from a jeweled eye, and tiny diamonds gleamed like bits of frozen fire in the four quarters of the medallion's outer rim. A small gold loop was set in its top for attaching to a chain.

Longarm looked at Lee Shan and smiled to indicate his appreciation. Lee Shan's polished, oval face showed the pride he felt at being able to present something of this worth to the man who had saved his life.

"Thank you, Lee Shan," Longarm said. "I'll bet this here little elephant will bring me luck."

Lee Shan smiled broadly. "It will, Longarm. As it have brought you to my aid this night."

"May I see it, Longarm?" Doctor Thompson asked.

Longarm handed the medallion to the doctor. After a quick but thorough examination, the doctor passed it back to Longarm and asked Lee Shan how long the medallion had been in his family.

"Two centuries," Lee Shan replied, without batting an eye. "It have been a gift from the first of the Manchu princes—as a reward for my honorable ancestor's

13

loyal service. It have been in my family since that very long time."

Longarm looked back at the medallion, and then at Lee Shan. For a moment, it seemed to Longarm that Lee Shan was no longer alone, that the room was crowded suddenly with Lee Shan's father and mother, all his sisters and brothers, his ancient uncles and cousins, the graybeards, the hallowed ancestors back through time, all of them watching and smiling at Longarm, bowing their heads—as grateful to Longarm as was Lee Shan himself. It was just a momentary feeling, an odd idea he dismissed almost as quickly as it occurred to him. Yet it gave him a different picture of Lee Shan—and all the Chinese he had known in this city. They were an awesomely ancient people—part of a culture that was civilized when Longarm's own ancestors were trooping about the highlands in the skins of animals. And this made their treatment at the hands of white men here in Denver—and throughout the West these past years—all the more senseless and insupportable.

"Well, thanks," Longarm said. "I'll take good care of this, then." Moved in spite of himself, Longarm busied himself by taking out his handkerchief and wrapping it carefully about the medallion, then placing the handkerchief back into his breast pocket.

"Guess I'll be on my way," he said then, touching the brim of his hat and stepping to the door.

The doctor accompanied Longarm and pulled the door open for him. "As soon as I settle Lee Shan in," the doctor told Longarm, "I'll report to the roundsmen and see what I can do."

"You'll be needed, it looks like," Longarm replied, stepping out through the door. "And I'd be obliged if you'd tell Lee Shan I'll be back in a couple of days, to see how he's getting on."

The doctor smiled. "I'll tell him that."

Longarm found the night clammy, the air filled with

14

the smell of burning things—not at all like the odor of burning leaves to which he had grown accustomed in this mile-high city. He reached the sidewalk, and soon found himself caught up in the swarm of fleeing Chinese as he headed for the nearest station house to see what he could do to stem this night's madness.

The pink-cheeked stripling playing with the typewriter outside Marshal Billy Vail's office glanced up at Longarm as he pushed through the outer door. This was George Linden Carver, Vail's clerk-secretary, the "GLC" appended to Vail's signature on the terse telegrams sent out by the chief marshal to deputies in the field.

"The chief's been looking for you," he said, barely able to conceal his pleasure. "All morning. I'll tell him you're here."

Longarm patted the fellow gently on his cheek. "You caused me a speck of trouble just a little while back. Remember that election case in Kansas that those Russian nesters were involved in?"

George nodded. "Sure I do."

"Sure you do," Longarm echoed with an edge of sarcasm. "You know you damn near got me shot?"

The young man gulped and started to say something, but Longarm continued, "The next time I wire this office about a wanted man, do us both a favor and check with Billy before you wire me back to let the jasper go. If I happen to live through another mistake like that, I can purely guarantee you won't be so lucky. Now, you go right on playing with that machine there, old son, and I'll just right in."

Longarm was already through the door after a short, quick rap on it, and was pleased to see Marshal Vail leaning back with his feet on the desk, a half-empty glass in his hand, a bottle of whiskey standing on the desk blotter. As he closed the door behind him, Long-

15

arm took off his snuff-brown Stetson and winked broadly at the chief marshal.

"Starting pretty early in the morning on that hooch, ain't you, old son?"

"Don't give me that 'old son' routine!" Vail retorted, hastily swinging his legs down from his desk. "Don't you ever wait before coming in? I've got a secretary, damn it! And where the hell have you been?"

Longarm slapped his hat down on the corner of Marshal Vail's desk and slumped down into the chief's red leather armchair. "I'll need a little of that medicine of yours, Chief, before I can answer all those questions. I've had a hell of a night."

"*You've* had?" Vail bellowed. "What in tarnation kind of a night do you think *I've* had? Half the city in flames! Washington calling! The streets filled with crazed Orientals! Why do you think I need this morning tonic?"

"Sorry, Chief. I thought you needed it because you were a lush. I didn't realize you were out in that business last night, too."

"You're damn right I was." He squinted at Longarm. "And I'm no lush. Just for that, you can pour your own."

"Thank you." Longarm poured himself a hefty belt, then sat back down and sipped the libation gratefully.

"Is it all right now if we get to work—if I give you your assignment, you hulking son of a bitch?" Vail asked sweetly, smiling. Alcohol always brought out the best in him. "Or would you like to tell me the sad tale of your wanderings last night? You didn't set that damn fire, did you?"

"No, I didn't. I'd like to catch the son of a bitch who did, though."

"So would I."

Longarm looked at the chief carefully. "There are

16

some folks right outside this office who figure it was a fine night's work. You don't agree?"

"It messed up my private life, Longarm, and injured a few firemen, and Washington is wondering what the hell's going on. You can just hear those congressmen now, yelling about the Yellow Peril. They look upon this fire as one more good reason for not letting any more Chinamen in. So, hell, no. It wasn't a fine night's work."

"You don't agree with the politicians?"

Vail grimaced distastefully. "Who wants to agree with *them*? But you got to admit, Longarm, there's a lot to what they say."

"Is there?"

"Hell, Longarm! They only came here to take what they could get and then hightail it back to China. That's what they *said*. But they stay here and multiply like rabbits. They conduct all their business with their own families and kill each other with impunity. That Tong warfare is really something. They show no mercy, believe me." Vail shook his head. "They don't *belong,* Longarm. All they do is cause trouble and work for next to nothing. Worst damn scabs in the world, and that's trouble we don't need—not with all this labor unrest cropping up. They ain't citizens, Longarm. They've got their money. Now they should go home, like they intended in the first place."

Marshal Vail was out of breath. He took a hefty swallow from his glass.

"Finished?" Longarm asked.

"Yeah, I'm finished, Longarm. Now, why the hell were you so late getting in here?"

"I was at a jewelry shop."

Longarm took out the medallion Lee Shan had given him and swung it on the gold chain he had purchased for it. Vail was impressed. Longarm let him examine it while he explained to Vail how he happened to have it.

17

Handing the medallion back, Vail said, "So now I suppose you're on their side."

"I'm on the law's side, Chief. I'm a lawman. So are you. What happened last night had nothing to do with keeping the peace. In addition to those firemen you mentioned, forty-three Chinese were killed, and the rest are homeless."

"All right, all right. You don't have to get up on a soap box with me. No one likes what happened last night." Then he looked at Longarm with one upraised eyebrow. Longarm knew that look. Billy Vail had suddenly had a bright idea. "But just so you don't get all carried away with your new love for the Chinese, maybe I'll make a change in assignments. Just for your own education, that is." He grinned malevolently and started pawing through the blizzard of folders and dodgers that littered his desk. "Yes, sir. This is all going to work out just fine."

"What are you up to, Chief?"

Still searching for the folder he wanted, Vail glanced up at Longarm, his eyes gleaming. "I was going to let this assignment go to the California office. Washington wanted me to handle it; I told them I didn't have the men for it. But it looks like Washington is going to have its way." He found the folder and pulled it toward him, a pleased smile on his face. He looked like the little farm boy who had just finished the whole pie, the one he had found cooling on the windowsill. "Yes, sir. The great Custis Long will see to this personally."

Longarm leaned back in the chair. He had opened his mouth once too often, and now his superior was going to make him work some. But Longarm wasn't upset at all. Whenever Vail dug out these assignments to shut Longarm up—or to show him who was boss—they turned out to be more fun than a sackful of wildcats. After all, there was only one thing worse than being trampled to death, and that was being bored to death.

Vail had opened the file and was now studying it carefully. He read through it quickly; then, satisfied, he leaned back in his chair and looked at Longarm, his face quietly grim. "You don't remember Hitch Scally. I knew him. One of our best deputies—just a mite too careless at times. Well, it cost him, this time. He was found a week ago, cut down by one of the Chinese Tongs, from the way it looks."

Longarm could see that Vail was more interested in making his point about the Yellow Peril than he was in giving Longarm the information he needed. "Now, let's just eat this apple one bite at a time. Where was this fellow killed? Here in Denver?"

"In Slab City, Washington. Up near the Canadian border."

"Go on."

"They're smuggling coolies in over the border."

"Who's 'they'?"

"The Tong." He looked quickly back at the folder. "The Ong Leongs. That much Hitch found out before they riddled him. Washington wants you to go out there, stop them from smuggling any more of their yellow brothers into the United States—and nail the bastard who killed Hitch." Vail leaned suddenly toward Longarm and fixed him with an icy stare. "And that's what *I* want too, Longarm. I want that man, whoever he is. And I don't care if he's yellow, black, or white, just as long as you get him."

Longarm got up. The banjo clock on the wall said it was close to ten-thirty. The westbound train was to pull out late that afternoon, which would give him time to look in on Lee Shan before he left. "I'll catch the next train for San Francisco," he told his boss.

Vail leaned back in his swivel chair and nodded. As Longarm pulled open the door, Vail said, "You just be careful of those hatchet men and slant-eyed females, Longarm. You may be the most bullheaded son of a

19

bitch on my staff, but you're also the best damn poker player in Denver. Take care, hear?"

Longarm touched the brim of his hat to the old tyrant and pulled the door shut behind him. He had no doubt that part of Billy Vail's touchiness was the result of the old lawman's frustration at not being able to lift his ass out of that chair and chase a few hard cases himself, the way he used to in the old days. But that time was past and Vail knew it, and the knowledge just didn't sit well with the man.

Hell, Longarm remarked to himself, *it wouldn't sit well with me, either—if it ever comes to that.*

Emerging from the building, he stuck a cheroot in his mouth, restrained the impulse to light it, and headed down Colfax.

Doctor Thompson pulled open the door to his office, recognized the deputy at once, and quickly stepped aside, reaching his hand out to shake Longarm's.

"You're here to see about Lee Shan, I have no doubt," the lanky man said.

"How's he doing?"

"He's gone."

Longarm's eyebrows rose. "Already?"

The doctor's lean face crinkled into a smile. "Come in here. I have something to show you! You know what they say about these inscrutable Orientals."

Longarm followed the doctor into his office and saw, sitting with brilliant serenity on the man's desk, a golden Buddha not more than four inches high. The doctor picked it up in his hand, hefted it, then gave it to Longarm.

"Feel the heft of that," the doctor said.

Longarm took it. He looked at the doctor. "That's solid gold, looks like."

As the doctor took the Buddha back from Longarm and set it down on the desk, he smiled and said, "In my greed, I chipped away at the back of it. It could

20

be lead, you know, covered with gold leaf. But I found that it was solid gold, as you say, all the way through. An impressive gift, you must admit."

"How did you get it?"

"Lee Shan left this morning without so much as a by-your-leave. I thought I had seen the last of him. Then there was this knock on my door. When I opened it, the only one in sight was my golden friend here." The doctor beamed.

"Lee Shan's all right, then," Longarm said, striding back out of the doctor's office. "That's what I came to find out."

"He's evidently in very good hands, Longarm. And he has left me the wherewithal to pull out of this dank Western metropolis and move back East, to New York, possibly. A practice in that wealthy community should assure my success." His voice grew resonant with hope. "Out here one competes with the quack and the snake-oil salesman. Not so in New York."

Longarm shook the man's hand. "I'll be off, then. I'm glad things worked out so well for you."

"And you, Longarm—the best of luck to you!" the man said, as he pulled the door open. "It was a lucky thing for me that you happened along to save that Chinaman from the mob."

Longarm nodded and left the doctor. Once out on the street, where the smell of last night's fire still lingered on the wind, he wondered at the capriciousness of fortune. To some, that ugly business had meant ruin, terror, and death. To Longarm, it meant an assignment far from Denver. And to Doctor Thompson, it meant a new lease on life—a chance to begin anew in an Eastern city more in keeping with his talents.

As Longarm started down the street to his lodgings on the other side of Cherry Creek, he felt the warmth of the medallion as it rested on his chest under his shirt. For some reason, the feel of it comforted him.

And he would not have preferred a gold Buddha.

The stage rocked and groaned as it wound through the pass on the last leg of its journey north from Klamath Wells. Longarm, wedged in close to the window, found some relief from the stage's grueling discomfort by looking out through the open flap at the towering firs, the dank, lush growth of this wooded land. The contrast to the West as he had always known it was more than startling. It was humbling.

Clouds hung low over the land and the rain was almost interminable. And when it wasn't raining, there hovered in the air a kind of dankness, a miasma filled with the smell of growing—and rotting—vegetation. The big trees had been left behind, well below the pass the stage was now traversing. What Longarm saw now between the large fir trees were knee-high ferns, gleaming from the moisture that dripped from the firs, and beyond them—dim in the misty air—hellish tangles of vines and rotting barriers of windfall. In the few clearings or burnoffs, he caught sight of riotous ground maple and grapevines. He saw a thick, dank, inhospitable wilderness. It would not, he realized, be an easy thing to prevent Chinese from slipping through this forest undetected. But with the sky and the sun out of sight beyond the canopy of branches and clouds, anyone using this route would need a pocket compass and experienced guides to make it through to their destination—that, and not a little luck.

"Magnificent country, isn't it?"

Longarm turned from the open window and looked at the man who had just spoken. He had gotten on the stage at the last stop and made himself comfortable directly opposite Longarm. The only other passenger was a drummer, now asleep, with his arms folded around his sample case. His sleep was labored, punctuated every now and then by piglike snorts that carried the faint stench of sour whiskey—he was the polar opposite of the fellow who had just addressed Longarm.

Despite the damp, clinging humidity that kept the wood and leather surfaces of the coach's interior damp to the touch, the man across from the marshal was wearing a high, starched collar, white cuffs, a light alpaca jacket, white linen trousers snug about the calves in the latest fashion, a black silk cravat, and highly polished boots. He wore no hat. His hair was parted in the middle, brushed smooth, pomaded to a shiny gloss. His ears were prominent, as was his nose, and his sharp eyes peered at Longarm through severe steel-rimmed spectacles. He was not impervious to the awesome humidity, however. Two large beads of perspiration were rolling down his high, narrow forehead, and another was dripping off his lantern jaw.

"Permit me to introduce myself," the fellow said. "I am Charles Swinburne Spittles."

"Custis Long," Longarm replied. He intended to enter Slab City without identifying himself as a lawman. Working undercover in this investigation, he felt, would give him an edge he might need in this wild and somewhat remote country.

"I am the editor and publisher of the *Slab City Citizen*. Are you on your way to Slab City on business, sir?"

Longarm nodded almost imperceptibly. "Sort of."

Spittles waited for more, and when it was not forthcoming, he straightened his narrow frame and stared boldly and inquisitively at Longarm. "A salesman, sir?"

The drummer beside Spittles awoke suddenly, blinked blearily about him, reached into his case, and pulled forth a fifth of whiskey. Unscrewing the cap, he offered the bottle to Spittles, who shook his head. Longarm also declined the offer. The drummer took a long, thirsty swallow, screwed the cap back on, plunged the bottle back into his case, and was asleep again almost instantly.

Spittles had waited patiently for Longarm's reply through all this. Now he raised his eyebrows. "You are a salesman, then?"

"Reckon you might say that."

"Might I, now? And what might you be selling?"

"You want this here information for that paper of yours?"

"Of course."

"That's just what I figured," Longarm said, pulling his hat down over his eyes and slumping back in his seat. "Think I'll get me some shut-eye."

He closed his eyes and managed to drop off for a brief time, as the stagecoach's almost level passage through a marshy stretch gave him some respite from the grinding, jolting ordeal they had experienced earlier climbing through the pass. It was the crack of the stage driver's whip and a sudden, jolting turn that brought him fully awake a few moments later. He glanced out the side window. The stage was pulling into a tiny hamlet—a collection of log buildings and frame dwellings all but lost in the towering firs and the foggy, sodden air that hung over everything. The driver braked the coach to a halt in front of a long, low, frame-built way station.

"We're just stoppin' for passengers!" the driver called down.

Longarm saw the jehu hop down, his shotgun rider dropping to the road beside him with his double-barreled weapon cradled in his arm. As they slogged away through the mud toward the station, a small Chinaman and what appeared to be his daughter approached the stage, both of them stepping carefully across the sloppy ground.

It was the daughter who pulled open the coach door and stepped aside for her father to enter. The old Chinese ducked his head and stepped up into the coach. Longarm moved closer to the window to give him room beside him. The old man saw this, though there was no change at all in his expression, and sat down beside Longarm. His daughter entered and sat in the seat facing Longarm, between Spittles and the drummer.

Spittles's face had gone ashen when the two Orientals had entered the coach. Now he pulled himself up to his full height and hissed, "Get out of here! Both of you! You sit on top, not in here with white men!"

The drummer stirred himself, straightened, and looked blankly across at the old man. His eyes widened. He shook himself suddenly, as if he couldn't believe what he was seeing. Then he looked to his side and saw the old man's daughter. At once, he pulled himself away from her—a movement that revealed an instinctive, gut-deep revulsion. The man might have been pulling back from a leper. "Go 'way," he murmured thickly. "Get out . . . here. Sit topside!"

Wearily, but with infinite patience—as if they were taking a survey of some kind—the old man and his daughter looked to Longarm. It was obvious that his word would be the one to decide the matter, that if he agreed with the other two whites, the Chinese couple would haul themselves out of the coach and ride on top between the baggage rails.

Longarm smiled thinly at the old man. The Chinaman's face was round and plump and shrewd. There was a straggle of thin white whiskers on his chin. He wore a dark, close-fitting cap on his head; his coat was a dark cloak with what appeared to be sable lining; his trousers were of blue satin. It was a shame to see so much mud on what were obviously finely tooled, exquisitely fashioned high-button shoes.

Longarm touched the brim of his hat to the old man's daughter. There was a subtle change in the expression around her almond eyes, but little else to indicate that she acknowledged his greeting to her. She was small, not much more than four and a half feet tall, Longarm judged. Her face was a tiny oval, its

25

perfection emphasized by shining jet black hair that was pulled straight back from her temples and forehead. She was, to Longarm's sight, disturbingly dainty. In a wild land like this, she seemed impossibly frail and vulnerable.

He looked at the drummer, and said, "Go on back to your bottle, or you'll find yourself lugging that sample case on your back all the way to Slab City."

There was enough command in Longarm's tone to convince the drummer. He started to say something, thought better of it, then shrugged and hauled out his fifth. Spittles, however, did not roll over so easily.

"I see," the man pronounced icily. "You are taking the side of these two yellow heathen. Is that it?"

"This here little girl and her old man would have a devil of a time up there on that baggage rack. If you're so all-fired anxious to see someone riding up there, why don't you climb up there yourself?" Longarm smiled then, to take the heat out of his words. "Relax, Mr. Spittles. There ain't anything to be afraid of with these two. Seems to me they add a touch of class to this coach."

"I can only conclude, sir, that you are a stranger to the West Coast—that you have little or no comprehension of the enormous issues that are being raised by the unceasing influx of these yellow heathen!"

"No, but I'm sure you are about to tell me."

The man took a deep breath. "Your education is sadly deficient, sir. But I will allow circumstances to fill in your ignorance. You will soon see—once you arrive at Slab City—just what squalor and decadence these people bring in their wake!"

Longarm looked at the old Chinaman and smiled. "This here pen pusher's letting his mouth run away with his brains, I'm thinking. You just relax. If he doesn't shut his noisemaker pretty soon, I'll stuff it shut with one of my boots. So you just pay him no

26

never-mind. His mother didn't bring him up to be polite to strangers, looks like."

Longarm had no idea whether or not the old Chinese could understand a word of what he had just told him, and there was no change of expression in the man's eyes as he regarded him. But that was not the point. Charles Swinburne Spittles had heard every word. Longarm touched the brim of his hat to the Chinese doll, then leaned back in his seat and smiled at Spittles.

Spittles started to say something, then clamped his thin, defiant mouth shut, and turned his head to look out the window. The driver and the shotgun guard mounted the stage. A whip cracked, and in a few moments they had left the town behind.

Longarm pulled his hat down over his eyes again and tried to get more sleep.

The horses were struggling up a grade so steep that Longarm came awake suddenly and reached out to brace himself. The Chinese girl was keeping herself in place by some kind of magic, while the drummer—in a drunken stupor by this time—had rolled off the seat and was coiled up in a small ball at the old Chinaman's feet. Spittles had braced both of his feet against the boards under Longarm's seat. The driver's whip was cracking furiously, and the sound of his heavy voice urging on the horses came to Longarm clearly. Endearments and blandishments were alternated with long strings of poetic, highly imaginative blasphemies. It worked, and somehow the laboring brutes pulled the stage to the crest. The stagecoach was moving at little better than a crawl by this time.

Longarm glanced out the window. Trees and thick underbrush crowded close upon the road. The clouds hung as heavily as ever. At this height they had a smothering effect, and Longarm could feel the moisture beading on his face. It had not rained since morning,

27

yet he felt that it must come soon—the air was so laden with moisture that it must burst at any moment.

The stage driver swore violently. Longarm felt the coach pull to a halt and heard the horses stamping, their traces jingling. A rough, surly voice cut through the damp air with startling resonance:

"Keep your hand away from that shotgun, mister! And tell them passengers to get out, slow and easy-like!"

Longarm ducked his head out of the window and saw, standing in the road in front of the stage, a weird-looking figure armed with a double-barreled shotgun. The highwayman was wearing a floursack mask with two ragged eyeholes and a soiled white linen duster that concealed his clothing and build.

"Throw down that shotgun!" the figure commanded.

Longarm saw the shotgun go tumbling to the ground. The highwayman moved closer to it and kicked it into the bushes.

"Now tell them passengers to get out, and throw down the box."

By this time Spittles was also leaning out of the window. He gasped and turned to look at Longarm. "Black Bart!" he cried. "It's him!"

The highwayman had seen Longarm and Spittles by this time, and had moved close enough to them so that his shotgun was covering them both.

"Better get out," growled the stage driver. "All of you. This here son of a bitch ain't satisfied with just this here money box."

"You are damn well right I am not," the highwayman said, his voice coming with surprising resonance and clarity through the flour sack. "Now get out! Every damn one of you! I ain't got all day."

As Longarm got out of the stage, the box hit the ground. The highwayman stepped back behind it and kicked it once with his boot. When the top did not fly open, he brought his shotgun up and aimed it at Longarm and Spittles as the two of them came to a halt before the stagecoach. Longarm watched the highwayman closely. He seemed cool enough, and his finger was resting on the triggers of his shotgun.

From behind Longarm came the sounds of the old Chinaman and his daughter as they left the stage also. He glanced back at them. The old man positioned himself just a little behind Longarm, his daughter on the other side, as far from the highwayman as he could get her.

His shotgun trained on them, Black Bart came closer to the stage and peered in. "What the hell's the matter with that fellow still in there?" he demanded.

Longarm said, "He's drunk."

"Haul him out, damn it! If he's got whiskey, that's something I can use, too."

Longarm started back to the stage.

"Wait a minute!"

Longarm pulled up.

"Turn around slowly, mister."

Longarm did as Black Bart told him.

"Put your hands up!" As Longarm raised his hands, the highwayman looked quickly around him. "All of you! Put your hands up and keep them there!"

As everyone, including the old Chinaman's daughter, raised their hands to the sky, Black Bart stepped toward Longarm, reached into his coat, and pulled out his Colt. "That's a nice cross-draw rig you got there, mister," he said, tossing the revolver into the brush. "Let's see who the hell you are, anyway."

The highwayman pulled Longarm's wallet from the inside pocket of his frock coat. Opening it, he caught sight of the badge at once. "Well, well!" he exclaimed, pulling from it what folding money Longarm carried and handing the empty wallet back to him. "Looks like we got a lawman this time—a deputy U.S. marshal!" A chuckle came from under the sack. "Good thing I saw that bulge under your jacket."

"You still want that drummer, old son?" Longarm asked, pocketing his wallet.

"You heard me, Marshal. Drag him out."

As Longarm reached in for the drummer, out of the corner of his eye he saw the highwayman wave down the driver and the shotgun guard. Longarm grabbed the drummer by the collar of his jacket and tugged him across the coach's floor. The fellow's eyes popped open just before he hit the ground. With a groan, he rolled over onto his hands and knees. For a moment Longarm thought the drummer was going to get sick. The stench of whiskey hung over him like a curse.

Longarm stepped back. The highwayman moved closer to the drummer and kicked the man viciously in the side. The drummer flipped over onto his back and looked with suddenly wide eyes up at the highwayman. He was instantly sober. Scrambling to his feet, he thrust both hands into the air, his stubbly chin quivering with indignation, his red-rimmed eyes wide with fear.

"Go back in there and get that sample case, drummer," the highwayman said. "Now!"

As the drummer scrambled back into the stage, the highwayman chopped at the lid of the strongbox with a small ax, kicked it open, and began stuffing the bags of gold coins it contained into the pockets of his linen duster. He was as alert as he was greedy, and kept his finger on the triggers of his shotgun and the shotgun trained on all of them. Not the slightest movement on the part of the passengers, the driver, and the guard escaped his notice.

Nevertheless, Longarm considered this highwayman the most incompetent he had ever witnessed—and it had been Longarm's misfortune to watch a few of the best in action. This one, the marshal had long since decided, was not the notorious Black Bart, as Spittles had contended. The highwayman seemed to have planned nothing. His instructions were spur-of-the-moment. There was no order to the robbery. It was, in effect, a hopelessly amateurish effort—and it was this very fact that gave Longarm pause. A nervous amateur most likely committing his first robbery with a flour-sack over his head and a loaded double-barreled shot-gun in his hand was as dangerous as a lighted match in a gunpowder factory.

With everything of value in the strongbox now bulging the pockets of his duster, the fellow straightened up and waggled his shotgun at them. "Line up in front of the stage. All of you!"

The driver and the guard took their places beside Longarm and Spittles, while the drummer dropped his bag in front of the highwayman and backed witlessly into the old Oriental and his daughter.

"Let's see purses, wallets, rings, watches—all your valuables!" the highwayman commanded in his reso-nant voice.

They all began digging into their pockets. With a bitter curse, the driver lifted his watch from his vest pocket and handed it to the highwayman. The stage driver was unfastening the gold chain from the watch when the robber yanked the watch—chain, fob, and all—into his hands.

"None of that!" the fellow said. "I want all you got!"

As he took a silken purse, heavy with coins, from the old Chinaman and dropped it into one of his al-ready bulging duster pockets, he turned his head toward Longarm, then took a step closer to the law-man and brought the two muzzles of his shotgun to within inches of his face.

"What's the matter with you, Marshal? What are you waiting for? Give me that watch!"

"It ain't a valuable watch, but it's a good one, and I'd like to keep it, if it's all right with you, old son."

"Give it here, damn you! What makes you so spe-cial? This here's my robbery. I'll run it the way I want."

"The watch fob too?"

"Of course, damn you! Quit your stalling!"

31

"Well, if you'd step back some and take that shotgun out of my face, I might be able to pull the watch out easier."

The hooded figure hesitated a moment, then took a step back—the twin muzzles of his shotgun still yawning up at Longarm's face. Longarm lifted the watch carefully from his vest pocket, hefted its solid weight for a moment in a show of reluctance, then handed it to him with his left hand while he kept his right over the other vest pocket—the one containing his twin-barreled derringer. A somewhat bulky watch fob, at this moment its solid heft was a great comfort to the lawman.

As the highwayman took the Ingersoll watch in his hand and glanced swiftly down at its face, Longarm said, "You goin' to want the watch fob too, old son?"

"You're stallin', mister!" the highwayman said, steadying the shotgun. " 'Course I do! Hand it over!"

There was a small metal clip fastening the chain to the butt of the derringer. With his left hand, Longarm unclipped the chain and, in the same motion, lifted the derringer from the pocket, his big right hand concealing its brass gleam from the highwayman. The fellow saw the chain fall free and looked suddenly up at Longarm, his eyes narrowing, the shotgun wavering. He had not yet seen the derringer. Longarm stepped quickly closer. With his left forearm he knocked the shotgun's barrel up and away. At the same time he thrust the derringer in under the fellow's linen duster. Longarm felt the twin barrels poke into the man's gut, and fired.

The highwayman was flung backward. As he dropped to his knees, Longarm strode quickly forward and kicked the shotgun out of his hand. The weapon detonated harmlessly as it landed in the road.

Longarm snatched the floursack off the highwayman's head. The fellow had a rat's nest of red hair. His face was bone white, his eyes wide in shock. "I'm gutshot, Marshal!" he cried. "You've murdered me!"

"Give me back that watch."

"I can't! Gawdamighty!"

"I said give it here. And don't drop it!"

A dark, pulsing stream was pouring out from under the man's linen duster. There was an odd, greenish shine to it. With a low groan, the highwayman handed Longarm his watch. Longarm took it from the man's trembling fingers, clipped the chain to the butt of the derringer, and replaced the watch and chain in his vest. The highwayman looked up at Longarm.

"You got to help me! I'm gutshot, I tell you!"

"There ain't much I can do about that, mister, unless you want me to put another bullet in you. You'd go a little faster, then."

"You ain't got no heart, Marshal! You're a murderer!"

"And you're a lousy holdup man. You should have stuck to what you were doing before you got this bright idea."

Longarm turned to the others. The girl had her back to the wounded highwayman, her face resting on her father's shoulder. Spittles was watching the man on the ground with a shocked countenance; he looked somewhat green around the gills. The driver and the shotgun guard were pleased. The drummer was reaching for his sample bag; he was obviously in need of more booze.

"Get your valuables out of this fool's duster," Longarm told them. "We'll soon enough be using it for a shroud."

The stage driver, a broad-shouldered fellow with a powerful gut, wasted no time in pulling the duster off the wounded highwayman. Swiftly, deftly, he took the bags of gold coins from the pockets and tossed them back into the strongbox. The old Chinaman left his daughter and, with quick fingers, retrieved the bulging purse the highwayman had taken from him. Longarm waited until the others had picked the duster clean before he claimed the folding money the highwayman had stashed in his inside coat pocket.

Then he looked down at the dying man. He was curled up on the road like a large worm some giant had stomped on. His eyes were closed, and the blood was no longer pulsing through the hole in his gut. His face was the color of old newspaper.

"You killed him!" Spittles said to Longarm. "You killed Black Bart! There's a reward! Eight hundred dollars!"

"This ain't Black Bart."

"Yes, he is. I've been reading about him now for years. This is the way he operates. A linen duster, a shotgun, and a floursack over his head."

"That's right. And cloth wrapped around his feet so he won't leave footprints. Black Bart stays afoot. He's some walker, he is. Last summer they tracked him sixty miles before losing him—and he was on foot all the way. Now look here at this fellow's feet. Boots and spurs. And if we look around, we'll find his horse, more than likely."

"Then . . . who is he?"

"Some clerk who thought he'd cash in on Black Bart's reputation."

The stage driver and the guard were bent over the highwayman. The stage driver looked up at Longarm. "He's gone, the poor son of a bitch. Dead as a doornail."

"Wrap him in that linen duster then and dump him in the boot. We've got a ways to go yet, ain't we?"

The men nodded.

As Longarm went searching for his Colt, the driver and the guard rolled the dead robber into his linen duster and dropped him into the rear boot. Longarm found his Colt undamaged, and returned to the stage. The two men had not been too particular in their disposal of the highwayman. One foot was sticking up in plain sight, the spur gleaming dully in the moist air.

Longarm ducked into the coach and pulled the door shut.

The old man's daughter looked quickly away when Longarm caught her eyes on him. The drummer had developed a bad case of bottle fever and was making short work of a fifth. Spittles, his face still pale, regarded Longarm with a mixture of horror and admiration. Longarm sighed and looked out the side window.

Any chance he might have had of arriving in Slab City quietly and going about his business with a minimum of fuss was gone now. Hell, the editor and publisher of the town's only newspaper was sitting across from him at that very moment. Longarm could imagine already the headline Spittles was preparing in his mind for tomorrow's edition of the *Slab City Citizen*. Longarm tugged his snuff-brown Stetson down over his eyes, leaned back, and tried to get some sleep.

But the thought of that sixth passenger riding behind him in the boot made that impossible.

Chapter 2

As Longarm left Slab City's Redwood Hotel dining room the next morning, a fresh, unlit cheroot in the corner of his mouth, he was suddenly confronted by a man as tall and broad-shouldered as himself.

"No doubt about it!" the fellow cried, a pleased smile creasing his handsome face. "You must be the deputy U.S. marshal who saved the stage!"

The man stuck out his hand. Longarm took it and felt the fellow's huge hand swallow his own in a steaming grip. The man's dark eyes gleamed like wet anthracite. From under the wide brim of his white, high-crowned Stetson hung long, dark hair that just reached his shoulders. The hair shone lustrously and was well combed out. He was dressed impressively in a vested suit of sparkling white linen, and his boots were highly polished cordovan leather.

"Name's Duff Ryan," the fellow boomed. "Pleased to meet you, Marshal. Come over special to congratulate you myself. Figured I owed you. The money in that strongbox was my payroll—along with Helga Jensen's. Much obliged!"

"The name's Custis Long," Longarm said, moving the cheroot to the other side of his mouth.

"Marshal Long." Ryan nodded. "You've just breakfasted, have you?"

"Yes."

"Well, then. Allow me to show you about our thriving little metropolis."

"I'd appreciate that."

Ryan steered Longarm out through the lobby, his hand resting in friendly fashion on Longarm's shoulder as they stepped out onto the hotel's wide verandah.

"Let's stop right here, Marshal," Duff Ryan said. "The better to get our bearings." He waved a huge hand toward the settlement spread out before them. Unlike the day before, the sun had broken through, revealing a startlingly green prospect. The mountains that hemmed in the valley seemed to hang in the air, their foothills lost in the early morning mist. "The site of Slab City," Ryan resumed, "is a narrow but fertile crescent locked within the loop of the Nooksack River. You see how it gleams there in the morning light? Beautiful, is it not?"

Longarm nodded assent hastily. The man sounded like a carnival barker—yet his enthusiasm and obvious sincerity prevented Longarm from taking offense. Despite himself, he found he was warming to the man.

"Mean though Slab City may appear at first glimpse, Marshal, it bears within it the seeds of future greatness—and better than that, wealth. Mark my words. Before too many years, Slab City will be a metropolis tapping the richness of the vast timberlands of the interior and utilizing for its manifold industries the abundant—I might say, the *super*abundant—water power of this region. On its way already to tap this wealth is the Northern Pacific, and soon after that, the Great Northern!" Ryan looked with sheer jubilation at Longarm. "It is God's truth, Marshal Long. The Great Northern and the Northern Pacific are both on their way."

"Well, that should make a difference," Longarm

37

allowed. "Yesterday's stage ride to Slab City was a mite long—and just a bit bumpy, at that. Nothing got broke, but I seem to have loosened a few nuts and bolts."

"Well said!" Ryan boomed. He slapped Longarm on the shoulder. "You have a way with words, sir! And a becoming modesty, as well. No mention at all of that unpleasantness you handled with such brutal dispatch. Admirable."

Longarm clamped his teeth down on the cheroot. If there was one thing he did not like, it was some flannelmouth slapping him on the back and howling in his ear about what a great man he was. But Longarm kept his composure. Duff Ryan meant only good fellowship by his manner, and Longarm was intrigued by him. The fellow was sure enough outsized, but if that was a crime, the deputy would have had to arrest himself long ago.

"And now for that look around I promised you," Ryan said, starting down the porch steps. "There will be quarters, I'm afraid, where you will be well advised to hold your nose while passing through. The Chinese quarter. Chinatown, we call it. Ah, they are a most troublesome race, Marshal, swarming in like locusts. Ubiquitous, you might say. Ubiquitous and treacherous. An unwanted yellow tide of cheap labor that will soon destroy all of us if it is allowed to continue. The heathen will soon reduce all of us to a standard of living equal to theirs, if this invasion continues. I am a businessman, but I side with the laboring man on this issue. The yellow tide must be brought to a halt. Forces are already at work to do just that." Ryan looked sharply, shrewdly at Longarm. "I assume you are here, as an arm of the federal government, to put a stop to this illegal tide."

"Guess you might say that."

"Capital! That is precisely why I am so pleased at your arrival here in Slab City, and from what I gathered from Charlie Spittles—you really shocked that pen pusher, you know—you are just the man for the job—if courage, quickness, and resourcefulness are any indication.'

"I'm also as quick as a rattler and just as cold-blooded," Longarm added slyly, "when I see an old man and his young daughter told to ride on a baggage rack while fat white men ride inside. And whether this tide you're talking about is yellow, green, or purple, it doesn't make a bit of difference to me. All I care about is whether it's illegal."

"Of course! Of course! Spittles told me all about that." Ryan chuckled heartily. "He also told me what you threatened to do with your boot if he didn't shut his mouth! Admirable! I like your style, Marshal. We should get along famously."

They were passing a bank at that moment.

"Mine," said Ryan, waving a hand at it almost negligently.

They continued on to a huge saloon that took up the rest of the block and extended well around the corner. It was called the Skidroad Palace. A legion of aproned Orientals were swamping it out. The batwings were open, and Longarm caught a glimpse of a long, gleaming mahogany bar, rows of bottles, green table tops, and florid paintings of pink-fleshed nudes on the walls.

"That's mine also," Ryan said as they moved around the corner past the saloon and started out into the street.

The broad street was clogged with heavy morning traffic. Great wagons piled high with freshly cut timber, pulled by huge Belgian workhorses, thundered past them as they picked their way across the street. The drivers of the wagons and the few loggers Longarm saw on the street were white men. They were dressed in the traditional stocking caps, bright woolen shirts, heavy water-repellent pants, and big, studded boots of the logger.

Gaining the other side of the street, Longarm found himself walking alongside a huge general store. Ryan did not have to tell Longarm who owned it. Duff Ryan's name was painted in bold green letters across the false front. Glancing into the emporium as he passed, Longarm saw the many Oriental clerks Ryan had hired to wait on customers. The pattern was getting pretty obvious to Longarm by now; Duff Ryan and others might protest the Chinaman's willingness to work for next to nothing, but this would not stop these same men from hiring Orientals in order to squeeze just that much more profit out of their enterprises.

They were close to the river now.

A huge sawmill and, beside that, a great, yellow pile of sawdust blocked momentarily Longarm's view of the river as they approached. Next to the sawmill, and extending well down the muddy street, there was a solid line of two-story frame dwellings, in and out of which poured a steady stream of Chinese.

"Helga Jensen owns this sawmill," Ryan said, a note of faint disapproval in his voice, as if it galled him to think of anyone else in Slab City owning anything of substance. "And this entire Chinese quarter as well."

Soon Longarm and Ryan were moving through the throng of diminutive Orientals. They moved in a kind of quick shuffle, their heads slightly bent forward, great, broad hats covering their heads, their long, braided queues hanging down their stooped backs. Longarm had the queer impression that he was looking down upon a sea of bobbing hats. The very few women he saw were dressed in long skirts slit up the side to reveal pleasing ankles and incredibly small feet. They walked up on their toes, in a dainty, mincing motion that came very close to a trot.

"Smell it?" Ryan growled.

The smell Ryan had warned him about earlier was indeed noticeable. It was compounded primarily of smoke from woodburning stoves mixed with the odor of food cooking, food foreign to Longarm's taste. And those smells were combined with the inevitable stench that came with crowded human habitation. Longarm had encountered it often enough on Indian reservations, where the normally clean, nomadic Indians were forced to live packed together with little or no provision for their sanitary needs.

Both sides of the street were now lined with these tenements, all of them teeming with humanity. There were shops, run by Chinamen. Laundries, bootmakers, cigar makers, tailors, and open markets, where the smell of fresh fish, rice, and greens smote Longarm's nostrils with the force of a physical blow. He had walked into another world. Here in Slab City, hemmed in by towering peaks, was a tiny piece of China.

"See what I mean, Marshal?" Ryan demanded.

Longarm nodded. He knew what it was that offended Ryan—and all the others who railed against this sudden, overwhelming explosion of Oriental culture in their midst. Its strangeness was what frightened them and aroused their hatred. The smells, the crowding, the bent, seemingly servile Chinese. Perhaps the two most disturbing elements of their presence, Longarm realized, were their high, sing-song language—more like singing than speaking—and the profusion of the thoroughly incomprehensible ideographs of their written language, plastered on signs and walls everywhere.

The strangeness of these people intrigued Longarm, but he could see how others might be confused and frightened by it. He could not understand, however, why a man like Duff Ryan should be so concerned. He did not appear to be either frightened or confused.

They left the Chinese quarter behind, and cut up a narrow street toward Main Street. When they reached the corner, Ryan planted himself securely in the middle of the wooden sidewalk and looked back down the side street, already lost in shadows. He shook his head. "As I told you, Marshal, that woman owns it all. She's a shrewd one, all right. There is no doubt in my mind that she is a moving force behind the continued illegal importation of these Chinese."

He looked sharply at Longarm, and said, "Did you see those Chinese women?"

"Yes. But there weren't many, I noticed."

"Not many, perhaps. But a damn sight more than there were last spring. That's what they're importing—women. And in those narrow, foul-smelling quarters they will breed like rats."

"Women? That's all they're smuggling in?"

"Coolies too, I have no doubt." Ryan looked sharply at Longarm. "Helga Jensen has a Chinese foreman. And there have been rumors that this Chinaman does more than satisfy her needs at the mill." He frowned and looked away from Longarm. "But of course that is very difficult to believe—of *any* white woman."

"I think I'd like to meet this Helga Jensen."

"You will, soon enough, I'm sure. But I'd like you to walk down a few more blocks and see Spittles. I am afraid he made a poor impression on you yesterday. And I would like you to see my newspaper and allow Spittles to acquaint you with the situation hereabouts. He's a fine reporter and a shrewd man, though I admit he dresses like a headwaiter most of the time."

"I'd like to oblige you, Duff," Longarm said. "You've been real helpful with this tour of your metropolis, and I sure do appreciate it. But I think I better just eat this apple one bite at a time. The man I want to see right now is Rolf La Tour, your town marshal. You'd be doing me a real service if you'd just point me in the right direction."

"Of course, of course," Ryan said, smiling. "Rolf's our town marshal, all right. But he contents himself exclusively with drunks and malcontents. The traffic in illegal Chinamen, he does nothing whatever to discourage."

"I guess that may be so, Duff, but I was told to get in touch with him. One of our men was working with him before he was found dead."

"Ah, yes. Scally. Terrible thing, that murder. Had the look of the Tong about it. None of us in town had any idea that Hitch was working for the federal government—until his unfortunate death, that is."

"La Tour knew."

Ryan frowned. "Yes, of course. That's right. He must have, at that. The trouble is, Rolf La Tour has not been in his office for the past couple of days. Rumor has it that he's, shall we say, on the town? In this case, Chinatown."

"Then I'll just go to his office and wait for him."

Duff Ryan rocked back on his heels and looked coolly at Longarm. "I know you'd like to get about your business, Marshal," the man said. "And I guess you're about ready to start eating that apple, as you put it. But believe me, Spittles is a fine reporter. I am sure he can help you find La Tour—and he can help you with much more, besides."

Longarm found it impossible to take offense at Duff's eagerness to help. He smiled suddenly and said to the man, "Lead on, Mac Duff."

Spittles was at one of the presses, nervously monitoring the work of a young Chinese, over whom he towered. When he saw Longarm and Duff Ryan enter, he looked distractedly back at the Chinese, then abandoned him to the press and hurried across the pressroom to meet them. He was still a sartorial marvel, even though his fingers were black with ink. His high collar was immaculate, his dark cravat neatly tied. He still wore his vest, every button buttoned, with bright blue garters on his shirtsleeves to keep his cuffs from wandering. His pants still hugged his calves, just as the latest fashion dictated. Charles Swinburne Spittles was a real swell, all right, and Longarm found it difficult to share Duff Ryan's confidence in his abilities as a reporter. The man belonged on a stage, not out gathering news.

"I'd shake your hand, Mr. Long," Spittles said, "but my hand is filthy, as you can see."

"That's all right. We already met."

"Of course."

"Charlie," boomed Ryan, "I want you to help the marshal. You know this town better than most. Right now he's looking for that no-account town marshal. After that, I'm thinking he'd be interested in your view of the smuggling that's been going on."

"Sure thing, Mr. Ryan."

Ryan turned to Longarm. "I'm leaving you in good hands, Marshal. This fellow knows Slab City. He knows where the bones are buried." He winked broadly. "Just don't you let the way he dresses fool you. You can't tell a book by its cover." He laughed heartily at that, slapped Spittles on the back with enough force to rattle the fellow's back teeth, then strode out of the place.

Spittles looked coldly at Longarm. "Do not be misled by my dress, Mr. Long. I simply see no reason at all why I should not look the very best I can whenever that is possible. You would be surprised at the doors that are opened to me in this town as a result of the way I dress." Spittles smiled thinly. "After all, they think, what is there to fear from such a silly fop?" He turned then, and beckoned to Longarm. "Today's front page has already been set," he said. "Come see for yourself. You are mentioned prominently."

He pulled up in front of a high table, unrolled a freshly printed page proof, and showed it to Longarm, pointing to the first column. Longarm read:

44

ATTEMPTED HOLDUP AT RUSSIAN NOTCH

HIGHWAYMAN FATALLY WOUNDED

DEPUTY U. S. MARSHAL SHOWS COOL COURAGE IN FOILING ROBBERY ATTEMPT

Under the headlines, Spittles had written a pretty accurate account of the attempted robbery and its aftermath. After reading through it swiftly, Longarm looked up at Spittles. The man had a pleased look on his face. He was obviously proud of his account.

"I don't suppose I could talk you into not printing this?" Longarm asked.

"That's out of the question, Mr. Long. Haven't you ever heard of freedom of the press?"

"Guess I have, at that. The thing is, I was hoping to keep my ass down in this town while I went about my business. This kind of publicity I don't need."

"I am afraid word of your exploit will have preceded this modest account's arrival on the streets, Mr. Long. Rumors, I am sure, are already flying. This news story will only nail down the facts. Surely there is no harm in that."

"Guess not." Longarm took out a cheroot. As he lit it, he said, "Your boss told me you could help me find the town constable."

Spittles frowned. "He's on one of his periodic visits to Chinatown, I believe."

"Where in Chinatown?"

"If you'll wait a moment, I'll go with you."

"You don't need to do that. Just tell me."

Spittles smiled. "You will never find him without me, Mr. Long. I understand these people. And they understand me. And respect me."

"You *think* you understand these people, and you hate them."

45

"To understand them *is* to hate them, Mr. Long," Spittles said, shrugging into a maroon jacket and reaching for his bowler hat.

With barely a nod to the old Chinaman sitting on the narrow stairs sewing shoes, Spittles ducked into a tenement and turned to Longarm. "You see that?" Spittles said, as he led the way down a long, narrow corridor. "That old man will have twenty pairs of shoes finished by noon today. And this is his work area, this stinking hallway."

Longarm did not reply. He was intrigued by the fact that Spittles was able to find his way with relative ease through a stifling passageway that was almost pitch black, past countless apartment doors from under which the fumes of opium and exotic incense leaked. Spittles was obviously not a stranger to this side of Chinatown's life.

At the end of the hallway, Spittles descended a flight of rickety steps. The odors of musty clothing, oil lamps, and boiling rice were mixed with the stronger odor of damp earth. Longarm followed Spittles through the darkness across a dirt floor for a while, turned to the left, and felt raw boards under his feet. They turned twice more in the dark, and then Spittles was leading Longarm up a flight of unplaned wooden steps into a hall that was comparatively well-lit by a couple of oil lamps sitting on shelves along one wall.

At the end of this hall there was a door. Spittles stopped before it and knocked sharply. There was a few seconds' wait, and then a tiny peephole appeared in the doorway. Whoever was on the other side recognized Spittles, and after a rattle of locks and the sound of a beam being slid back, the door swung open.

The man at the door was a mountain of a Chinaman—obviously not a Cantonese, as were most of the Chinese working in the West. He was bull-throated, thickly muscled about the shoulders, gorilla-armed,

46

leather-skinned. The Chinese god that had fashioned him had had plenty of material to work with, and had given it time to harden.

He stepped aside for Spittles. Spittles nodded to Longarm and stepped into the room with the lawman on his heels. The room was large and cubical, its doors and windows—if there were any—hidden behind tattered and dusty velvet hangings of green and blue and silver. The few pieces of furniture in the place were cheap and battered. Cones of incense burned on little red tables in the corners. The tables were decorated with Chinese characters in gold paint.

The big Chinaman poked at one of the wall curtains, swept it aside, and vanished. A moment later, a tall woman entered, nodded silently to Spittles, and pointed to two upholstered chairs. Behind her followed a small servant with cups of steaming tea on a black-lacquered tray. The little man was noiseless on slippered feet, and vanished behind the wall curtains after placing the tray on a small table in front of the chairs, into which Longarm and Spittles had already eased themselves.

Longarm watched the tall woman ease herself gracefully down onto a corner of the sofa facing them. He had not taken his eyes off her since the moment she had entered the room. She was obviously Eurasian, possibly a mixture of Mexican and Chinese. She was probably close to thirty, broad-shouldered, deep-bosomed, wearing a black silk dress, the severe lines of which did much to enhance her slim figure. Her Oriental lineage showed only in the black shine of her long hair, pinned up with lacquer combs, in the pale yellow of her unpowdered skin, and in the folds of her upper eyelids at the outer corners. But there was no slant to her eyes, her nose was almost aquiline, and she had more chin than most Cantonese he had seen.

"This is Deputy U.S. Marshal Long," Spittles said to the girl. "He has come here to speak with Constable La Tour."

Her dark eyes flicked with sudden appreciation at Longarm. Spittles was right, Longarm realized. His reputation was already abroad in this town. She smiled suddenly at him, revealing incredibly white teeth.

"I'm Lillian M'Ling," she said to Longarm, "since this clerk has not seen fit to introduce me to you."

Spittles went pale. "It was just an oversight, Lillian," he protested.

She looked back at Spittles. "Of course."

"Is the constable here?" Longarm asked the woman.

She rose almost regally to her feet. "Drink your tea," she told Longarm. "I will see what I can do with Rolf. I am sure he will want to meet the deputy U.S. marshal, the hero of Russian Notch." Bowing slightly to them, she turned and disappeared beyond the wall curtains.

Spittles leaned forward and took the cup of tea sitting on the tray in front of him. Longarm took his cup, also. The tea was weak and did little for him. He drained the cup and sat back.

"Incredible, is it not?" Spittles said, shuddering delicately as he looked about him. "You know where you are, of course."

"A Chinese cathouse?"

"That and *worse,* Mr. Long. It is the most notorious opium den north of Seattle. Didn't you smell that opium on the way in here?"

"Guess I did, at that."

"You see, then, why I feel as I do—and why Duff Ryan agrees with me. They prefer to live in close quarters such as these, not coarsely filthy—like the ignorant and besotted Irish—but with an enthusiastic, inherent, and refined uncleanliness that is far more disgusting. I must say, Mr. Long, that their whole civilization impresses me as a low, disciplined, perfected sensualism. Everything in a Chinaman's life and habits seems cut-and-dried, like their disgusting food. There is no sign at all that any of them seem capable of any

48

emotion, any passion—good or bad. None of the finer instincts. None. Only a depraved lust to satisfy the moment."

"If you were running for office, Spittles, I'd say that'd be a fine speech—for all those hotheads who want to run the Chinese out of this country. But right now, all I'm interested in is getting ahold of this here town constable."

"Are you threatening to shut me up with one of your boots again?"

"Hell, no, Spittles. I'll just wrap you one on the back of the head with this here Colt. Wouldn't want my boots to get eaten away by all that snake venom you keep spitting out. I suspicion it'd curl my boots right up."

Spittles drew himself up to his full height, his face growing almost as white as the starched collar that was tucked so stiffly up under his chin. An umbrella salesman, Longarm thought suddenly. That was what Spittles reminded him of, now that he thought of it.

Lillian M'Ling appeared suddenly before them, the coffee sheen of her face drained to an unpleasant paleness. Behind her, the giant Chinaman towered. "You had better come," she said. "Both of you. There is trouble!"

Spittles looked nervously at Longarm, then got reluctantly to his feet. Longarm stood up and found himself on a level with Lillian M'Ling's wide green eyes. He looked into them and saw genuine fear.

The burly Chinaman led the way along a narrow corridor, then down a twisting stairway that seemed to go on forever. Spittles was just ahead of Longarm, and behind the marshal was Lillian M'Ling. He could hear the faint rustle of her silk dress. Foul-smelling, guttering candles set on narrow beams gave the only light as they continued down into what Longarm was sure must be a cellar, well below street level. With each step, the stench of opium smoke grew stronger.

At last they came to the bottom of the stairs. A narrow passageway, shored up by rough timbers, yawned before them, with a tiny, flickering pinpoint of light over a door at the far end of it. As they moved on down this passageway, Longarm heard the scuttering of tiny feet in the darkness. Rats. That and the increasing dampness led him to believe they were close to the river. As they got closer to the door, Longarm saw another heavily built Chinaman, standing with folded arms in the shadows beside it, as silent and impassive as a Buddha.

When they reached the door, the guard stepped out of the shadows and pulled it open for them. Ducking his head low, Longarm stepped through the doorway and found himself in a long, narrow den with another door at the far end of it. Fish-oil lamps cast a dim yellow glow over the place. The dirt floor was puddled in spots from the water that seeped through the ceiling and darkened the overhead beams. He was barely able to stand upright as he passed through.

The air reeked with the sweet smell of opium smoke. Longarm had little doubt that he could have himself a happy little pipe dream from the smoke alone, if he stayed down here long enough. The walls on both sides of the den were fitted with tiered bunks, four bunks high, with very little space between them. Each bunk held a man who was either in the act of doping up his opium pipe or was already deeply asleep, wrapped in blissful dreams. The nightmares, Longarm knew, would come later.

And all of the smokers were white men.

"You see!" said Spittles in a fierce whisper back over his shoulder at Longarm, "this is how they contaminate the Western races! This is how they will destroy our land! Many of these white opium addicts were once respected merchants and citizens of Slab City!"

Longarm made no reply. They were at the other door now. The big Chinaman opened it by removing a sturdy beam that lay across it. He stepped aside, allowing Spittles and Longarm to enter. The air in this second, much smaller den was heavy with not only the smell of opium smoke, but with the stench of raw whiskey as well.

There were no bunks in this room. A bedraggled sofa was against the far wall, with a man sitting on it, bare from the waist up, with a crazed look on his face, his boots before him on the dirt floor. A small Chinese girl was curled up in a tight ball at the foot of the sofa. She was naked except for a broad, black silk sash wound around her waist. She stared at them fixedly as they approached the sofa, a glazed look in her eyes. There was a smoking opium pipe on the dirt floor at her feet, within reach of her small hand.

Spittles pulled to a halt in front of the man, his narrow shoulders thrown back in haughty contempt as he gazed down at the man.

"Constable La Tour," Spittles said, "I have brought a deputy U.S. marshal here to see you, since this is now your place of business, apparently."

"The name's Custis Long," Longarm said, stopping beside Spittles and looking down at the constable. "As soon as you're fit, I'd like to have a word or two with you about Deputy Scally. I understand you were working with him when he was killed."

La Tour nodded dully. His lean face was cadaverous, his yellowed, drooping mustache adding a touch of comedy to the wild light in his bloodshot eyes. His ribs showed through the greasy white sheen of his sunless flesh. His neck was scrawny. If this was the man poor Scally had been counting on, Longarm thought grimly, no wonder Scally had ended as he had. Longarm bent closer to the man.

"You hear me, La Tour? You ready to snap out of it? The holiday's over!"

The town constable appeared to be in some kind of shock. Longarm assumed it was the combination of opium and whiskey, and was about to shake the man, when the fellow stuck out a bony hand and opened it, palm up. Beside Longarm, Spittles gasped. La Tour was holding in his hand a tiny, intricately jeweled chest. With trembling fingers, La Tour opened it. Inside, sitting like a jewel on a tiny piece of velvet, Longarm saw a small ivory hatchet.

Longarm was about to ask La Tour what the significance of the ivory hatchet was when he heard a sharp, painful grunt behind him, coming from the doorway. He spun, his Colt already out and covering the door, and saw the big Chinaman sagging to the floor —a long, narrow, scimitar-like sword buried up to its hilt in the man's stomach, its wicked, dripping point poking out through his back. Lillian M'Ling had already flung herself into the corner beside the doorway, her face hidden, her arms covering her head.

In the doorway stood two Chinamen, their short-barreled sixguns gleaming in the dull light. A shot lanced past Longarm at La Tour. Longarm heard the bullet's impact. Another shot disintegrated the single oil lamp. Longarm flung Spittles to the ground over the huddled Chinese girl and crabbed swiftly to the wall, flattening against it in the darkness, his own gun now spitting back at the fiery flashes in the doorway as the two Chinamen continued to empty their guns at La Tour. Longarm's .44 silenced one gunman. The other returned Longarm's fire. As flames sliced toward him from the doorway, Longarm pumped back two quick shots—one high, one low—then flung himself flat.

There was a gasp, followed by the sound of a heavy body falling. Yellow light streamed in from the other den, catching the thick, coiling black powder smoke that now filled the room. The acrid, choking fumes tore at his eyes, and his ears were ringing like firebells from the detonations in this closed-in space as he hurried toward La Tour. Spittles, apparently unhurt, was getting to his feet.

"Get some light in here!" Longarm called back to Lillian M'Ling. He heard her stepping over the bodies in the doorway, and turned his attention to the wounded La Tour.

Even in the semidarkness, Longarm could see how the bullets had torn him. One slug had caught his face, another his right shoulder. His midsection was a dark, shining mess. The man's sphincter muscles must have given way. A foul stench was rising from under him, filling the room.

"Who did this, La Tour?" Longarm asked. "Do you know who it was?"

The man reached up and grabbed Longarm's vest, pulling him down toward his shattered face. Lillian M'Ling was over them by this time with a smoking oil lamp. "*China Belle* . . . see Scott! Tell him . . . *China Belle* . . . "

The man choked on the blood welling up from his destroyed lungs, and then his head sagged to one side. He let go of Longarm's vest. His body seemed to settle into the cot.

Longarm straightened and turned to Lillian M'Ling. He was astonished to see a small, highly polished Smith & Wesson .38 in her hand. Stepping back, keeping its muzzle turned on Longarm, she placed the lamp on a small table and cocked the single-action revolver. She appeared to have no difficulty at all in accomplishing this.

Only it was not Longarm she wanted, apparently. She pointed the gun at Spittles, her beautiful Eurasian features as cold and implacable as death. "You son of a bitch, Charlie Spittles. You brought them here! I trusted you!"

"No, Lillian!" Spittles bleated. "You've got this all wrong, so help me!"

For a moment she looked as if she might pull the trigger. But only for a moment. Reluctantly, she lowered her revolver.

Behind Lillian M'Ling, two of her heavy bully-boys stepped in over the two bodies in the doorway, and each was carrying a wig with a long Chinese queue dangling from it. Looking then at the two dead gun-men sprawled face-up on the floor, Longarm realized that he recognized both of them. They were not Chinese, but white men. He had last seen them in their bunks in the other den, smiling blissfully in their opium sleep. Only they did not need to pretend they were asleep now. This time it was the real thing.

And they were dreaming of a damn sight hotter place than this one.

Chapter 3

Not less than half an hour later, Longarm found himself in a surprisingly opulent apartment well above the smoke-filled dens and rat-infested warrens of Lillian M'Ling's empire, settling down onto a richly brocaded sofa to wait for her return. With a soft, sibilant urgency, she had insisted on her need to change into something more comfortable.

He had relieved her of her .38 caliber Smith & Wesson, allowed one of her remaining bully-boys to stand guard outside, and now settled back to wait. He had no doubt that she would return, and understood her need to absent herself from him. He had seen how hard—despite her stoic resolve—she had taken the death of the big Chinaman who had led them into La Tour's den. The man must evidently have been her favorite.

Spittles had left in a hurry to make his deadline, after explaining to Longarm the significance of the curious little ivory hatchet, and Longarm had seen to it that La Tour's body and that of the dead Chinaman —along with those of the two white men—were removed to the local undertaker's. Though Spittles swore he had never seen either of the two men before, Longarm was interested in seeing who—if anyone—would show up to view their remains. It would be interesting also to see which group of Chinamen claimed the body-guard's corpse so that it could be sent back to China for a proper burial. It might tell him who Lillian M'Ling's allies were.

As he thought once more of that grisly duel below ground, he found himself marveling at those remaining white men, lost in their opium dreams, secure on their narrow bunks, sleeping through the hell exploding just beyond them in the next room. Perhaps, Longarm mused, they had transformed those shattering detonations into the tinkle of soft bells and made it all part of their lotus-scented dreams. . . .

Lillian M'Ling returned. Parting the bamboo curtains with a single dramatic gesture, she stepped into the room, tall, straight-bodied, and proud. There was only the slightest trace of redness around her eyes to reveal the grief she had allowed herself to express in private, but that was not what Longarm noticed.

She was suddenly impressive—as if she had mastered every force in her vibrant personality to meet whatever threat Longarm presented. A butterfly-shaped headdress, spangled with the loot of some fabulous jewel box, exaggerated her already impressive height. Her gown was amethyst filigreed with gold above, a shimmering rainbow below.

If this bustling logging town in the middle of the Northwest wilderness were to secede from the rest of the United States and elect itself a queen, this woman would do superlatively. She smiled slightly at Longarm's reaction. Moving regally into the room, she made herself comfortable in a black inlaid chair close to Longarm. She crossed her legs and the slit in her skirt revealed a honey-colored calf and a portion of her thigh. The movement was deliberately provocative.

"You saved my life, Mr. Long," she told him. She

56

smiled swiftly, her perfect teeth flashing in her golden face. "If there is anything I can do to show my appreciation . . . "

Her meaning was perfectly clear. Longarm forced himself to remember the bodyguard stationed just outside the apartment door—only a hint of the powerful resources this remarkable woman commanded. He returned her smile. "Just tell me the truth, Lillian."

"Of course." Her English, he noticed suddenly, was as perfect as the gleaming teeth she occasionally flashed on him. And the intelligence now directed at him through her brilliant green eyes was almost intimidating.

"What was La Tour doing down there, Lillian—besides enjoying himself?"

"He was in hiding."

"From who?"

"The Ong Leong."

Longarm frowned. "Would you like to explain that?"

"The Ong Leong are one of the Five Families. I believe you whites call them Tongs."

Longarm nodded. On his way through San Francisco he had learned what he could of the Chinese on the coast, and had learned that five families—all from different regions of the Pearl River Delta in China—now controlled the Chinese in this country. They coexisted poorly, and their rivalry often came to violence. The claim of each family was that it was established solely to look after the welfare of its individual Cantonese members. In fact, they derived their income through control of prostitution, gambling, and the sale of opium—among other equally lucrative rackets.

"Why was the Ong Leong after La Tour?"

Her green eyes probed his for a moment as she carefully considered her reply. "I am not sure," she said. "Perhaps he was killed for the same reason Scally was killed. That too was a Tong execution."

"Did he get a little hatchet first, too?"

She frowned. "I don't know."

"What I can't understand, Lillian, is how La Tour got that little box. Someone brought it to him—right under the nose of one of your guards." He smiled and let her consider the implications of his suggestion.

She saw at once what he was driving at. "You think Rolf was set up—that I was behind his death?"

Longarm said nothing.

"That's nonsense," she went on. "Worse than nonsense. I was trying to *save* his life. You are too devious a man, Marshal, to understand."

"Am I? Why were you so interested in saving his life, Lillian? What was he to you?"

"He was my lover."

"Then who was that girl with him?"

Her composure slipped momentarily as he caught her on that. But her reply was cool and almost convincing. "That girl was in my employ. She was nothing to Rolf—a bone I threw him at times, to while away his loneliness."

"You mean his imprisonment."

"I do not know what you mean." She got quickly to her feet. The audience, it seemed, was at an end.

As if a bell had been rung somewhere, the wall curtains behind Longarm parted, and Lillian M'Ling's new bodyguard appeared. His flat, powerful face was impassive, but his small, slanted eyes regarded Longarm almost hungrily. He was undoubtedly eager to make good in his new role. Lillian looked past Longarm at the big fellow and smiled. "Just a moment, Ton. Mr. Long will be leaving soon. You may wait outside for him."

As Ton disappeared back behind the drapes, Longarm got to his feet. "I'll be wanting to talk to you again, most likely," he told Lillian. "That is, when I get the answers to a few more questions. I hope you won't mind seeing me."

58

"Of course not," she said, walking with him across the room.

When they reached the spot in the wall where the door was, Lillian leaned enticingly close to him as she parted the wall curtains. Longarm caught the faint whiff of an indescribably delicate fragrance that drew him almost hypnotically closer to her.

She was waiting, her face turned to his, her full lips parted slightly. He saw her tongue resting between the tips of her teeth. And then her arm was around his back, drawing him gently to her. The kiss was full and warm. There was a delicacy, and yet a passionate intensity to it—beautifully controlled and modulated; she exercised a skill that was beyond craft. For a second, as she pulled gently back, her teeth tugged gently on his lower lip.

She looked at him, her green eyes glowing softly. "Despite your suspicions, Marshal, I cannot be angry with you. You saved my life, and I thank you. Those bullets were meant for me as well as Rolf. Perhaps that small token of my gratitude will suffice for now."

She smiled enigmatically and rapped softly on the door. It was pulled open instantly. As Longarm stepped past the curtains and through the open doorway, he looked back. But the curtains had fallen into place and Lillian M'Ling was gone.

Spittles and Duff Ryan were sitting across from Longarm in a quiet corner of the Skidroad Palace. Ryan was leaning back in his chair, enjoying one of Longarm's cheroots, watching Spittles with an amused glint in his eye as the pen pusher held forth on the evils of the Chinese.

" . . . and not only that, Mr. Long, no American can do business with a Chinaman. They are universally dishonest and unreliable. The entire business life of China is permeated with the idea that every person who takes part in a transaction should take his share of the graft. They have no regard for the sanctity of an oath. Why else do you think that no court in this country is allowed to accept the testimony of an Oriental against a white man? That's the law of the land, Mr. Long."

"Just because I enforce the law, it doesn't mean I think all laws are right or just." Longarm looked at Duff Ryan. "Do you see it the same way as Spittles, Ryan?"

"As Spittles says, they have no regard for the sanctity of an oath, Marshal. What else could our courts do?"

"I seem to recollect a few of our politicians don't show too much enthusiasm for the sanctity of *their* oaths. Are you two saying graft is unknown in these here United States?"

"Of course not," Ryan said. "But we don't *approve* of graft."

"And with the Chinaman, Mr. Long," Spittles broke in eagerly, "it's a way of life!"

Longarm held up his hand. He was weary of the turn this conversation had taken. If there was one thing he couldn't abide, it was ganging up on a person —or a race. It always smelled, no matter how justified the action was alleged to be. "I get the drift. You gentlemen are in favor of keeping the Chinese out— and I'm here to see what I can do to slow down the flow of illegal Chinese being smuggled across the border. So I need your help."

"Anything we can do, Long," Ryan said. "You just tell us."

Longarm looked at Spittles. "You say no Chinaman came to claim the body of that dead giant who worked for Lillian M'Ling?"

"That's what I said. Very unusual."

"And no one knows who those two white men were who posed as Chinamen?"

"That's right," said Duff Ryan, "and they'll be

planted in boot hill tomorrow without a single mourner. Mark my words. And the town will have to foot the bill." He snapped that last off angrily, as if this were the worst aspect of the business.

Longarm looked back at Spittles. "Does this look like a typical Tong attack, Spittles?"

Spittles glanced nervously at his boss, then cleared his throat. Longarm waited, watching Spittles carefully. There was a lot that didn't make sense about this murder of Rolf La Tour. It would be interesting if Spittles tried to cover that fact up. "No," Spittles said, taking a deep breath. "I would say that this was not only not a typical Tong murder, it had nothing to do with a Tong."

"Why?" asked Duff Ryan, surprised.

"The white men posing as Chinese, for one thing. And that little ivory hatchet that La Tour showed us. The Chinese keep these formalities among themselves. A member of another Tong might receive such a warning, but never a white man." Spittles smiled. "We are barbarians, you see. We do not deserve the courtesy."

Longarm nodded. "La Tour was murdered, but not by a Tong. By someone who wanted the Ong Leong Tong to get the blame."

"I agree," said Spittles.

"That's not how it read in the paper, Spittles," Duff Ryan said, frowning.

Spittles smiled at his boss. "It will sell more papers this way, Mr. Ryan, and provide one more reason for legislation against Chinese immigration." He looked at Longarm then, a smug look on his face. "And if the one behind the murder of La Tour wanted us to blame the Chinese, why tip him off that we do *not* so believe?"

"I agree," Longarm said, reluctantly appreciating Spittles's good judgment in this matter. Spittles was a hard man to like, but that didn't mean he was without intelligence, Longarm realized. He continued, "Who is

61

this fellow La Tour mentioned before he died? Scott? And China Belle?"

Spittles shook his head. "I don't know any China Belle. Could be a local Chinese prostitute, but that's unlikely. Scott, however, is another story. He must have been referring to Scott McPherson."

"That would be Constable Scott McPherson of the Royal Mounted Police," Duff Ryan explained. "La Tour was working with him and his superior, Inspector Brock Wilde. You'll like him, Long. He's as big as you are—and just as tough. The two of them had been working with Rolf—and with Scally earlier—in an effort to find the route the smuggled immigrants have been taking."

"Where can I find them?"

"Chilliwack, Canada. Just across the border. I'd say a day's ride."

Longarm nodded and got to his feet abruptly.

"No need to hurry off, Marshal," Duff Ryan protested. "Have another drink with us."

"Thanks, Ryan. But I'm anxious to see what kind of horseflesh I can rent at your livery." He smiled. "And what you'll be charging."

"I'll go with you," said the man grandly, "and there will be no charge; I'll see to that. You're a federal officer, working for all of us, putting your skill and your life on the line to make this a better, cleaner place. It's the least I can do."

Longarm almost laughed aloud. With a line of bull-shit like that, Duff Ryan was a natural to make it big in politics—after he had finished taking over all of Slab City, that is. The two men left the Skidroad Palace together, leaving Spittles at the table to watch them go, an ironic gleam in his eye.

Walking back to his hotel less than an hour later to gather his gear for the ride north into Canada, Long-

arm was forced to pull up quickly as a tall blonde
Valkyrie stepped into his path.

"I am Helga Jensen," she proclaimed, arms akimbo.
"And I see also now who you run with already—that
octopus! So soon you are his man!"

Longarm realized he did not have to introduce himself to this woman. She knew already who he was, and
why he was in Slab City. This was the Helga Jensen
who owned the mill and most, if not all, of that
wretched real estate that made up Chinatown. She was
easily as tall as Longarm, and since she owned a
lumber mill, she obviously felt she should dress like a
logger. Her bright blonde hair was braided and worn
like a crown around her head. She wore a bright red
plaid cotton shirt and a heavy denim jacket. Denim
pants and high-laced boots completed her outfit. It
was strictly masculine garb, but the sight of an at-
tractive woman, thus attired, had a peculiarly arous-
ing effect on Longarm. He could not help but notice
the ample thrust of her breasts as they tugged against
the shirt's buttons, and the narrow hips and long,
smooth thighs revealed almost lovingly by the tight
denim pants. Even the boots, following the curve of
her calf muscle as closely as they did, enhanced her
striking, powerful figure.

Longarm grinned at her. "Why don't you let me
explain?" he suggested, taking out a cheroot.

She nodded briskly. "Ya! You explain to me how
you enforce the law if you are in that man's pocket.
How much already has he paid you? I see how he
lead you around by the nose. And a big man like you!
Ashamed, you should be!"

"If it were like that, Helga, I *would* be ashamed."

Her beautiful, sky-blue eyes narrowed. "You deny
this?"

"Helga, this is no place to talk," Longarm said, with
sudden impatience. "I am on my way to my hotel.
Maybe we can talk about this later."

"A real dude, that's what you are!"

Longarm had had enough. She was beautiful and striking and he did not want to make an enemy of her, but being browbeaten in public was not to Longarm's taste. He stuck his cheroot into the corner of his mouth, and with his left hand on her shoulder, pushed her gently to one side so that he could proceed.

She gave reluctantly, her face darkening, her blue eyes snapping icily at him. Two burly loggers, obviously Helga's lieutenants, had been keeping back against a storefront behind her. But the moment Longarm put a hand on Helga and brushed her aside, they leaped furiously into his path.

"Ain't no man goin' to handle Helga!" the nearest fellow growled; and suiting actions to words, he took a generous swipe at Longarm.

Longarm had expected the blow. He stepped inside it, blocked it with his forearm, and then brought his knee up into the man's groin, causing him to double over with a short cry, his face contorted in sudden pain. Longarm caught him once on the side of the jaw with a roundhouse right and the man spun, semi-conscious, to the board sidewalk. The other fellow immediately assumed a boxer's stance with his fists held low. He milled in a backward-leaning posture, striking out with rights and lefts, the onlookers that had swarmed from all sides cheering him on loudly. But as he continued to back-pedal, the cheers turned to jeers.

Longarm laughed at the man also, touched the brim of his hat to Helga Jensen, and continued on to the hotel.

The horse Duff Ryan had offered him—like everything else he owned, he had nothing but the finest horseflesh for rent or sale at his livery—was a big, powerful Morgan, a breed that had never disappointed Longarm. He found himself looking forward to the ride into Canada, and was not even bothered that he

would undoubtedly have to camp out overnight, starting out, as he was, this late in the day. He was anxious
to shake the tensions—and the smells—of Slab City.

On his ride north that afternoon, Longarm—following
the directions given him by Duff Ryan—found himself
cutting through a towering stand of firs. Only dim
patches of blue sky were visible through the thick
cover of branches. He was in a hauntingly quiet,
cathedral-like world, the silence of which was punctuated only by the echoing calls of the countless song-
birds and the sighing of the wind in the branches far
overhead that sounded to Longarm like surf breaking
on some distant shore. Occasionally he rode through
a slanting bar of sunlight that knifed through the damp
gloom of the place, transforming everything it touched.
    The spongy forest duff completely muffled the sound
of his Morgan's hoofs. Looking behind him, Longarm
saw no hoofprints. His passage through the woodland
left no trace, it seemed. It was as if he were moving
through water. Clumps of tall ferns, pearled with moisture, dotted the ground like potted palms inside the
lobby of some fabulous hotel. The few clearings he
rode through were covered with tangles of blueberry,
wild grape, and ground maple. The powerful whiff of
ripe blackberries baking in the sun whenever he crossed
these clearings impressed him with the abundance of
food that any smuggled Chinamen slipping through
from the border could count upon.
    But as Longarm had reminded himself when first he
had reached this dim, forested world, they would need
compasses to keep themselves on course. The sky was
as distant and remote as the stars themselves, and even
when the sky was visible, it was usually blanketed by
a heavy raft of rainclouds rolling in off the Sound.
And they had better be dressed warmly, too. The big
trees dripped moisture constantly. At times, Longarm

had the uncanny sensation that he was riding over the floor of a submerged world.

Still, if the smuggled Cantonese did dress warmly and did indeed make sure at least one of their number carried a compass, tracking them through this fabulous wilderness would be well-nigh impossible. Longarm began to realize then what a nearly impossible task poor Hitch Scally had been given. And La Tour, who was, after all, just Slab City's town constable. Longarm hoped these Canadian Mounties had a better way. Stopping the aliens long before they got this far seemed like the obvious solution. Why this famous new police force hadn't figured this out already, and acted on it, was something Longarm aimed to find out.

He felt the floor of the forest lifting under him steadily. Soon the heft and stature of the big firs grew less awesome. More and more light began to filter down through the branches, and occasionally the Morgan's shod hoofs struck through to the caprock underneath as the spongy ground cover thinned out. Twice he saw deer bounding off through the trees at his approach. The clearings were now more extensive, and were alive with berries and ground vines. Wildflowers appeared in bright clusters.

Once he saw the humps of feeding grizzlies browsing on the borders of a clearing. They were a female and her cubs, and she was on her hind legs in an instant, paws held before her in a prayerful attitude as she watched him through her tiny, nearsighted eyes. But it was her nose that told her what she needed to know. As Longarm pulled up cautiously and patted the neck of his mount to steady it, the big grizzly dropped to all fours and crashed through the brush and back into the cover of the forest, her cubs scrambling and rolling before her.

Longarm reached the pass he had been looking for soon after, rode through it and into the valley floor beyond. He came to the river he had been told to

66

watch for, and pulled up on its bank, looking for a place to cross. It was midsummer, but the water was running deep and fast. He saw a spot where he might be able to ford the river—a rocky ledge that extended under the water better than halfway across and was easily visible just under the water's surface. But beyond the ledge, the water swirled in black, powerful eddies that were snatching with a quick and savage violence at every twig and branch that swept by.

Longarm decided to move along the river, heading northeast and away from Chilliwack in an effort to find a safer ford. It soon became a matter of finding a trail between the river's bank and the timber's edge. He crossed several small feeder creeks and occasionally found clear going through natural meadows whose wild hay stood amber and tousled. The river quieted at last and made great roundabout loops on its way to the Sound. He crossed here and turned northwest, back in the direction of Chilliwack.

At times, the face of a cliff came down to block him, whereupon he took to the foothills, and using them, slowly crested the small range and dropped again into another river valley. The border, according to the directions he had been given, was across this river and just beyond the next range. He should be able to see the smoke of Chilliwack from the trail over the hills.

But it was sunset by this time, and he decided to camp by the stream for the night. He found a grassy sward on a bank overlooking the stream, started a fire, and cooked up bacon and coffee. He kept the fire going while dusk came on, and took out a cheroot and lit it. The occasion was too special, the weariness too complete to haggle with himself over whether or not he should smoke. He lit up and sucked the smoke into his lungs, stretched out his legs, and leaned back against his saddle. The hobbled Morgan was grazing on the lush grass a few yards downstream.

It had been a long ride through beautiful country,

and he was thinking of this as he sat back and puffed contentedly on his cheroot. It was too bad that a land as magnificent as this had to be settled by mealy-mouthed, tight-fisted boneheads who could think only of how much money they could get out of it. As Longarm had ridden through those corridors of giant firs, he had thought more than once of Duff Ryan's boasts —and he saw now how puny and inappropriate they were to the size of this land.

And surely there was enough room for a few more Chinamen. As there had been for the Swedes, the Irish, the Welsh, the Scotch, and all the rest.

A fish broke the river's surface, the sound carrying through the still air in a widening ripple of soft echoes, and somewhere a deer made a racket in the brush on its way to water. The crickets were setting up a howl. Dusk drifted in, thinly shadowing the world. His small fire brightened in the gathering darkness. The deer still stirred the brush, now closer. He listened to it for a moment, his mind only half on it.

He bent forward to drop another twig on the fire and heard the rustling progress of the deer in the brush once more. The disinterested part of his mind began to pay attention. The sound stopped, then began again. It grew nearer each time he heard it. Longarm glanced downstream to the Morgan. It was no longer feeding on the grass, but was looking behind Longarm, its ears tilted alertly forward.

Longarm was lying full-length with his back leaning solidly against the saddle, the cheroot glowing in his mouth, his head turned to the flames of his campfire. He moved his head slightly to watch the black edge of the brush and timber fifty feet behind him. At that moment he felt the wind sweeping off the river toward the timber. It raised his hair slightly in its gentle passage.

Hell, he thought. *That ain't right.* He was upwind of any critter moving out of that wood toward this

68

water. The smell of his fire, not to mention the human stench of his person, should long since have warned away any well-brought-up deer.

The fire was a small one by this time, burning on its last few branches. He sat up, his mind flooded with warning as it fully awoke. He swept his hand across the fire's ashes and flung wood and sparks in a shower through the shadows—then ducked his head low and rolled away from the saddle, snatching his Winchester out of its boot as he went.

The shot came immediately after, the slug nicking the top of his saddle and whining off across the river. He saw the flash of the gun in the thicket and rolled again, then steadied himself and squeezed off a shot. A return shot, from farther down the stream, snapped at him, and this one sliced the grass beside him, its passage sounding like an angry insect. He rolled again, momentarily losing his orientation on the thicket. He still could hear movement through it, and realized, from the heaviness and boldness of it, that he was up against more than one assailant.

The shadows were deepening rapidly now all along the meadow, and the Morgan was nickering nervously, edging back toward the river. He steadied himself, levered a fresh round into the chamber, and waited. The sound of moccasined feet pounding, the swish of grass being thrust aside by thrusting legs, came to him clearly. His finger rested on the trigger. He waited a moment longer and then stood up.

The Indian, wearing a bowler hat with a small feather stuck in the band, was caught by surprise. His eyes grew wide as he dropped his shoulder and tried to dodge to one side. Longarm fired the rifle from his hip, levered it rapidly, then flung himself to the ground. His round had slammed into the Indian just above the swell of his gut. He uttered a startled grunt and toppled into the grass beside Longarm and began to crawl toward him. Longarm fired at him through the grass and the fellow quieted.

Another shot came from upstream. The slug hit the ground just in front of him, spraying moist clods of dirt into his face. Keeping his head down, he sprinted back to where his saddle lay and dropped behind it, facing upstream. He levered a fresh cartridge into the firing chamber and waited for the next gunflash. It came almost immediately, piercingly bright against the dark line of trees. The round buried itself in the saddle's cantle, dangerously close to Longarm's temple. He swore softly, steadied his rifle on the spot where the flash had come from, and squeezed the trigger.

A muffled cry followed Longarm's shot. He heard something heavy and metallic drop through foliage to the ground, then the sound of a man running. Longarm was on his feet in an instant, rushing into the dark timber after him. The Indian was in full retreat before him, panting and grunting as he smashed through the brush deeper into the timber. At last Longarm realized the futility of the chase and turned back to the river. He found the rifle—an old Henry—where the Indian had dropped it. He smashed it against a tree, and hurled it into the brush. When he reached the river, he stood quietly for a moment to listen. He thought he could still hear the Indian in motion through the woods, apparently still circling away.

The Indian he had shot was lying in a messy tangle of blood-clotted grass, breathing shallowly, his eyes wide. Longarm knelt beside him, but in the now almost complete darkness, he found it difficult to see his face clearly or do much about his wounds. As he tried to turn the man slightly to examine his shoulder wound, the fellow's breathing stopped. There was an ugly, choking gasp, and the Indian's body seemed to shrink into the grass. Longarm stood up, looked for a moment down at the dead man, and decided to move his camp.

70

Chilliwack was a settlement of perhaps sixty houses built of logs and riven cedar shingles, all scattered along a sluggish creek and up the sides of the surrounding hills. The smoke from late breakfast fires drifted out of tin chimneys, and men strolled the streets in high-laced boots, deerskin jackets, and slouch hats with the brims turned down to keep off the intermittent rain. Riders drifted in and rode past, their horses clopping almost silently through the fetlock-deep mud. Longarm saw a pack train winding down through the hills toward Chilliwack from the west.

He rode past a pair of saloons and a big hay shed, skirted the general store, and rode up a sharp rise to a large log-and-shake cabin on a grassy bluff over-looking the town. There were two flagpoles before the building. The Canadian flag fluttered damply from one, the flag of the Northwest Mounted Police from the other. Longarm dismounted, dropped his reins over the hitch rail, and strode inside.

A corporal with a strange round hat perched on the top of his head showed Longarm into Inspector Wilde's office. Wilde got to his feet as the corporal closed the door behind them, and walked briskly around his desk to greet Longarm.

As he shook Longarm's hand, he smiled warmly and introduced himself. "Inspector Brock Wilde, Marshal. I'm pleased to meet you in this heathen outpost!"

Wilde's grip was a strong one, and Longarm found himself looking into a ruddy, freckled face and meet-ing the powerful, searching glance of clear blue eyes. Wilde wore his rust-colored mustache down well past the corners of his mouth. His hair, of the same color as his mustache, was clipped short, the temples clean.

"I'm Deputy U.S. Marshal Custis Long," Longarm replied.

"My pleasure, Marshal. Sit down." As the inspector went back behind his desk, he said, "You're here about

71

that poor devil Scally, I have no doubt. He was work-ing closely with us. A good man. That was a bloody shame."

"That's part of it, I reckon. Marshal Billy Vail in Colorado wants the scalps of the men who did it. He knew Scally—and like you, he thought he was a good man. But we've got a smuggling problem too, I hear, at the back of it."

"Indeed we have. But stopping that smuggling is easier said than done." He leaned back in his chair. "How was your trip from Slab City?"

"This country surprises a man. The trees are big—almost a mite too big, I'm thinking. And water. You get it underfoot and in the air."

Wilde leaned forward eagerly, his hands clasped be-fore him on the desk, a beaming smile on his face. "This is big country. Dwarfs a man, it does. Scales him down to his proper size. I love it! So the journey was uneventful. Good."

"Didn't mean to say that. Had some trouble last night, about sundown."

"Oh?"

Longarm told Wilde about the attack, describing in detail the appearance of the Indian he had killed. When he finished, there was a frown on Wilde's face.

"Some Siwash, most likely. After your horse and your weapons."

"Siwash?"

"Trash Indians. No bloody good, not a man jack of them. Coastal tribes native to this region. Untrust-worthy lot, for sure—either at your feet or at your throat."

Longarm nodded. That could have been all it was, of course. Just two Indians who had caught sight of him riding out of Slab City and thought they would have easy pickings once they caught him alone on the trail. Until he learned differently, that explanation would have to serve.

"Inspector, Town Constable La Tour is dead, killed supposedly by the Ong Leong Tong."

"You say 'supposedly.' "

"There are too many holes in that explanation, looks like."

"So he was murdered by parties unknown—like Scally?"

Longarm told Wilde what had happened in Lillian M'Ling's opium emporium. When he finished, Wilde leaned back in his chair.

"*China Belle*, is it? And La Tour mentioned Scott."

"That's right."

Wilde got to his feet quickly and walked to the door. He pulled it open and told the corporal to scare up Constable Scott McPherson on the instant. Longarm heard the scraping of a chair against the wooden floor, followed by the sound of a door closing. Wilde turned back to face the marshal, closing the door behind him.

"McPherson will be here soon, Marshal Long. You will have a few answers then, I am sure. He'll be glad to tell you about *China Belle*."

McPherson, a short, stocky fellow with almost jet black hair and thick eyebrows, made himself comfortable on Inspector Wilde's cot along the wall. He had been genuinely sorry to hear of La Tour's death, but his dark eyes had lit when Wilde mentioned what Longarm had told him about *China Belle*.

"*China Belle*," he told Longarm, "is the name of an old clipper that used to run tea from China. For a while it fetched guano from Peru, and supposedly that's what it's bringing in now." McPherson smiled. "But I doubt it, from what you just told me. They're bringing in a cargo that smells as bad, maybe—but it ain't guano."

Longarm looked at Wilde. "If you know the ship and you know what it's bringing in, why don't you stop it, send it back?"

73

"Until this moment, Marshal," explained a very pleased Wilde, "we didn't know which of the four ships moving up the coast was our target. Now, thanks to you—and poor La Tour—we can move." Wilde looked at McPherson. "Do you have any idea where it will be putting in?"

"Pirates' Cove. I'm sure of it this time."

Wilde glanced at Longarm. "The last shipment we guessed wrong, both as to which ship was smuggling the Chinamen and where they were bringing them ashore. Puget Sound is an ideal dropping-off spot for these smugglers—hidden coves, islands, clear beaches. But this time we'll be on hand to greet them—and send them right back where they came from!"

The inspector got to his feet, his face flushed with excitement. "We have until midafternoon before we pull out. Allow me to show you around this modest post and help you get settled."

Longarm got to his feet. "That's mighty nice of you, Inspector. I'd like a bath and some food, in that order, and a quiet place for a quick nap. I didn't sleep much last night."

"Would my quarters suffice?"

"That'd be right generous."

Wilde moved out from behind his desk and slapped Longarm warmly on the back. "You're a much taller man than Scally, Marshal—and obviously more sober than La Tour. I'm beginning to think that with your arrival, we're going to get a handle on this miserable business. It is a pleasure to have you!"

As the two men left the headquarters building with Longarm, he felt gratified that his arrival was bringing such swift action. But he was not as certain as Wilde that it was going to be all that easy from here on.

And he kept wondering about those two Indians. . . .

Chapter 4

"Here," said Inspector Wilde, handing the binoculars to Longarm.

Wrapping his reins about the saddle horn, Longarm brought the glasses up to his eyes and focused carefully. What he saw was an old three-masted clipper ship, most of its sails furled, moving into Pirates' Cove, just as McPherson had predicted. The ship rode low in the water. Longarm could see the crew moving up and down the rigging. The only sails the ship was using this close to land were the jibs and the spanker. As Longarm followed it with the binoculars, it was suddenly lost behind a forested headland.

He handed the binoculars back to Wilde. "I didn't see any Chinamen," he remarked.

"And you won't," Wilde replied. "They are kept well below, jammed together like sardines—without the olive oil."

Longarm nodded. The sailing vessel had reappeared on the other side of the headland. As he watched, its anchor splashed into the water.

"They'll be waiting until dark before unloading their cargo," McPherson said. He was sitting his mount just behind Wilde. There was a pleased look on his face.

This time he had guessed right concerning the cove the smugglers would use.

A rifle shot cracked in the damp air behind them. The look on McPherson's face changed abruptly, and Longarm saw a quick stain spreading on his shoulder, even as he clapped his hand over his tunic and toppled from his horse. Longarm wheeled his Morgan about and started toward the line of trees from which the shot had come.

"Take care of Scott!" Longarm called back over his shoulder as he raced over the ground. Another shot cracked. Longarm kept his head low and drew his Colt. The second shot had come from a clump of bushes just in front of a large fir. He sent a bullet into the bushes. A third shot snapped at him, cutting through the foliage and buzzing angrily past his right ear. Longarm sent another shot into the bush and this slug sent the marksman bolting from cover.

In a moment he was behind the fir, pelting for the safety of the woodland. Longarm passed the bushes and cut around the fir. The man was running with his rifle in his hand. He appeared to be limping slightly. The fellow heard the thunder of the horse's hoofs, turned, and went down on one knee. As he brought up the rifle, Longarm aimed carefully and squeezed off another shot.

The bullet caught the man in the forehead, slamming his head back so violently that it seemed to take his whole body with it. Dismounting on the run, Longarm ran up to the man and knelt beside him. The hole in his forehead was reasonably neat, with only a thin trickle of dark blood oozing from it slowly. The back of his head, however, was resting in a sodden mass of shattered bone and brain. It was the other Siwash, Longarm had no doubt.

He wore the same nondescript clothing as his companion: Levi's and a cotton shirt, a floppy hat with a lone feather stuck in its band. He had kept after Long-

76

arm, it seemed, to finish what he had begun the day before. Longarm picked up the Indian's rifle. It was a new one, still smelling of the oil it had been packed in —a Winchester .44-40.

Longarm got up onto his feet and, bringing the rifle with him, returned to Wilde and the wounded McPherson. Scott was back up on his horse, slumped over the saddle horn, his face a pasty gray.

"He'll be all right," Wilde said, "but we'd better get him back to the post."

Wilde reached over to clap the grim Scott on his back in an effort to buck up the man's spirit, but he succeeded only in causing the tight-lipped constable to groan slightly under his breath. Wilde appeared not to notice as he wheeled his horse around.

"I'll stay here," said Longarm, "and keep an eye on that ship down there."

Wilde nodded. "As you wish, sir. We'll be back before sundown. Plenty of time to catch those coolies." His face went grim. "I assume that shot was meant for you. Am I right?"

Longarm nodded and watched the two ride off. The plan, discussed earlier, had been to scout the cove in order to make sure it was the correct one, then go back for more Mounties. As Longarm watched Wilde and McPherson, he couldn't help wondering why the Mounties dressed in such outlandishly loud uniforms: bright scarlet jackets, steel gray riding breeches, gleaming black boots, white buckskin gauntlets, and white cork helmets with brass-link chin straps. So bright and resplendent did the two of them look that Longarm had no doubt that if that ship below them in the cove had anyone on lookout, Wilde and McPherson must already have advertised their presence.

Longarm shrugged and went back to get his horse. It sure as hell promised to be an interesting night, at that.

The four Mounties with Inspector Brock Wilde were crouched behind Longarm, who was himself peering over a massive boulder set in the sand about fifty yards from the shoreline. Longarm was not at all happy with Wilde for bringing only four Mounties, but Wilde had laughed off Longarm's objections, insisting that a single Mountie was worth a dozen coolies. The men were certainly well-armed. They all carried formidable long-barreled Deane & Adams revolvers and Snider-Enfield carbines, a firearm Longarm had heard about, but never fired. The new Winchester he had taken from the dead Siwash was leaning next to his own Winchester against the boulder beside him.

Long rowboats, the stroke of their oars flashing in the moonlight, had already left the *China Belle* and were nearing the beach. As the boats got closer, Longarm could see how heavily laden they were with their human cargo. They were riding so low that Longarm could see occasional waves breaking over the gunwales. There were six boats in all.

With sudden, powerful strokes from the oars, the first boat was driven well up onto the beach. Sailors jumped into the shallow water and steadied the boat as the coolies were quickly unloaded. They scrambled through the shallow water up onto the sandy shoreline, their speech filling the night with a sudden alien clamor.

"We'll just wait," Wilde said softly to Longarm, "until they're all ashore."

The marshal nodded. Brock Wilde was pleased. This time, he had promised Longarm, the Crown was going to have the pleasure of sending these coolies back to where they came from.

The first batch of Chinamen were now huddled in a shivering, chattering group a little way up the beach while they waited for their brothers to be landed. The boats drove into the beach, the coolies piled out, and soon the beach was shrill with the chatter of the ex-

78

cited Chinese and the surly barks of the sailors in charge. After the boats discharged their cargoes, they went back for still more.

Longarm was astonished. It was difficult to believe that this many living human beings could survive for so long packed beneath the decks of that single clipper ship. He remembered his look at the ship through the binoculars. He had seen not a single coolie on deck.

After two more trips back to the ship, all of the coolies had apparently been landed. Wilde tapped Longarm smartly on the shoulder, then left to join his men. He heard the inspector speak softly to his crouching men, and then watched as Wilde stood up and, with his carbine held at the ready, led his four resplendent Mounties in good formation out onto the beach.

Longarm held back a moment to watch as Wilde led his men across the sand toward the noisy hubbub about the boats. Then he stepped out from behind the boulder himself. Wilde and his Mounties must have advanced to within less than twenty yards before they were noticed amid all the confusion attendant upon lining up the coolies and arranging them into some kind of formation for the long march ahead of them.

One of the sailors, a large, burly fellow with a great black beard and a white cotton shirt under his sea jacket, spun to face Wilde, a look of pure astonishment on his face. He had been in the process of issuing orders, and it was obvious to Longarm that this was the sailor in charge. Abruptly, the seaman laughed.

Wilde halted. "You can just hold it right there, me buckos!" the inspector called to them, his voice cutting through the damp night. "You are all under arrest, in the name of the Crown!"

The Chinese quieted down suddenly, then crowded hastily together, forming a single, quivering mass of humanity, their appearance now utterly pathetic. Some began to wail in despair. Longarm could guess why.

They had just finished one grueling voyage, and were now facing another. But the huge sailor to whom Wilde had spoken pulled himself up to his full height, arms akimbo, and continued to laugh at Wilde, the seven or more sailors with him moving cautiously behind him. None of the sailors were armed, and Longarm had the sudden, uneasy conviction that the arrest of these smugglers and the capture of this cargo of aliens was proceeding much too easily.

Longarm glanced at the coolies. They were no longer as silent as before. The wailing had increased as others joined in. The sound of their excited, dismayed jabber sank to a low, steady pitch. If this was a trap set to close on Wilde and his Mounties, they had no inkling of it.

The big sailor waited until Wilde got closer before he spoke. "And who the hell is the Crown, mister?"

If this was meant to infuriate Wilde, it succeeded. "You'll see!" he cried. "And you will soon feel the lash of its justice—that you will!"

"No, he won't, Mountie!"

The voice was harsh and carried ominously above the murmur of the coolies—and it came from behind Longarm. The marshal spun about.

But he was not fast enough. A rifle butt caught him smartly on the side of his head and he went down. As he fell, he was struck again in the back by a well-placed calked boot. Flipping groggily over, Longarm saw a gang of hooded men, armed with rifles, stepping past him as they advanced on Wilde and his Mounties. The Mounties hesitated for just a moment, but that surprised pause was fatal. A fusillade of shots dropped three of the Mounties before they could get off a shot. Longarm saw Wilde fire point-blank into the foremost of the hooded men, and then receive a shot that sent him spinning to the beach. The remaining Mountie accounted for a second hooded man, and then caught a slug in his midsection and buckled to the ground.

Longarm, his knees like water, attempted to get back on his feet and bring his Colt around. A kick from behind caught him in the side, the heavy toe of the boot digging well in under his ribs. Longarm felt himself tumbling, his hat flying, and caught a momentary glimpse of hooded heads turning on him, rifles gleaming as they lifted to track him. . . .

The big, black-bearded sailor was taking Longarm's wallet from him. Through pain-slitted eyes, the marshal watched the man get to his feet and flash his badge to the other sailors standing beside him. Dimly, as if from a great distance, he heard their laughter. Two Chinese, obviously members of the crew, joined the encircling sailors, and Longarm then saw the captain step to the big sailor's side and take the wallet. Surprisingly, the captain was an Oriental—a large and impressive man who told the big sailor to put the wallet back. He spoke in a curiously clipped British accent.

"What'll we do with him, Captain?" the sailor asked.

"Leave him with the others."

"Liable to bring the whole damn U.S. Government down on us. He's a federal law officer."

The captain frowned; then a slight smile softened his heavy features. "Can you use any additional hands on the voyage back, mister?"

The fellow smiled quickly and nodded his head in sudden agreement. "Yes, sir, Captain, I sure as hell can. That hold smells like one big outhouse. Someone has to clean it out. This here son of a bitch is big enough, and that's a fact. I got a few other lubbers who need the exercise too. Hell, I might even put the poor bastard in charge. He's got the rank, sure enough!"

The captain nodded curtly. "Give him back his wallet and bring him aboard, then. I want to catch the tide. This has already taken longer than I planned."

As the captain vanished through the crush of sailors

still staring down at Longarm, the bearded sailor—obviously an officer on the *China Belle*—returned Longarm's wallet to his inside jacket pocket and then motioned to two sailors standing close by. Furious that he could not seem to command his limbs or fight back in any way, Longarm felt himself being lifted by the two men.

The starlit night spun dizzyingly above him. He heard the sound of feet splashing through water beneath him, and then he was swung through the air to come down heavily in the bottom of a boat. For a moment his head sank beneath the bilge water. He tried to lift his head, and felt the filthy brine flooding his nostrils, burning his eyes. Then a rough hand grabbed his hair and hauled him upright to deposit him with his back against a heavy coil of rope in the stern.

Longarm could still manage to keep his eyes open just enough to get some idea of what was happening around him. As the boat was pushed off the sand and then rowed away from the beach, he glimpsed the bodies of Wilde and the four Mounties lying untended on the beach—with no sign at all of the coolies or the hooded gang that had obviously been waiting on that shoreline for them—and for Longarm and the Mounties.

He found that he could open his eyes wider. Slowly, carefully, he clenched and unclenched his right fist. The wires were no longer down. He no longer hovered on the borderline of consciousness. The sense of nightmare passed, but he was in no position to make any sudden moves. His hat was back there on the beach along with his Colt and Winchester. But he was still wearing his coat and vest—and in his vest pocket still rested his .44 caliber whore pistol, fully loaded.

Feigning complete unconsciousness, Longarm made the sailors manhandle him up the treacherous rope ladder leading to the *China Belle*'s deck. They were not gentle with him, however, and he met the deck at last with such brutal suddenness that he almost lost consciousness a second time. He was then carried below decks and flung unceremoniously into a small cabin, where he found himself coming to life beside a bewhiskered and thoroughly drunk sailor curled up in a corner, his head resting inches from a foul-smelling slop jar. Longarm glanced at the door that had slammed shut behind him, and saw bars on a small, round window. A dim oil lamp smoked yellowly from a hook on the bulkhead beside the door. The brig. He had been thrown into the ship's brig.

He listened for sounds that might tell him how close they were to sailing. Soon the decks above his head seemed to have their full complement of running feet. He heard orders being given and then the sound of a great chain being hauled out of the water. They were pulling up the anchor. In a few minutes the ship began to ride somewhat higher, freer. He felt the ship heeling over as it put about. The shouting of orders continued, but the slap of running feet had all but ceased. The sailors were above the decks now, swarming about the rigging as they unfurled the sails.

Longarm gained his feet and prodded the drunken sailor awake with his foot. As soon as the man opened his eyes, Longarm kicked him gently in the ribs. The fellow opened wide his bloodshot eyes and shrank from Longarm.

"Get up," Longarm told him. "And scream your fool head off."

"What . . . what's that . . . ?"

"You heard me. Get up!"

The tone of command in Longarm's voice alerted the sailor. He moistened his dry lips and tried to push himself erect. He took an uncommonly long time about it, and, in exasperation, Longarm reached out and grabbed the collar of his filthy shirt and hauled him roughly to his feet. For emphasis, and in order to get the man's complete attention, Longarm slammed him none too gently back against the bulkhead.

"I am a desperate man," he told the sailor with quiet emphasis. "You got that, sailor?"

The man nodded hastily. "Sure, I got it, mister. But what the hell you got against me?"

"Nothing, if you do as I say."

"Listen, you just tell me what you want, that's all. You just tell me."

"Yell. Yell your fool lungs out. And kick on that door. Do it until you bring someone down here to tend to you. Make like you got the horrors, you hear me?"

"Hell, that ain't no bother at all, mister! I been doing that the whole damn voyage, mostly." He gave Longarm a sick smile and then hurled himself at the door.

The man's voice, raised to the pitch Longarm required, was like a rough saw cutting through Longarm's eardrums. The fellow had a fearsome enthusiasm for his task and it was plain that he was not a stranger to the real horror of delirium tremens. Removing the derringer from his vest pocket, Longarm unclipped the butt from the watch chain and flattened himself against the bulkhead beside the door.

When the sailor saw the weapon in Longarm's hand, he redoubled his racket. Wincing, Longarm waited as patiently as he could. At last he heard running footsteps approaching the cabin. A shout from the other side of the door, which told him his companion's name was Jib, only increased the sailor's pounding and caterwauling. It was a howl, to Longarm's way of thinking, that could drive a wolf to suicide. If this didn't do the trick, he was damned if he knew what would.

The fellow outside the door gave up trying to quiet Jib with threats. Longarm heard—above Jib's fearsome howl—the sound of the bolt being drawn, the

84

chain being unlocked. Still howling like a banshee with the colic, Jib backed away from the door and flattened himself against the opposite bulkhead. He was giving this performance all he had, and Longarm was grateful.

The door was pulled open and a burly sailor burst in, his face dark with rage. He looked neither to the right nor to the left as he went for Jib. Jib ducked away. The fellow grabbed his shoulder and hung on. Longarm stepped out of the brig, slammed the door shut, and shot the bolt. The key was still hanging from the padlock. He looped the chain quickly, locked it, turned the key, and headed for the companionway. Moving up it swiftly, he found the star-spangled sky suddenly blocked out by a burly sailor—with a marlinspike in his right fist.

"Now, what the hell're you doin' out of that—" he started to say to Longarm.

Then he saw the glint of Longarm's weapon and fell back swiftly, calling over his shoulder for all hands to help him. The prisoner was loose!

Bursting up onto the deck, Longarm looked quickly around and saw the sailors dropping to the deck from the rigging on all sides of him. Crouching, they started toward him. Longarm was in the center of the deck. His first thought was that if he could make it to the rail, he might be able to dive overboard and swim back to shore. But it was a suddenly forlorn hope as he saw the ranks of sailors closing in on him.

Abruptly he shoved his derringer out in front of him and slowly circled. "All right," Longarm growled, "I've got two rounds in this little fellow. Which one of you is going to be first?"

The sailors stopped, and some pulled back. Four Chinese sailors, however, pushed through the white sailors. Each one held a thin, curved sword in his hand. They were smaller in size than many of the white sailors, but were eager for the challenge, it seemed. As, crouching, they moved closer to Longarm, the other sailors let out a cheer and stepped back to watch. Nearing Longarm, the four Chinese spread out as if on some silent command, and surrounded him. He did not want to shoot these foolhardy men point-blank, but he saw no choice. It was obvious they did not believe he meant to shoot.

One Chinaman, braver even than his fellows, made a sudden lunge for Longarm, his blade slicing at him with a speed that made it almost invisible. Longarm drew back and fired into his assailant. With a loud screech, the Chinaman fell to the deck, clutching at his midsection. To Longarm's astonishment, he found his vest and the shirt under it hanging in tatters, a thin red line tracing from just under his chin all the way to his belly button. He did not have time to contemplate this, however, as another eager Chinaman drove at him, his long blade cutting the night air like heat lightning.

Again Longarm fired, and again his slug caught a Chinaman in his stomach, and once more he looked down to see his jacket and shirt hanging in bloody ribbons from his upper torso. This time he had been struck in the side, and the blade had sliced deeper. But now he had no bullets left, and as he spun to face his attackers coming at him from the rear, the rest of the sailors surged forward and sprang upon him. Countless hands grabbed at him. Men were shouting in his ear. But his bloody torso was making it difficult for anyone to get a good hold. In their excitement, they got in each other's way, and the remaining Chinamen were unable to use their deadly blades in such close quarters.

Spinning furiously, Longarm sent his would-be captors stumbling from him. Thoroughly angered by this time, Longarm picked up one of the Chinamen and hurled him at those sailors closest to him. They went down like tenpins. Another jumped on his back from behind, his forearm about Longarm's throat. He was pounding furiously on Longarm's chest, and his weight was causing Longarm's knees to buckle. Reaching back, Longarm grabbed the man's head and, burying his fingers in his hair, pulled him forward onto his shoulders, and then began to spin. The fellow soon went flying into a crowd of sailors—and the way seemed clear for Longarm to reach the ship's rail and dive over.

He dug for it, but was more exhausted than he realized. His boots slipped on the blood-slick deck and he went down. At once he was swarmed over by a pummeling, enraged crew. He felt his face being driven into the deck. He struggled furiously just to turn his head so that he could breathe.

A clipped British voice cut sharply through the uproar. It was the captain, ordering everyone off Longarm. The weight eased. He found he could lift his shoulders. Almost beyond exhaustion, he rolled over and glared up at the circle of his tormentors, wishing he had two more rounds—and his derringer still in his hand.

One of the two remaining Chinamen darted close to the captain and spoke to him in hurried Chinese, pointing, as he did so, to Longarm's ribboned chest. The two talked animatedly for a short while, and it seemed to Longarm that the sailor was the one protesting, and that finally he had his way. The captain nodded curtly to the sailor and looked down at Longarm, a barely perceptible smile on his Oriental face.

"This, it seems, is your lucky day," the captain said to Longarm. "I am informed by my countryman that this good fortune is deserved. I must admit, it is bloody strange that a minor official of your country should be so endowed, but there is no way to deny the imperatives of our ancestors."

The captain's remarkable speech—its content, as well as the British accent—left Longarm completely

87

astonished. What the man seemed to be saying was that they were not going to string him up to the nearest yardarm and strip his hide from him inch by inch after all, despite the havoc he had just wrought to a couple of his compatriots.

Longarm pulled himself wearily to his feet and stood before the captain. "You don't mind if we go through that again, do you? I'd like to take that speech of yours one bite at a time."

"One bite at a time?"

Longarm nodded. "What's my luck got to do with your ancestors?"

"Never mind." The captain smiled coldly. "Perhaps you are not all that lucky, at that. We are at least a mile from shore by now."

The captain stepped back and, with a casual wave of his hand, indicated that Longarm should be tossed overboard. He turned his back on the marshal then, and that was the last Longarm saw of the man as he was surrounded, lifted quickly, and then carried rapidly toward the ship's side. He was launched into the night with great vigor. He felt the salt air buffeting his hair, and then he struck the heaving water shoulder-first, knifing well below the dark water. His lungs were close to bursting before his face broke the surface. Treading water, he caught sight of the black bulk of the *China Belle*, its square sails bellying out with the wind, pulling rapidly away from him.

Treading water, he saw the dark line of the timbered coast. It looked to be an enormous distance away, and with each heave of the waves, it vanished from his sight. Reluctantly he ducked beneath the surface, wrestled off his boots, let them sink, then struck out for the shore. The thought of losing his boots—as well as his derringer—infuriated him. Some day he'd catch up to that slant-eyed Britisher and his bearded officer.

And then he forgot all about those two as he realized he was fighting the outgoing tide.

The salt water had cleaned out his superficial chest and side wounds pretty well by the time he crawled ashore on his hands and knees—and collapsed. When he awoke, it was close to dawn. Lifting his head, he saw that he was in a rocky cove with less than a foot of clear sandy beach under him. As the birds awoke in the trees farther inland and the sky lightened noticeably, he got to his feet and looked around.

But he could see nothing until he climbed farther inland and positioned himself on a small bluff that gave him a clear view of the coastline for miles in either direction. He sighted the beach where the coolies had been put ashore, well north of him. The dark stain on the white sand where Wilde and the four other dead Mounties lay was barely visible.

He started up the rough coast and was almost halfway to the beach when he was greatly relieved to see Inspector Wilde struggle to a sitting position, then stagger to his feet. For a moment, Wilde looked in bewilderment around him. Then he staggered over to one of the fallen bodies and went from one to another in growing anger and despair. He was about to leave the beach, more than likely heading back to where they had left their horses, when Longarm came within hailing distance. The man halted at Longarm's shout and began striding swiftly toward him.

It was a grim-visaged man who shook Longarm's hand warmly. A raw, sore-looking crease in the man's scalp ran from a point just above his left eyebrow all the way back past his ear, ending in a bloody, coagulated mess of sand and hair. The bullet's force had knocked Wilde out; fortunately it had not broken through his skull, but the man would bear the visible reminder of this past night's business for the rest of his life.

At that moment, however, Wilde was caught up in astonishment at Longarm's condition. "Cut to ribbons, you are. Why, man, you're a bloody mess. And no boots!"

Longarm explained about the boots. When he finished the account, he remarked, "At least I'm no longer bound for China. Most likely I'd have spent the whole damned voyage on my hands and knees scrubbing down the filthy hold where they packed in all those coolies."

"Mighty strange," the inspector said, shaking his head in wonder, "their letting you go like that. And it's a bloody good thing you can swim." He turned about, looked back at the beach, and sighed. "But for now, Marshal, we've got a melancholy task ahead of us, I am afraid. Three of those men are dead. One is pretty close to it—and judging from his condition, he probably wishes he *were* dead. I would be grateful for your help."

"You've got it."

"I'll see to the horses, then. Stay with that poor lad I told you about. See if you can quiet him down some. He's beginning to rave."

Longarm did not have to quiet the young Mountie down. By the time he reached the constable's side, he was dead, his face resting in the battered crown of Longarm's snuff-brown Stetson.

Four hours later, riding the Morgan, with a dead man's boots on his feet and a riddled scarlet tunic over his lacerated shirt and vest, he rode into Chilliwack beside Brock Wilde. Behind them, draped over their horses, came the four dead Mounties. As they trailed through Chilliwack, the sight of them brought activity to a halt among the cluster of shacks and log buildings that lined the main drag. Riding past the biggest saloon, Longarm heard the tinkle of the tinny piano inside stop abruptly as their sad procession emptied the place.

Once the four bodies were handed over to the quartermaster for burial, and Longarm was able to take his leave of the very despondent Brock Wilde and Scott McPherson, he cleaned himself off in a steaming tub and allowed the post surgeon to take a look at his wounds. The man, a poker-faced breed who spoke only French, seemed to delight in scraping off the scabs that had already formed over the lacerations. He poured liberal amounts of raw whiskey into the newly reopened wounds, and followed that with extensive bandaging wound tighter than a corset around Longarm's torso.

The next morning, Longarm rode out of Chilliwack with what was left of his coat, shirt, and vest rolled neatly inside his bedroll. He wore a buckskin jacket, his battered, snuff-brown Stetson was on his head, and a dead man's boots were still on his feet as he headed back to the beach, determined to pick up the trail of those coolies.

Wherever that trail led him—and he didn't care if it took him into the jaws of hell—he would follow it and nail to the nearest tree those responsible for the atrocity through which he and Brock Wilde had managed somehow to live.

Chapter 5

Longarm had little difficulty picking up the trail the coolies took after they left the cove. Feeling secure from pursuit after the way they had left things on the beach, the smugglers made little effort to cover their tracks as they hustled the coolies across the dripping landscape. For four days Longarm followed their trail. To his surprise, it led not south to Slab City as he had expected, but southwest instead, crossing the border well to the south of Chilliwack. From there on, the trail led along bottomland, through a low pass, and then down into a rugged expanse of timber.

The coolies and those driving them were on foot, and Longarm was mounted. He was gaining on them steadily. But they had close to a two days' start on him, counting the nights, and he was never able to catch up to them before they reached, on the fifth day, what Longarm realized at last was their destination: the bustling Great Northern railhead, Top Gap.

Longarm was high in the foothills of the Cascades by this time, only a few miles west of the railhead, when he came across Chinese laborers busy filling a ravine with small wheelbarrows of dirt. He pulled up on a rise, crossed his arms over the pommel of his saddle, and watched intently as the seemingly scrawny coolies labored. Most of them were dressed in blue cotton blouses, broad trousers, and either wooden shoes or oversized boots. Every one of them wore a great, broad, circular hat with a single jet black queue hanging down behind. They pulled their small barrows with a steady, jogging motion, looking neither to the right nor to the left. When they reached the edge of the ravine, they turned like tiny toys that some kid had wound up, and dumped the contents of their carts down the steep incline; then, almost without pause, they trotted back again to the side of the mountain, where others were diligently hacking away at the dirt and gravel and shoveling it into waiting carts, some using only their bare hands as tools. The result was a steady stream of wheelbarrows leaving the embankment with loads of dirt to be dumped into the ravine, each one returning empty almost immediately to begin the whole process over again. It would take a long time, Longarm realized, to fill that ravine for the trestle waiting to span it. But they would get it done.

Riding past them, he picked his way through the pass and came across other gangs of Chinese preparing the track's roadbed. He began counting them as he rode past, and at last he gave up. There must have been thousands of coolies working just this stretch of the Great Northern track alone. Those smuggled coolies he was trailing were probably already at work, lost in the shuffle of Chinamen that filled the area.

Just before entering Top Gap, he passed six enormous railroad bunkhouse cars on a siding. They were swarming with Chinese. The smell of rice, fish, and boiled tea filled the air. Top Gap itself was a narrow, constricted town spread out on both sides of the railroad that sliced through it, and was hemmed in on the north and south by towering cliffs. The town had no place to expand except to the east and west along each side of the tracks. Longarm rode a distance alongside the tracks before he came to the construction office of the Great Northern. It was located, he noted, on the second floor of a frame building, over a saloon.

He dismounted in front of the saloon, dropped his reins over the hitch rail, and was about to mount the outside stairs leading to the Great Northern office when he heard a loud, pleased voice booming his name. Longarm paused on the stairs and turned to see Duff Ryan, who was just leaving the saloon and striding toward him with another gentleman, a heavyset fellow in tweed jacket, trousers, and high-laced boots. He wore a short-billed cap on his head, and his rugged face was clean-shaven.

"Well, well, Mr. Long," Ryan said, "this is indeed a pleasure, meeting you here like this! Let me introduce you to Cyrus MacRae, the Great Northern's assistant chief engineer."

The engineer shook Longarm's hand and said he was pleased to meet him. His voice was soft but powerful, with a rich Scottish burr to it.

"Now tell me, Marshal," Ryan demanded. "What in blazes are you doing here? I thought you were in Canada, joining forces with the Mounties."

"I was on my way up to see Mr. MacRae here," Longarm said. "Reckon you can come along too, if you've a mind."

"Of course," MacRae said. "I've got some good Scotch in my office—a darn sight better than that rotgut you just purchased for me, Ryan. I'd be delighted, Mr. Long. By all means, let's go right on up."

Longarm followed the engineer up the stairs and into his office, Duff Ryan coming after them and pulling the door shut. Longarm found himself in a well-lighted room with more than the usual number of windows. A surveyer's transit stood in one corner, and a long table along the inside wall was covered with survey maps, large and small, weighted down with T-squares and slide rules. A battered and untidy roll-top desk stood in the far corner. There were enough chairs to go around, and as Longarm and Duff Ryan sat down, MacRae pulled a bottle of Scotch out of a desk drawer, blew the dust out of some glasses, and poured their drinks.

"Now, then," said MacRae, sitting with his back to his desk. "What can I do for you, Marshal?"

"That depends. I'm trailing a pretty large contingent of newly smuggled coolies, and I followed them to this railhead. What do you know about them?"

MacRae sent a startled glance at Ryan, then looked back at Longarm. "Smuggled coolies, you say?"

Longarm nodded. "They were smuggled ashore six nights ago. I took after them as soon as I was able, but I was never able to close the gap. Most likely they're out working on your railroad now."

MacRae shook his head. "If you took any time to camp, those nights you were on their trail," he said, "you never really had a chance of overtaking the slant-eyed devils. They march right on through the nights, you know."

Longarm had begun to suspect that much. He took a sip of the Scotch, found it excellent, and glanced back at the engineer. "Is there some way I can trace those coolies? Or would you prefer to keep them hidden? I should tell you they are witnesses to murder. Four Mounties were shot down in cold blood on the beach the night they were smuggled ashore."

MacRae's eyebrows shot up in sudden alarm. Ryan seemed equally astonished. It was he who spoke up next as he turned quickly to MacRae.

"You see, Cyrus! It is what I have been telling you all along. This is dirty business. I don't care how you value their services, this traffic in coolies can only bring disaster down upon you and the Great Northern!"

MacRae looked at Longarm with troubled eyes. "I am sorry to hear of that, Marshal," he said. And the man seemed sincerely affected by what Longarm had just told him. "However, I *need* those coolies. Consider! Not one of them weighs much more than a hundred and ten pounds—and that's sopping wet—yet those small, wiry bodies seem capable of prodigies of strength and endurance. Moreover, they learn quickly, they are slow to complain and ready to start work when the whistle blows. I admit, they bicker shrilly among themselves, and there is occasional bloodshed between different clans, and they love to gamble. But their headman takes care of everything without bothering me. They hire their own Chinese cooks and stay to themselves. They are not strikers, do not get drunk on payday, and do not shoot up the whorehouses along the right-of-way."

"Come now," Ryan broke in, with a short laugh. "They can't be perfect."

"For my purposes, Ryan, they are. They do have an outrageous habit of bathing every day, and they seem to drink prodigious quantities of boiled tea, but I notice that with all the tea they drink, they don't get sick nearly as often as my white laborers, whom I've seen reach down with their filthy paws and scoop up raw ditch water to drink. One more thing. I have yet to describe a task they have been unable or unwilling to tackle. We've been through some rough country, Mr. Long, and I couldn't have made it without them."

"Yes, you could have," Ryan snapped, no longer so easygoing. "It would have taken you a little longer, that's all. And you would have had to pay decent wages to white men. Perhaps it is that which sticks in your craw, MacRae."

The man did not allow himself to get ruffled by Ryan's remark. He was obviously used to Duff Ryan's prejudices concerning the use of Chinese laborers, and had long since decided not to take offense at the man's more belligerent outbursts. He looked down at his drink, lifted it to his lips, and took a long swallow. Then he turned his attention back to Longarm.

"But of course, what you tell me puts a different light on things, Marshal. Can you tell us what happened?"

Longarm told them.

When he had finished his account, Ryan leaned forward and asked, "You say you felt it was a trap?"

"Yep. With the coolies as the bait."

"It could be, of course," MacRae said, frowning. "But if so, it was a foolish move indeed. I am sure Ottawa will not be happy to hear of the death of four Mounties. They won't let that pass without some form of action."

"Good!" Ryan said. "It's about time they took this smuggling seriously. I am sorry for what happened to you and those men, Longarm. But if this is what it takes to alert the Canadian government to their responsibilities in this matter, then I must say I am gratified." He turned to address MacRae. "This journey I have taken to plead with you to stop using Oriental labor may have some effect after all, it seems. Surely, MacRae, this last shipment of cheap labor has come at too high a price. Even your flinty heart can see that!"

MacRae considered Ryan's remarks for a moment, then he downed his drink and slapped the empty glass onto his desk. "Sometimes you go too far, Duff Ryan. Too far. It is the shortsighted, narrow view of white bigots like yourself that forces us to resort to smuggling in order to obtain the laborers this railroad must have if its mission to open the Northwest is to be fulfilled! I will have those men. I will see this line completed—and on schedule!"

Duff Ryan pulled in his horns. He held out a hand placatingly, and smiled at MacRae. "A difference among gentlemen," he said, "can always be settled peaceably. Perhaps I was a bit harsh, MacRae."

MacRae poured himself another drink, his sandy brows canting slightly, his blue eyes twinkling. "And besides, it wasn't just the yellow devils that brought you to Top Gap. You want a decision on that route. You're a man cut from my cloth, Ryan, however you try to deny it. Money, that's what drives you. And the power it gives you. Well, if you can convince that crazy Swede to let you purchase that tract, we'll be laying rails through it before the snow flies. But I must have that route available to me before another week has passed. Otherwise, I'll have to start surveying other routes. And that's my last word on the subject."

"Two weeks, MacRae. Give me two weeks longer."

The man considered this for a moment, his jaw out-thrust, his eyes determined. Then his face softened. He shrugged and said, "All right, Ryan. Two weeks it is. But that's all the time you'll get."

Abruptly the two men glanced over at Longarm. So intent had they been on their own business that they seemed to have momentarily forgotten his presence; like gamblers rolling for high stakes, they had become lost in their own world.

Longarm said, "Then I can expect no help from you, MacRae?"

"Help?"

"In tracking down those smuggled coolies and the men who brought them here."

"I assure you, Marshal, I would like nothing better than to help you. But those coolies were more than likely delivered to local Chinese headmen, whose crews are strung out for miles along the tracks. And the men who brought them here have long since been paid off and are already well away from Top Gap. You may question the crew chiefs and those headmen working under them, but I can tell you from experience, you will get nothing but insane jabbering and much shrugging of the shoulders."

Ryan chimed in, "He's right, Marshal. Trying to

gct anything out of those foreign devils is next to impossible. I should know."

It was about what Longarm had expected. He rose wearily to his feet. He was looking forward to a steaming bath and a hot meal. "Well, I reckon I can thank you for this Scotch, Mr. MacRae, but I'd listen to Mr. Ryan here, if I was you. The next time you let a crew of smuggled coolies go to work for the Great Northern, you just might consider the blood on the hands of those who delivered them to you. And maybe the stockholders in this here company should consider on that, too."

MacRae stood. "I'm sorry I can't help you, Marshal. I know how you must feel. But I think, in all fairness, you should realize that our stockholders couldn't care less how we complete this railroad—just so long as we complete it on schedule and begin to show a profit."

Longarm touched the brim of his hat to both men and left the office. As he started down the stairs to the street, he found a cold anger building slowly within him. The deeper into this business he got, the sorrier it became. He had lost his Colt and his derringer, along with his Winchester. His boots were at the bottom of Pirates' Cove. His suit was a tattered mess and his upper torso was wrapped so tightly that it caused him to sweat every time he took a deep breath—and it was sore. Four good Mounties were dead. La Tour and Scally were dead. And still the smuggled coolies kept pouring in across the border. For one of the few times in his life, Longarm felt almost pure helplessness.

He reached the street and dug out his watch to see what time it was. But as he looked down at it, he swore softly to himself. The watch was ruined—had been since that long swim to shore the other night. It hadn't been working since that night, but habit died hard and he had clung to the fool watch in hopes of a miracle. But there wasn't going to be any miracle. He thrust the watch back into his side pocket, his anger and frustration making it difficult for him to think clearly.

Watching the steady stream of men swarming into the saloon beside which he was standing, he decided that what he needed was another Scotch, and then maybe a few more besides. *No! What you need, old son, are those sons of bitches who bushwhacked you on that beach!* Suddenly Longarm remembered something from that night which had been sitting quietly in the back of his mind, waiting to come forward. It was nudging him now, and he was remembering vividly the way those hooded men had swept out onto the beach, knocking Longarm to the ground and moving past him to open up on the Mounties.

And what he had just remembered might damned well go a long way to telling him who they were, and who they were working for. Longarm thrust his shoulders back and decided he would get that steaming bath and the hot meal first, and *then* have himself another Scotch. He had a long ride ahead of him—back to Slab City to finish an argument Helga Jensen had already started.

Those hooded men had worn the calked, spiked boots of loggers. And the biggest logging operation in this territory was being run by that big blonde Valkyrie. Maybe those men had been her way of finishing that argument.

Four days later, after having slept that night in his hotel room in Slab City, Longarm descended to the lobby and asked the desk clerk where he could find a first-rate watchmaker, gunsmith, and tailor. Visiting the watchmaker who had been suggested to him, Longarm left his watch with the man, even though the fellow seemed none too enthusiastic about his prospects for success in repairing the Ingersoll. The gunsmith, however, had just what Longarm wanted—including a solid brass derringer, .44 caliber. He told the man

100

how he wanted the small loop to be soldered to the derringer's butt, then left with his new Colt resting snugly in his cross-draw rig. It had taken only a few minutes for the gunsmith to file off the front sight.

The moment Longarm entered the tailor shop that had been recommended, he recognized the round face with the thin straggle of white whiskers that looked up at him from the sewing machine behind the counter. At once the little Chinaman grinned happily. He seemed enormously pleased to meet once again the tall lawman who had saved them all from that highwayman, and he and his daughter from riding on top of the stage.

The man jumped up from his chair and came swiftly around the counter to greet Longarm. Clasping his hands before him, he bowed quickly—once, twice, three times. Then he looked with great happiness up into Longarm's face.

With sudden, surprising clarity he spoke up. "I am doubly honored! It was only my inability to believe that one possessing Your Excellency's heaven-born splendor would waste his time on so mean a clod as myself that kept the least of your slaves from visiting your hotel in person and thanking you for your mighty labors in this miserable person's behalf." He sobered. "Now you have come to me. It is an honor—to me and to all my ancestors!"

Longarm was too astonished at this incredible outpouring to say anything. The man's speech and attitude were in startling contrast to the silent Oriental who had sat beside him on the stage.

The old man plucked at Longarm's buckskin sleeve and drew him gently through the curtains behind the counter and into a small room. From a further curtained doorway emerged his daughter, as exquisitely proportioned and as delicately attired as he remembered her, wearing a black silk jacket that reached to

101

her knees, with trousers of the same material beneath, her tiny feet bound in lavender slippers.

But a subtle change seemed to have come over her. Her olive complexion was flushed. Her eyes, as he remembered them, had been veiled in a soft, delicate light before. Now they were a gleaming black, burning with an intensity that seemed to contradict her frail, delicately fashioned body. Her glance, which swept over Longarm in an instant, seemed to ignite him. Yet all this occurred in a single instant, and as soon as she passed through the doorway, she was her father's obedient, submissive servant.

The old Chinaman gave her swift orders in their own tongue. She bowed and left hastily. The old man turned to Longarm. "If the Terror of Evildoers will honor one of my deplorable chairs by resting his divine body upon it, I can assure him the chair shall be burned afterward, so no lesser being may use it."

"Don't burn it," Longarm said, smiling. "I might want to come back and sit in it again."

He sat down in the chair that had been offered him, and placed the bundle he had brought on the floor beside it. The chair was a little small for his frame; its arms and backs were draped with costly-looking material. He glanced around the room and found it surprisingly spotless, the walls covered with dark curtains, the usual shrine in the corner containing the tiny urns, statuettes, and other relics of departed ancestors. It was not a gaudy room—nothing at all like Lillian M'Ling's place—but seemed impressive nevertheless. It gave Longarm a sense of wealth easily attained and casually used. He glanced back at the old man, whose eyes had been watching him shrewdly.

"My name is Long," Longarm said. "I'm sure you know that by now. If you like, you can call me Longarm. But you got the advantage of me. I didn't see your name on the store front outside."

"Chang Li Chang," the fellow replied, smiling mildly

102

over his whiskers and bending his head almost to the top of the small ebony table before him, "your humble servant."

The daughter appeared with a dazzling tea service and set it down soundlessly on the small table before Chang. The old man paid no attention whatever to the delicate creature as she poured the tea for Longarm and passed him the small, incredibly light cup and saucer. There was a small candy on the saucer beside the cup. She poured her father's tea then, ladling in an astonishing amount of sugar. Without so much as a glance in Longarm's direction, she retreated swiftly, silently back through the curtained doorway.

Longarm sipped the tea—he found it bitter—then put the cup and saucer down on a small table near his chair. "I came in here because I need a tailor, Chang. All this fine hospitality makes me wonder why we don't have more Chinese tailors in Denver."

Longarm picked up the bundle and passed it across to Chang. "That's what is left of my suit coat, vest, and shirt. The shirt is a lost cause, I reckon, but I'd like for you to see what you can do with the coat and the vest."

The old man's hands untied the bundle swiftly. He held up first the coat, then the vest, examining both with expert eyes. Then he turned to the shirt. The heavy broadcloth was in tatters. Longarm had washed as much of the blood from it as he could, but he had no illusions about being able to wear it again.

"A shirt," Chang said, "finer than this is already yours, and this vest and coat will be fashioned once again as fit for the giant who wears them."

"That's fine," Longarm said. "How soon can you have it?"

"By sunrise tomorrow. These treacherous fingers can work no faster, and the evil spirits have robbed my eyes of their youth. They are unworthy of your needs.

103

But your humble servant shall work through the night until your raiment is ready once again."

"No need to go through all that," Longarm protested, no longer so amused by Chang's overblown words. If it was a game, it was one that Longarm could do without. When it came to using the king's English, he was a meat-and-potatoes man. And the only people he ever complimented openly were gamblers and confidence men he was getting ready to surprise. "I won't need the coat and vest for a while, anyway. Take your time, Chang."

He got up then. Chang got up also. "If the Emperor of Lawmen would remove his buckskin, I would measure him for his new shirt."

Longarm shrugged out of his buckskin. He had torn off the top of his longjohns, since they too had been slashed along with his shirt and vest. He had removed the heavy bandages as soon as he had reached Slab City. He had been pleased to note that soon the scars would fade away almost completely, so well had they been dressed by that breed doctor; but at the moment, the cruel network was not a pretty sight.

And now Longarm saw a subtle change in Chang's manner. The wordplay before had been accompanied by a barely perceptible twinkle in the old man's eyes. At the sight of Longarm's chest and side, however, the light left his eyes and Longarm had the conviction that he was now—for some reason—a different person in the eyes of Chang Li Chang. Slowly, with infinite care, Chang lifted the chain holding the jewelled medallion over Longarm's head. Placing the small trumpeting elephant almost reverently down on a nearby table, Chang produced a tape and began measuring Longarm's chest and arms, his eyes continuing to regard Longarm's scarred torso with something approaching awe.

Finished, he stepped back. "My poverty is even

greater than I had supposed. Does the King wear rags? Can a humble tailor transform sackcloth into ermine? I will leave the Giant of Law-enforcers here while I search out a material worthy of such a hunter of men."

He bowed swiftly, called something to his daughter in the next room, and vanished out the door, his tape measure still about his neck.

The girl entered the room the instant the outer door closed. She stopped in surprise at the sight of Longarm standing naked to the waist in the middle of the room. But her astonishment lasted only a moment. She came to him quickly then, her tiny hands suddenly on his chest, her fingers tracing lightly the course of his scars. There was a scent about her hair that clouded his senses.

She looked up into his face, and he was impressed once again by the delicate beauty of Chang Li Chang's daughter. Gold earrings swung beside her smooth cheeks, and a jade butterfly was in her hair. Her black silk jacket, he saw now on closer inspection, was alight with tiny, glittering stones.

Suddenly she threw both arms around Longarm and rested her cheek against the curly hair on his chest. She seemed to take an impish delight in moving her cheek back and forth over it. She lifted her oval face to his, and the command in her eyes was almost impossible to deny. He lowered his face to hers and she kissed him, her small lips opening under his with a fierce directness that aroused him almost instantly. Her hands moved swiftly down his back, her fingers sliding in under his waist and moving around—and all the while her lips clung to his, her tongue darting and catching at him, drawing him closer. She began to pull him into the other room.

He felt himself moving with her willingly, caught up in the eager, almost childlike lust of this dainty creature. Only as he felt the curtains over the doorway brushing against his naked shoulders did he pull back and regain his senses. He could not disport with Chang's daughter in this fashion. It was unseemly—a wicked breach of old Chang's hospitality. She saw his reluctance and her face lost its flush and became almost white, the eyes cold, scornful.

"What matter?" she demanded in a fierce, sibilant whisper. "You no like Li Fan?"

"Of course," Longarm protested. "You are a very pretty little girl, but—"

"No little girl!" she cried heatedly, her face suddenly livid. "Li Fan is woman. She has desire like woman. She has skill like woman. Li Fan make good professional woman!"

Longarm held up his hand in an effort to placate her. Before he could soothe her, they heard the outside door opening. Her right hand snaked up and slapped him sharply; then, in a tottering, hopping run, she vanished behind the curtains.

Longarm turned to see Chang hurrying, head down, through the doorway, a heavy, fawn-colored bolt of broadcloth over his arm. He must have seen the still-swinging curtains, and should have noticed where Longarm was standing, but his crafty eyes did not change expression as he approached.

"Feel this!" he demanded, holding up the fabric.

Longarm felt of it and was impressed; it was warm and pliant to his touch, yet not too heavy. He nodded, pleased.

Chang rocked back on his heels, even more pleased than Longarm. His white whiskers ruffled in a smile that was grandfatherly in its benign delight. Longarm felt warmed by it. "The Destroyer of Outlaws deserves only the best. A cloth of gold would be more suited to such a knight as yourself. Accept my abject apology that I could not create such a cloth." The twinkle was back in the man's eyes now, Longarm saw.

106

He smiled down at him. "I accept your apology, Chang. This will do nicely, and I thank you. How much is all this going to cost? The government I work for doesn't place the same value on my services as you do."

"Price!" the old man was horrified. "It is a gift! A feeble, unworthy gift in payment for your valor." He paused then, significantly. "And for protecting Li Fan and your humble servant from the evil prejudice of salesmen and barbarians of little education." This last was a reference to Spittles, Longarm had no doubt—and it was spoken with a resonance that led Longarm to believe that the old tailor wanted him to hear this not as playful banter, but as a serious statement.

Chang bowed. "Tomorrow morning, return. The Prince of Lawmen will have raiment worthy of his calling."

Longarm picked up the medallion and shrugged into the buckskin shirt. He didn't like his cross-draw rig so visible, and would be pleased indeed if Chang could mend his coat and vest well enough for him to be able to wear them once again. The old man accompanied him to the shop door, bowing as he closed the door behind Longarm, his thin chin-whiskers fluttering.

Later that day, dressed in fresh Levi's, the buckskin shirt, his snuff-brown Stetson, and a new pair of boots, Longarm went searching for Helga Jensen. She was not at the mill. Her Chinese foreman said she might be at one of her logging camps. Longarm got directions from the fellow—it was not the easiest thing in the world to understand him—saddled his Morgan, and rode west, following the Nooksack River.

After traveling for close to ten miles, he came upon a skidroad that led from the river deep into the magnificent stand of Douglas fir that by this time crowded the river's bank. The road created a kind of green-walled canyon. It was fashioned of felled trees sunk crosswise into the soft, moist ground. The completed skidroad looked to Longarm like ties laid for some gargantuan railroad.

Following the directions of Helga's mill foreman, Longarm turned onto this skidroad and was soon well into the echoing quiet of this astonishing timber. After less than a mile he heard the loud, clear call of a bullwhacker's voice echoing down the forest road. Soon he heard the clank of chains and the straining and wailing of oxbows as a team of heavy oxen came into view, hauling a massive load of huge logs. The bullwhacker was walking beside the six yokes of oxen, a goadstick resting lightly on his shoulder. Behind the oxen, just in front of the logs, a small Chinaman was bent over double as he continuously daubed thick oil on the skid poles to keep the logs coming. It was backbreaking work, but the little Chinese never looked up once as Longarm guided his Morgan well to the side and watched the bullwhacker and his team of oxen pull the squealing, jingling logs past. Every now and then the bullwhacker would erupt in a violent oath and bring the steel brad at the end of his goadstick down hard on the stolid backs of his oxen.

When the logs were past, Longarm guided his horse back onto the still-smoking road and continued on until at last he came to some of Helga's loggers cutting a swath through the big trees. Occasionally he heard a tremendous thump that would shake the ground and cause his mount to shy—another big one coming to earth. Riding past these downed titans, Longarm marveled at how shrunken the big men clambering on their calked boots over these great trees looked in comparison to the giants they had felled.

The stumps that remained, Longarm noted, were sometimes as much as sixteen feet high, so that Longarm felt he was riding past the living headstones of

108

giants killed in battle. The ground around these stumps looked as if clearing it had been a day-long job in itself. He pulled up to watch one of the loggers standing on a springboard while he chopped away at the tremendous girth of the tree he was attacking. The board was a piece of nearly flat wood, at least five or six feet long, with an iron lip on one end of it, the lip resting in a notch on the tree, well above the floor of the forest.

The man worked steadily, metronomically. Great white chips were flying, a steady run of pitch flowing from the growing wound. The logger, like most of the others working about him in the timber, was wearing thick, water-repellent clothing that must have been stiff enough to begin with and looked positively iron-clad by this time. Longarm had heard the loggers referred to as "tin pants" and he could understand why. On their heads most of them wore stocking caps, and on their feet those heavy, calked boots. This man had taken off his stocking cap, however, and Longarm could see great, grimy beads of sweat rolling down his face. He didn't look down once.

Longarm rode on through the timber, looking for the crew chief. He was told to try the main camp farther into the timber. As Longarm rode, he noticed quite a few Chinamen at work, most of them busy at menial tasks. He passed a cookshack and found it staffed almost entirely with Orientals. The thick slash that covered the ground was being picked up and carted away by silent, industrious gangs of Chinese. Their mute, concentrated effort was most impressive. The division of labor was obvious to Longarm. The big loggers—Swedes and other Scandinavians, with a smattering of heavyset Irishmen—were busy with felling the trees, debarking and skidding them to the various skidways where the bullwhackers and their teams were waiting for them. The Chinese were kept busy doing menial chores: running for new axheads, carrying water, tending to the oxen. But there were a great many of them, and their role, Longarm could see, would soon and easily expand. It was inevitable. They were quiet, industrious, and eager to learn.

At the moment, Longarm saw no friction between the Chinese and the white loggers. The Chinese were keeping to their tasks, and the loggers enjoyed the services of such docile and industrious helpers. It was easy to see how quickly they—as well as Helga Jensen—had gotten used to the Chinamen's labor. Like Cyrus MacRae of the Great Northern, they would soon find the coolies indispensable, and the continued illegal importation of them a necessity.

Longarm came at last to the main camp and was told by the crew chief that Helga had already left for Slab City. He expressed surprise that Longarm had missed her. The man spoke in a thick Scottish accent, and Longarm could not miss the slight edge of derision in his tone. He could not be sure, of course, but he wondered, as he turned his mount around, if he had not been deliberately misled. But he said nothing to the crew chief and headed back to Slab City, arriving there well after sundown.

He left the Morgan at the livery, supped at a small, heavily frequented restaurant run by a jolly Chinaman and his family, then steered clear of the Skidroad Palace and went to his hotel. He was intent on a second good night's sleep between clean sheets.

The matchstick he had slipped between his door and the frame had dropped to the carpet in front of his door. It gleamed softly in the light that filtered through the crack under the door. Whoever was in there waiting for him was making little or no effort to conceal his presence. Longarm continued on past his door without pause. At the far end of the hall, he removed his boots, and holding them in one hand and his drawn Colt in

110

the other, he returned without a sound to his door and kicked it open.

Helga Jensen was sitting up in his bed, combing out her long blonde hair.

Chapter 6

Longarm stood in the doorway, astonished.

Stroking her hair without pause, she glanced at him, her blue eyes warm now, playful—and just a mite challenging. "Well? Is it all you want, to stand there and gape like school boy?"

Longarm closed the door behind him and, smiling, walked closer to his bed and gazed appreciatively upon her. She had pulled the covers up to her waist, but had done nothing to conceal her great, round, high-riding breasts. Across her milk-white shoulders and past her breasts, flowing over and around them like silken gold, spilled her gleaming yellow tresses. As he watched her, she continued to comb out her hair. Like something alive, it seemed to grow more beautiful, more opulent with each long, flowing stroke.

"No doubt about it," Longarm said, taking off his hat and shaking his head in wonder. "There's something mighty fetching about watching a woman comb her hair."

"Ya! It is why I do it. For me it is good thing too." She glanced over at the carved oak highboy next to the window. There was a framed oval mirror attached to the top of it. On the shelf below the top were a washbasin and a pitcher, with a small piece of soap on a dish beside them. Towels and washcloths were folded neatly on the highboy top. They did not belong to the hotel. She had brought them herself, Longarm realized. "First you clean yourself," she said, "then join me. I will let you comb my hair, maybe. After we talk."

Longarm shrugged. It was the best invitation he had received in a long time. As for talking, Helga seemed in no mood to wait. As soon as he stripped to his waist, poured the lukewarm water into the bowl, and began lathering his hands, Helga started talking to him.

"I am sorry I was rude to you on the street. But all the same, it was nice to see how you handle them two big fellows. Very nice. I guess then that big man like you not need to run with any man—even that octopus, Duff Ryan!"

Drying off his face, he glanced back at her and grinned. "Thank you, Helga. I accept your apology."

"Yes, I apologize." She looked at him sternly then. "Now take off your pants and your underclothes and clean yourself off there too. What you think?"

Longarm held up his hand. "All in good time. I have to work myself up to it."

She put her brush down beside her on the coverlet. "You want I should give you a hand? Like mother wash little boy in tub on Saturday night?"

Stepping out of his Levi's and then pulling off his longjohns, he shook his head. "That's all right, Helga. I can handle it."

"Yes," she said, eyeing him appreciatively. "You should handle it. You have much there to handle, Longarm." Her handsome face brightened in a brilliant smile. "That is a fine name for you, I think."

Longarm blinked, slightly surprised; he had not told anyone in Slab City his nickname. Once again, his reputation seemed, if not to have preceded him, at least to have followed close on his heels.

"You go back to that lovely hair of yours," he told

her, "and I'll just finish up here. I'm getting a mite chilly."

"Ya! You hurry and I warm you good."

Longarm hurried, then climbed in beside her. The sheets, as he had hoped, were crisp and clean and warm. Helga seemed to radiate sunlight. He leaned back to take her all in. It took him a while.

She put down her hairbrush, reached to the floor on her side of the bed, and brought up a bottle of golden Scotch and two large tumblers. Balancing both glasses in the palm of one hand, she filled them to within a whisker of the top. Her deftness was a marvel. As was the amount.

"You fixing to drink that, Helga, or take a bath in it?"

She smiled, and, without a word, down it went like tap water.

"Take another," Longarm suggested, grinning and still holding the glass she had already handed to him.

"Don't mind if I do," Helga rasped hoarsely, catching her breath and patting her chest between those two magnificent breasts.

He watched her pour and drink. He took a good healthy belt of his own drink, swished it around in his mouth, and sent it trickling down, savoring its tingling warmth.

"Save the rest of that until later, Helga," he suggested, his eyes beginning to water. "We've got the whole night ahead of us, don't forget."

"Ya!" she said. "Maybe you are right. But first I must explain."

"You don't need to explain."

She put down the bottle and the glass. Then she turned to face him, her large, impudent breasts driving him wild. "But yes, I do. It is so important you understand why Helga hate this man Ryan. I call him octopus. And that is what he is. He own everything in town. And he hate me because I own much also. I am

114

his rival. And he hate my Chinese workers. And now he wants my land! He—now it is clear to me—make offer to Great Northern—for Helga's land! But it is *my* land. I file on it! Soon I will supply Great Northern with all its lumber, its ties, its telegraph poles. But Duff Ryan wants my land to give to the railroad, and wants my sawmill. He is octopus, I tell you. You must help me!"

"I'll help you, Helga."

She beamed. He thought she was going to reach out and pull him onto those lovely erect nipples. But she didn't. Longarm held himself in check, aware by now of a distressing urgency building within him. She saw the bedclothes rising, and smiled. "Thank you, Longarm. I knew you would help. You are too big, too strong, to lean on such a one as that Ryan and his reptile, Spittles!" She looked at him admiringly. "Chang Li Chang told me how you handled that snake in the stage on the way here." She leaned maddeningly close. "All of Chinatown knows it!"

"The tailor? You know him?"

She nodded conspiratorially. "Ya. I am his landlady. He is not only tailor, you know."

"What do you mean by that?"

She shrugged elaborately, causing her breasts to do wonderful things. "You will find out, maybe. Enough of him. You promise to help me. Good." She patted the bed beside her. "You help me and I help you."

"I'll help you, Helga, as soon as you explain a few things."

"A few things? What few things?" She was immediately on her guard.

"I want to know about the death of Scally—and what you had to do with that ambush at Pirates' Cove."

"Me? Ambush? This is crazy, way you talk! Ya! I think maybe you sick. I think maybe I better not give myself to you after all. A suspicious man like you would not appreciate such free passion!"

"Nothing's free, Helga. You know that. You need coolies to run your operation—you and that railroad. You're the last person who would want to see the flow of coolies stopped. Pretty soon you'll have them cutting your trees. You're already got yourself a Chinese foreman at the mill. It's good business, Helga—stopping me, that is. By the way, those two Siwash you sent after me won't be coming back to Slab City."

"You talk crazy, I tell you." She looked at him narrowly. "You are wrong, I tell you. But I understand," she told him with sudden magnanimity. "Duff Ryan is pulling wool over your face."

"Over my eyes, you mean."

"Yes. You see? You admit it!"

Certainly Longarm found himself admitting at least that it was difficult to sit in bed alongside a naked woman as well-endowed as Helga Jensen and continue to insist that she was the evil genius behind the hell breaking loose in this portion of the Washington Territory. He not only found it difficult to believe; he found he didn't *want* to believe it. *Now pull yourself together, old son,* he told himself. *This is what happens when you mix business with pleasure.*

"Did you know Scally?"

She nodded. "He was nice man. Foolish, but nice. Not like you. You are nice, but you are not foolish." She smiled. "At least you try to be not foolish."

"Scally was foolish?"

"Very foolish man. He think he fall in love with Chang's wife."

"Wife?"

"Li Fan."

"I thought she was his daughter."

She laughed. It did wonders for Longarm. The sound of it was deep, intimate, throbbing. He was finding it more and more difficult to keep his mind on the business at hand. But he kept going doggedly. "Scally had an affair with Chang's wife?"

116

"Ya! Only it was not quite that way, you see. Li Fan have affair with *him*."

"And Chang found out?"

"Perhaps. Chang Li Chang does not tell me his business."

"How close did Scally get to finding out who was behind the smuggling?"

Again she shrugged. It was maddening. She saw the sweat breaking out on his forehead and tipped her head back and laughed, a delightful, deep chuckle. Then she turned her face to his. "I will tell you all I know," she said. "Later. I am beginning to flow like one of them big trees when the first big ax cuts deep. Do you understand that, Longarm?"

That was all she had to say. He understood perfectly.

He moved closer and felt the length of his body against hers. She was incredibly warm, the entire length of her. She patted his cheek. Her hand felt soft on his tough, weathered skin. Leaning close to her, Longarm kissed her hungrily, at the same time pulling himself still closer to her. Her breasts pressed hard against his chest. He could feel them heaving as her breath came faster.

Breaking the kiss, she reached her hand down, placed it on one of his buttocks, and pulled him hungrily closer. She began caressing him then, gently at first, then more vigorously, raising him to rigidity— pulsing, throbbing, and ready to drive. But she had no desire to end this at that moment. It was for her, he could tell, too delicious not to want to prolong it.

Her fiery fingers traveled up the small of his back, then across his heavily corded, deeply bronzed neck to his shoulders, and down his chest. She kissed his shoulder; then he felt the heat of her moist tongue licking it lightly, back and forth across its breadth, sliding downward to his nipple, flicking it, licking it hungrily, hardening it. Then she lifted her face from his chest

117

and, with wide mouth, searched out his own. Their lips came together in a moist, searing kiss that charged Longarm with an inchoate desire that rolled him swiftly over onto Helga.

His hand flew down to the hot, seeping moisture of her, and he could hear her groan as their grinding kiss continued with mounting fury. . . .

What the hell!

A rough, callused hand was tugging violently on his bare shoulder. Someone else had ripped off the covers. As Longarm turned his head to see what was going on, a clenched fist caught him on the side of his face, sending him rolling across the bed. He slipped backward, scrambling off the bed, and came down heavily on his back.

A setup! Helga Jensen was playing the old badger game!

Longarm could hear her screaming, calling for help. He pulled himself furiously to his feet and met his first attacker head on, parrying the man's flailing fists, boring in ruthlessly and cuffing him about the head and face, first from one direction, and then from the other. As he struck at his assailant, he kept moving him back. The fellow's knees appeared to wobble, his head no longer resisting the force of Longarm's brutal pounding.

Longarm's anger at his situation, and at himself for allowing it, sent him into a transport of fury—a fury that made him not less, but more efficient, cold, merciless. As he saw the big logger in front of him begin to buckle, he stepped swiftly closer, grabbed a handful of his hair, and slammed the man's face down onto his rising knee. There was an explosion of blood and cartilage as the man's nose met Longarm's knee. The man groaned and sagged drunkenly to the floor, a bloody froth breaking from his broken lips. The logger shook his head feebly and spat out some teeth, then rolled slowly to the floor, supporting himself on his hands and knees.

Helga was sitting up in bed, wide-eyed, terrified. The second man, crouching in readiness beside the bed, seemed to flinch as Longarm turned to him. Then he charged Longarm, a heavy goadstick held at the ready. Longarm ducked to one side, reached out, and caught the fellow's wrist. Twisting suddenly down and away, he heard the logger gasp. Then, astonishingly, the logger sank his teeth into Longarm's shoulder, just behind his neck. With a cry of rage, Longarm bent down the fellow's wrist and twisted. The goadstick dropped to the floor. Longarm flung himself around then, loosening the logger's grip on his shoulder. But still the man hung on. The pain was fierce as the man's teeth sunk still deeper into the muscle.

Longarm dropped swiftly to one knee. The fellow's teeth let go. Longarm grabbed the man around the waist and flung him onto his bleeding shoulder. Rising to his full height, he began to turn, slowly at first, then faster and faster. As he whirled about, the logger on his shoulder, his arms now flung out with the force of the momentum, Longarm stepped out through the wide-open door and flung the man bodily down the stairs.

Halfway down, he struck the bannister and broke through, still tumbling. There were screams from the lobby below. Ignoring them, Longarm turned back to his first attacker. The fellow was trying to crawl out of the room. Longarm placed himself behind him, grabbed him in the crotch and the back of his shirt, and heaved him out the door and down the steps after his companion.

Then Longarm slammed shut the door and turned to Helga.

"You are bleeding," she said. "Come. Let Helga fix."

"Ain't you fixed enough, Helga? Those two were your men, come to finish what they started on the

119

street the other day. It'll take more than your bully-boys to stop this here investigation, Helga. Now get out!"

"But I know nothing of those men! I did not bring them, Longarm! It is not what you think. I swear it!"

"Swear all you want, Helga, but I'm not about to believe a word. They were both loggers, and that means they work for you. Now get out!"

She became suddenly modest. She snatched up the bedclothes and held them over her breasts. Her eyes became icy now, her beautiful features hard. *Hell hath no fury like a woman scorned,* Longarm reminded himself. "Get out of here, Longarm, while I dress. I will be gone from this room as soon as I am dressed. And ya! I will not soon return. You will see!"

Without another word to her, Longarm dressed swiftly and left the room, deciding, as he descended the stairs and noted the shattered bannister, that he might as well try Duff Ryan's saloon after all. Maybe the Skidroad Palace had something in its pharmacy that could quiet a man, simmer him down a bit. He flexed his shoulder angrily, hoping that the logger with the tenacious bite wasn't rabid.

He was still working this thought over in his mind when he reached the lobby floor and saw a thin, gangling fellow, with a mustache that extended past his long chin, hurrying over to confront him. There was a tin star on his open vest. His white shirt was begrimed, and its collar was missing. His eyes snapped nervously at Longarm; so pale a blue were they that it almost appeared as if the man had no eyes at all.

"Wait!" he cried. "Hold up, please."

Longarm held up. Looking casually past the gawky lawman, he saw blood on the carpet in front of the desk. The desk clerk, his face pale, was looking at him with wide eyes.

"I'm the new town constable," the tin star told

Longarm hastily. "Tim Curry, and I want to warn you that this hotel will tolerate no more rowdyism. I believe you are responsible for the actions which injured those men, are you not?"

"That's right, Constable. Where the hell were you when all this was going on? What kind of a town is this, where a man has to wear his gun to bed? Have you locked those men up? They attempted to murder me and my lady friend, while we were discussing the weather in the privacy of my room. What kind of a town you running, mister?"

The small crowd that had gathered in the lobby looked with delight at the startled surprise on Constable Tim Curry's face. "Now, see here, mister . . ."

"No. You see here. How'd you get this job, anyway?"

"Mr. Duff Ryan. He suggested my name to the town council, and I decided I would take the job."

"You did, huh?"

The man moistened suddenly dry lips. "Yes, and now that I've heard your side of the story, Mr.—?"

"Long. Custis Long, deputy U.S. marshal."

"Oh . . . "

"That's right, Constable. But don't let that fact faze you. You just go right ahead and arrest me if you've a mind to. But I'd like it a damn sight more if you'd see to those two loggers who broke into my room and caused all this damage. Breaking and entering and assault and battery would be the charges I'd start off with—if I had them in my custody, that is. You got them in custody, have you?"

"No . . . as a matter of fact, they're . . . "

"Shit," said Longarm, and he walked on past the constable and out the door of the hotel, leaving the abashed constable standing in the middle of the lobby, looking helplessly around him at the grinning faces.

In the Skidroad Palace, Duff Ryan was holding forth

121

at a back table with what appeared to be a few of the town's movers and shakers. Spittles was there as well, sitting attentively at his master's elbow. Ryan looked up at Longarm's approach and smiled warmly.

"Marshal!" he cried. "Join us! By all means! What are you drinking?"

"Maryland rye. Neat."

A place was made for him at the table, and after the introductions were made, Longarm leaned his elbow wearily on the table and pushed his Stetson back on his forehead. "Where'd you find that new constable, Ryan? He acts like he's got a splinter for a backbone."

Ryan leaned back and chuckled. "You don't like him?"

"It ain't that. I figure he's nice enough to his ailing mother, but it doesn't look to me like he's worth a pitcher of warm spit when it comes to throwing a rope over this town. Was he your idea?"

"Marshal, after the way La Tour died, do you have any idea what we had to go through to get a grown man to put on that star? We have two very unruly elements in this town, the loggers and the Chinese, and both of them take orders from that blonde she-devil Jensen. And nobody wants to tangle with her. Hell, there's some talk that she's the one behind Constable La Tour's death, after all. I wouldn't put it past her." The men at the table nodded sagely at this. Spittle's pinched face grew even more pinched as he contemplated the evil of Helga Jensen.

"She thinks rather highly of you too, Ryan," Longarm drawled, taking the glass of whiskey the barkeep handed him. "But it looks like you still ain't got a grown man to wear the badge." He threw the contents of the glass down his throat with one quick motion.

Duff Ryan grinned. "You want the job, Marshal? In addition to your other duties? I am sure I could arrange it with the members of the town council." He looked around him at the men to whom he had just introduced Longarm. "Here they are right now—perfectly willing to make the change."

A few of the men laughed in agreement.

"Ryan, you know what I want," Longarm said impatiently. "But I sure as hell can't expect much help from that poor cull. He's so scrawny he could take a bath inside a shotgun barrel, and he has all the get-up-and-go of a chambermaid. You want those coolies stopped, or don't you? I'm going to need a posse and a man to lead it when that next shipment of coolies starts south."

"Of course I want them stopped. Everyone at this table does. But why in tarnation doesn't Washington send us more men like you? I know you can't do it all by yourself, but Tim Curry is the best of the pickings in this town, and that's the plain and unvarnished truth."

"Thanks for the drink, Duff," Longarm said, getting to his feet.

"No need to rush off, Longarm. Stay awhile. Join us."

"I guess I ain't in the mood for palaver."

As Longarm moved away from the table, he took out a cheroot and lit it. He felt vaguely uneasy. It was difficult to believe that the relaxed man he had just spoken to while surrounded by his cronies was the same man he had heard railing almost in a steady stream about the dangers of the Yellow Peril. That new constable was going to be no help at all, and Duff Ryan knew it.

He left the saloon and stood for a moment on the boardwalk. The wind coming from the river brought with it Chinatown's pungent smell of boiled vegetables, fish, and wood smoke. He turned up the street to his hotel.

The desk clerk was talking to a Mountie, whose back was to Longarm. The clerk saw Longarm and said

123

something to the Mountie, who turned. Longarm recognized Scott McPherson. His right arm was still in a sling, but the arm didn't seem to be bothering him much. Scott smiled in relief when he saw the tall lawman, and hurried across the lobby toward him.

The short, stocky fellow shook his head. "Thought I'd have to bail you out of the local jail," he said. "This here desk clerk seems to think you created quite a disturbance not too long ago—and then resisted arrest."

"Guess you could say the clerk has a general idea what happened. He's a mite off on a few particulars, though. What brings you to Slab City, Scott?"

Scott's dark, bushy eyebrows moved together in a frown as he looked quickly around, then lowered his voice and said, "Another shipment."

"When?"

"Tomorrow night. If we leave first thing in the morning with a posse, we'll be able to intercept them at *our* pleasure."

"Now, that *would* be a pleasure."

Scott nodded quickly. "That's what Inspector Wilde thinks, too. How much of a posse can you get together?"

Longarm did not have to think hard on that one. "No posse, Scott. Just you and me and maybe one or two others. Think we can handle it?"

The man nodded quickly, but his sudden paleness betrayed him. It was obvious that the prospect did not exactly set him afire with eagerness, but he'd go along. He had no choice.

"You got a room here yet?" Longarm asked.

"Not yet."

"Get one. We'll leave at dawn tomorrow."

Longarm left Scott and went up the stairs past two carpenters repairing the bannister by lantern light, kicked open his door carelessly, and strode into the room. The lamp was still lit, and he saw that Helga

124

had thought to make his bed. He yanked down the sheets in case she had left him any surprise under the covers—like a rattlesnake, maybe—then chuckled at his own lack of faith in womankind, and got ready for bed.

He slept with small pieces of rolled-up paper strewn on the floor between his bed and the door, and his hand under his pillow, resting lightly upon the butt of his new Colt.

Chapter 7

It was twilight of the following day, and Longarm—crouched behind a massive, moss-laden windfall—was watching the sullen line of coolies plodding toward him from the beach. He was alone. He had sent Scott around to the rear of the coolies, and the two loggers he had dragooned into joining him early that same morning were positioned about fifty yards on either side of the trail, crouching, like him, down among the damp foliage.

The great silver pan that was the Pacific was to Longarm's left, and the masts of the bark that had brought in this load of Chinamen were just visible above the headlands. Not all the coolies were visible. The line ran all the way back to the beach. The plan was to wait until the coolies had left the shore well behind and had established a solid trail through the giant timber before moving in. The Chinese were not what Longarm was worried about. It was their escort he wanted, and the escort was not yet in sight.

The faces of the coolies were only indistinct blurs in the gathering dusk, as their broad-brimmed, circular hats bobbed in unison to their steady march. As usual, they were dressed in somber dark blue cotton pants and jackets, with many of them carrying their few possessions hanging on each end of eight-foot-long bamboo tote poles balanced on their shoulders.

A shot rang out.

It came from well behind the column, its single crack shattering the wet, hanging silence. For a split second the line of coolies froze. Then, almost as if all of them were on a single fish-line, they turned about and ran, still in formation, back toward the beach. Swearing furiously, Longarm jumped up and ran out of his cover after them. The two loggers appeared then, looking apprehensively toward him.

"Which one of you fired that shot?" Longarm demanded.

Both men shook their heads vigorously, and indeed, even as Longarm asked the question, he realized that the shot had come from well beyond those two men. From Scott, more than likely.

"Come on!" Longarm called, as he raced toward Scott's position.

Topping a gentle rise on the edge of the timber, the two loggers beside him, Longarm saw Scott bolting through the tangled brush toward them. He was zig-zagging frantically as a pack of grim-faced sailors raced swiftly after him, each one armed with a rifle. Longarm went down on one knee and brought up his Winchester, levering a fresh cartridge into the chamber as he did so.

His first shot caused the pursuing sailors to pull up hastily, then disperse swiftly to the right and left, but still running forward, hidden now by the thick forest undergrowth. They were intent, it seemed, on pressing the attack. Sighting them, Scott raced toward Longarm and the two loggers, his head and ass as far down as he could get them.

Longarm retreated cautiously behind the massive trunk of a Douglas fir, the two loggers sticking close beside him. One of them was called Gus Mullen, the other answered only to Stokey. Stokey was short and bulky, with a red face and a round nose and black buttons for eyes. Longarm couldn't be sure if he squinted or just smiled a lot. His buddy—the fellow Longarm had found sleeping beside Stokey on the tavern floor—was taller and more raw-boned, and saw the world through clear blue eyes that crinkled often as the man laughed. Stokey said little, but he was obviously unhappy at finding himself part of the federal government, while Gus Mullen appeared to be enjoying himself hugely—until this moment, at least.

Panting loudly, Scott reached the tree and flung himself down behind it. The three men stepped back as the Mountie pushed himself to a sitting position. Through frightened eyes, he looked up at Longarm.

"They're everywhere, Longarm. There must be ten of them. And they're all armed!"

"How's your shoulder?"

"Practically useless now. I fell on it when I was hurrying back. That's when my rifle went off. I couldn't help it, Longarm."

"There ain't any sense in crying about that now, I reckon. We'd just better give as good as we get and try to outlast these bastards. But it don't look like we're going to catch ourselves any coolies tonight."

"What should we do?"

"Split up."

Longarm turned to Gus Mullen. "Help Scott, here. Make for the coast, then work south until you come to our horses. Take off as soon as you reach them." Then Longarm looked at Stokey. "Hightail it south right through the timber, Stokey. Don't wait for anything, but don't go for the horses if there's anyone close on your tail. You got that?"

The man nodded.

Scott rose to his feet, his face pale as he clung to his right arm. Darkness was falling fast, but Longarm had little difficulty in seeing the lines of pain etched on the Mountie's face. "Good luck, Scott. I'll hang back here some to give you fellows a running start. Now, git!"

They slipped off quickly, silently through the damp woodland. Longarm waited a decent interval, then moved out from behind the great tree and, keeping low, began to edge through the heavy underbrush toward the line of sailors he could hear now crashing recklessly through the woods toward him.

Swinging wide, Longarm ran back toward the slope he had crested earlier. He kept going over the top of the slope, then swung back again, aiming to come in behind the sons of bitches. He ran until a sharp stab of pain flared in his lungs, then kept on running regardless, forcing himself not to feel it, his soft-soled boots making little sound in the spongy fir needles. He was out of breath by the time he reached the timber behind the sailors. He slowed and squatted behind a thick clump of bushes and waited until he could breathe without pain.

Then he moved out from behind the bush and began to trot slowly, his rifle at the ready, into the timber. By this time, he hoped he was on the heels of the sailors. He saw a dim splash of color as a red-shirted sailor left the cover of a clump of trees and darted across a small clearing. Longarm stopped, aimed low to maim, not kill—and fired. The sailor stumbled forward for a few staggering strides, then collapsed with a cry into a thick patch of undergrowth. There were sudden shouts on all sides of Longarm. Men were calling to each other, trying to find out who had been shot, and who was doing the shooting.

Longarm dropped full-length upon the spongy turf and waited. A figure darted close by through the gathering murk. He tracked him with his Winchester and squeezed the trigger. The bullet hit low. He heard the *thunk* of the slug as it burrowed into bone and sinew, the muffled cry of pain and surprise as the sailor pitched forward.

"Two," he told himself softly, remembering that Scott had warned him of ten sailors, at least.

There were more shouts, from ahead of him this time, and Longarm could hear the sound of running men as they pounded about in the gloom of the timber in something bordering on panic. Longarm levered a cartridge into the firing chamber, and got quickly to his feet. He ran softly past the still-flopping sailor toward the sound of another one of them plunging recklessly through the underbrush. Increasing his speed, he drew closer to the fellow, though he was unable to see him yet.

And then he broke into a small clearing, the running sailor just ahead of him, less than ten feet away. The fellow heard Longarm's footsteps and started to turn. Without stopping, Longarm fired. The slug caught the man in the thigh. Longarm could see the explosion of blood erupting from the fellow's tight, dark pants as he tumbled forward onto the ground.

"Over here!" the sailor cried as he rolled frantically away from Longarm. "The son of a bitch is over here, behind us!'

Longarm overtook the man, silenced him with one downward thrust to the skull with the stock of his rifle, then grabbed him by the collar and dragged him into a deep clump of evergreen and fern. He looked quickly about him in order to place the spot securely in his memory, and then took off his shirt and hat, folded the shirt neatly, placed his hat on top of it, and thrust them in under a low, ground-hugging branch of evergreen. Snatching off the sailor's dark stocking cap, he pulled it down onto his head and yanked off the sailor's dark, bulky sea jacket and shrugged into it. It was a mite tight, but it would have to do.

All this had taken but a few minutes, yet the woods were rapidly coming alive with the pounding and shouting of sailors answering to their downed companion's call of a moment before. Longarm stood up and walked out from his cover. By this time darkness had pretty well fallen. Even if it hadn't, the close cover of the high trees overhead made it dark enough.

Three men appeared out of the gloom. At sight of him, they changed direction to make for him. Another two sailors approached him from behind.

"That you, Simon?" one of the men approaching from the rear called.

"Over here!" Longarm cried, muffling his voice as he waved his arm. "The son of a bitch is in here!"

Longarm then trotted into a dark pocket of trees and fallen timber. The going was rough, but he kept himself well ahead of his companions. They followed him obediently, still suspecting nothing, while Longarm kept his eyes and ears open for the rest of them. There should be three or four more, according to Scott's count.

The sailors behind him were catching up to him. In a moment they would notice his height, perhaps—or the Levis he was wearing, and the boots. Longarm kept going, hoping the increasing darkness would forestall his discovery. Shouts came from his left.

The sailor pounding close behind Longarm shouted back to the two sailors stumbling out of the brush, "This way! Over here! Longarm's gone this way! We're on his tail now!"

Longarm's gone this way!

Those four words hit Longarm with the impact of a gun butt. They knew who he was! They had been waiting for him. It was *him* these bowlegged sea dogs were after!

Just ahead of Longarm, the great, needle-straight trunk of a Douglas fir loomed, its base clothed in a thick tangle of vines, tall ferns, and evergreen brush. By this time, he figured, he had led this pack of assassins far enough inland to give Scott and the others all the time and distance they needed. It was about time for Longarm to show his hand.

Sprinting quickly ahead of the sailors, he shouted as unintelligibly as he could and pointed off to his left. He hoped they would interpret his garbled shout as meaning *He's over there!*

"What the hell's the matter with you, Simon?" the same sailor who had called to him before shouted. "I don't even see the bastard yet!"

But the two newcomers who had just recently joined them, along with the other five, veered off in that direction, passing within five or six feet of him in the wet, smothering darkness of the timber. Their panting and stumbling told him how exhausted they were by this time. Exhausted and no longer alert—except for that sailor who hadn't seen the bastard Longarm yet. . . .

Longarm pulled up suddenly, ducked back into the shadow of the big fir, and allowed the sailors to crash through the brush and on past him. As soon as all their backs were to him, he dropped to the ground and crawled on all fours into the thick brush at the base of the fir. For a few moments longer, the sailors staggered on into the dark woodland without him. Then Longarm heard that same smartass calling to the others to hold up—that Simon was gone.

Listening intently, he heard the rest of the sailors, their voices raised in sudden queries. In a short while there was a general consensus, and one of their number raised his voice in a shout.

"Hey, Simon! Where the hell are you? Simon! You all right?"

Longarm waited, and waited some more. He did not answer, of course. Once more the same fellow let out a yell, after which there was a sound of low, muffled palaver. It was dawning on them who it was who had led them this far into the timber. Longarm heard sharp, surprised exclamations.

And then there was only silence. They were backtracking cautiously through the timber, wary now, alert. And perhaps just a mite abashed at how close they had come to having that bastard Longarm by the short hair.

As they returned, they passed within a few feet of him. While they went by, Longarm counted them. There were seven, all right. Scott had been right in his original count. Ten sailors from that bark had been sent after him. And meanwhile, of course, the coolies were well on their way to the U.S. border and either the Great Northern Railroad or the timberland of Helga Jensen after that.

Longarm swallowed his mortification as well as he could, and kept himself quiet. He was cold. The dampness of the bushes seemed to have seeped into the very marrow of his bones. Cold rivulets of moisture trickled down his back. His toes were icy and his long legs ached from keeping such a cramped position. But still he kept himself quiet, not moving a muscle. The sailors had long since passed, and he could no longer hear their passage through the woodland; but he knew that meant absolutely nothing. They sensed he was around, that he could not have gotten far without making so much noise that they would have to have heard him. He was close by, they realized, and they were right now in the process of seeking him out.

Occasionally Longarm heard a damp twig snap, followed by angry, muffled whispers. The sound of wet saplings and bushes releasing their accumulated moisture as a body brushed past them came to him more than once. And then, for a long, long time Longarm heard nothing. The woods were as silent as death, waiting like him.

When Longarm was finally convinced they had all passed well beyond and were perhaps now trudging from the woodland on their way back to the cove and their ship, he began to count—very slowly—to a hun-

133

dred. When at last he had finished, he came slowly to his feet, his nearly numb legs protesting with assorted creaks and snaps. He felt like he had almost rusted away, and what bolts and hinges were still serviceable needed a bit of oil to get them functioning smoothly again. Cautiously he stepped out of the shadow of the great fir tree and looked about him. There was now very little light filtering down to the forest floor, but he was determined to return for his hat and deerskin shirt. He had grown almost as fond of the damn shirt as he was of his Stetson.

He moved swiftly along. The sailors had broken so many branches and trampled through so many bushes that he had little difficulty in finding his way back. He had gone not more than a quarter of a mile when he halted suddenly.

He couldn't be sure, but he thought he heard something off to his left. It could have been a deer, a bear, or even a big cat. Cougars, they were called in this part of the world. Longarm kept himself as still as the young tree beside which he stood. The darkness about him seemed to deepen, as if the moss-laden Paul Bunyan who owned this timberland had pulled the windowshades down for the night.

The sound came again, and this time he knew which animal it was: a member of the human species. He dropped to one knee, turning in the direction of the sound as he did so. The darkness twenty feet from him exploded in a roar of brilliant orange. Something smashed hard into the tree beside him.

Longarm fired back, rolling away from where he had just been, as another shot flared out of the blackness. Then he heard the sound of heavy feet crashing through the brush, moving closer. He crabbed sideways and fired toward the sound of footsteps, not expecting to hit anything. An answering shot lanced out of the darkness toward him. He rolled again, cranked his Winchester's lever, and sent a shot at the flash, not really expecting the sailor to be anywhere near it by then. This man was a savvy gunfighter and an excellent tracker who had almost taken Longarm.

A broken twig betrayed the fellow's next move, and then the sailor began to run. He was moving to his right—as most men under fire do naturally. Longarm levered swiftly and got off a shot. He heard the slug shearing through the branches. Again the sailor fired, and this round thudded heavily into the tree beside him.

It had missed Longarm completely, but he was tired of this game; it was liable to get dangerous. He slumped heavily to the ground, letting his rifle fall, and set up a wild, painful groan. Thrashing on the ground, he drew his Colt, but kept it under his rolling body. At last he lay still, waiting.

Something snapped in the dark—a damp twig, more than likely. Longarm lay quietly. After what seemed like a whore's lifetime, he heard another crunching sound just beside his head. For a sailor, this fellow moved very quietly through woodland. He was probably not a sailor, Longarm realized.

He sensed the dark presence leaning over him and heard the loud cocking of a single-action revolver. Longarm decided playing possum had done him about all the good it could for now, and that he had better try something else a mite more active. He rolled swiftly over onto his back, lifting his double-action .44 and firing blindly in the direction of that last ominous sound. He kept moving away, crabbing sideways into the darkness, and snapped off still another shot. The return fire came swiftly. Longarm noted the bright wink of the other's revolver and fired again, not at the flash this time, but to its left, as once again his quarry moved instinctively to his right. He heard the sound of his round plowing into flesh, followed by that of a metal object crashing through brush to the ground—

135

then thrashing noises and a series of low, guttural curses. After that there was only silence.

Still he waited. This gent could be as shifty as Longarm had been a moment before.

Then he heard the fellow's harsh, labored breathing. If the man was acting, it was a damn fine job. Longarm stood up and moved cautiously over the ground toward the sounds, his Colt held out and ready, trained on the ground in front of him. In the inky darkness, the fellow was like a dark hole in lighter darkness. He moved slowly, twisting in awful pain.

Longarm rested the muzzle of his Colt against the man's temple. "Stay quiet. One twitch and this here weapon might go off, old son."

"You've done me in, you son of a bitch!"

"Who are you?"

"Go to hell."

"Seems likely I will, when the time comes. The way it looks now, though, you'll be there ahead of me, tending bar."

"Very funny, you bastard. You've done me, good and proper!"

Longarm pulled the muzzle of his revolver away from the man's head and stood up. "Stay here and I'll come back for you."

"Like hell you will. Do anything you want; I ain't goin' anywheres. Not now, I ain't."

The man groaned then, and twisted over onto his stomach. The darkness was so complete that Longarm could not see where the man had been hit, but the faintly sweet smell of fresh blood hung about the spot like a curse.

"Before I go, I want to know who put you and the rest of those sailor boys onto me."

All Longarm got from the man was a dim, garbled mutter. He nudged the fellow's body gently with the toe of his boot. There was no response, none at all. He went down on one knee beside the fellow again, groped for his shoulder, and pulled him gently over onto his back. The man's dim face—his eyes black, lustreless coals—glowed palely, lifelessly in the darkness.

Longarm had asked his question just a mite too late, it seemed.

Standing up, he gazed down at the dim figure in the grass, trying not to feel as badly as he did about the demise of a fellow human being. After all, he told himself, this wasn't Shiloh, and the fellow at his feet wasn't that fourteen-year-old boy he'd killed among the cherry blossoms. He shook his head to clear it of the image that sometimes bubbled up unbidden at moments like this, and steeling himself, he bent once again and fished quickly through the dead man's pockets. He came up with a small plastic package of sulfur matches, a plug of chewing tobacco, and a fistful of silver. And that was all. There was nothing to help identify the man.

He kept the matches and tossed the chewing tobacco into the night. He thought for a moment about the silver dollars, then shrugged and pocketed the heavy coins. Striding off through the wet darkness, he held his forearms up in front of his face most of the time to ward off the dripping bushes and giant ferns. In all that rushing about he had lost his way completely in this Stygian darkness. All he could hope for now was a clearing that would give him some glimpse of the night sky. When—and if—the moon and stars became clear enough for him to read, he might be able to find his way back to that tree where he had left his hat and shirt, and after that, to where his horse was waiting.

He was still plunging through the hellishly wet gloom when the sound of a rising wind alerted him. He pulled up, cursing. Another rain. It came softly at first, like the gentle clapping of a thousand hands. And then, as if someone had knifed an enormous water sack, great, ropy gouts of water began cutting down through the darkness. There would be no moon and no stars this night.

Cursing powerfully with his lips clenched tightly to keep out the torrential rain sluicing over him, Longarm found shelter of a sort among the roots of an enormous Douglas fir, pulled his legs up under him, hugged himself—and began to shiver. Eventually, for want of something better to do, he closed his eyes and went to sleep.

The last thing he told himself was that on his return to Slab City, he was going to see if he could make some new friends. His old ones—and that included Scott McPherson—weren't getting him anywhere at all.

Chapter 8

It was late the next day when a soggy, sodden Longarm rode into Slab City. Leaving his mount at the livery, he visited Chang Li Chang's tailor shop, where he picked up his mended frock coat and vest. It was a remarkably fine job. Though Chang refused payment, Longarm pressed upon him some of the dead sailor's silver. After that, he returned to the gunsmith for the derringer, dripping water where he stood as he examined the small loop the man had attached to the butt. Next, he picked up his repaired watch and found a barber shop.

After that, a steaming bath and a hot meal topped off with two glasses of beer put him in a slightly better frame of mind. Slightly. He was still about ready to box the ears of a grizzly as he entered his hotel room and slumped wearily down on the bed.

The sounds of Helga's loggers in the streets below came to him dimly through the closed window. A few desultory shots were fired somewhere in the distance. There was whooping and hollering. That new constable was not going to have an easy night of it. But that was not Longarm's concern. This is what he told himself as he examined closely, for a second time, the mended frock coat and vest. It was amazing how that little Chinaman had matched the weave of the frock coat. And the vest was almost as good as new. At least he would be decently attired for the remainder of this miserable, wet mission.

He stood up and yanked off his boots. Like his earlier pair, they were low-heeled cavalry stovepipes. He had bought them a size too small, and the soaking rain of the night before had done to them precisely what he had wanted. They had dried out these past hours and molded to the shape of his feet. In these tightly fitted boots he could outrun any man—especially any logger—his size.

He peeled off the Levi's he had worn, and after that his longjohns, then put on newly purchased balbriggans and his brown tweed pants, now thoroughly cleaned and pressed and fitting as slick and close as a second skin. He shrugged into a new brown flannel shirt. After strapping on the supple, cordovan leather gunbelt, he withdrew the Colt from his cross-draw rig and proceeded to examine it closely.

He had been lucky enough to find another .44 with walnut grips, and he liked the feel of it against his palm. He swung out the Colt's cylinder, dumped its cartridges on the bed, and triggered the revolver. Earlier he had cleaned away the gummy deposits left by the black powder after his gunfight with the sailors. Now, catching the hammer with his thumb rather than letting it snap on an empty chamber, he was checking out the action. It was a new weapon and he wanted to be sure of it. Satisfied with the action, he reloaded the Colt, checking each cartridge before sliding it into the cylinder, and dropped it into his high-riding holster.

Then he checked out the derringer, carefully inspecting the tiny loop soldered to its butt and loading it just as carefully as he had the Colt. Clipping the gold watch chain to the butt of the derringer, he dropped the watch and derringer to the bedspread, pulled on a fresh pair of woolen socks, and over them his boots, and stood up. The vest and frock coat were next, and into the left and right pockets of his vest went the watch and the derringer respectively, the bright gold chain gleaming as it draped between the pockets.

In a moment he was ready for the street, a clean linen handkerchief tucked into the breast pocket of his frock coat. Snatching up his Stetson from the bedspread, he positioned it carefully on his head, dead center and tilted slightly forward, cavalry style, the hat's crown telescoped in the Colorado rider's fashion.

Longarm hadn't minded wearing that deerskin jacket, but he felt more at home dressed in his accustomed way.

And besides, he had decided to call on Lillian M'Ling. She hadn't told him all she knew, he was certain of that. And then, of course, there *was* that parting kiss. . . .

Longarm was almost across the lobby on his way to the door when Duff Ryan entered the hotel, his eyes lighting with pleasure at sight of the lawman.

"I was beginning to get worried about you!" Ryan boomed, wringing Longarm's hand in a warm handshake. "After what those two shiftless loggers with that sad Mountie told me, I was about ready to hunt up a posse of my own and go after you."

"Nice to know you were thinking of me. Where are they?"

"The Mountie is on his way back to Canada, licking his wounds, I imagine. Those two loggers you dug out of my saloon are back in the Palace, making up for lost time."

"Cuttin' their wolf loose, are they?"

Duff Ryan grinned suddenly, like a possum eating yellowjackets. "I guess they got a little damp out there. They're making more noise than a Mexican revolution. If you want to talk to them, you'd better hurry. They won't be on their feet much longer."

"I'm just relieved they got back all right," Longarm replied.

"Good. If you've got the time, I've got something to tell you. Something that might make this mission of yours a bit easier."

"I'd appreciate that, Duff. So far I've been about as successful as a skunk at a lawn party. What have you got for me?"

"Follow me. I'll tell you as we walk."

Longarm shrugged and fell in beside Ryan as the man led the way out of the hotel and down a back alley that led to another alley running parallel to the street. As they proceeded, evidently heading toward Ryan's general store, Ryan told Longarm what he had. He started off by asserting that he now had proof that Helga Jensen was behind the smuggling.

"You have proof, you say?" Longarm asked.

"You heard me correctly, Longarm."

"What kind of proof?"

"One of her own Chinamen. He has told us everything. Once you hear what he has to say, you'll have no recourse but to apprehend that hellcat." He looked at Longarm. In the darkness, Longarm thought he saw the man's eyes gleam. "Then we'll see to that dung pile they call Chinatown. We'll burn it off the face of the earth. Clean up this town once and for all. I've got plans for Slab City, Marshal—but they do not include Chinese, or any who push their cause."

"I see." Longarm took out a cheroot and clamped down on it, hard. This was the man Longarm had come to expect. But he was a damned sight more agitated than he had been before Longarm took out after that last shipment with Scott. The man was obviously quite changeable in his moods.

"Where have you got this fellow? In jail?"

"Of course not. He's an informer. Once it became

142

known he was telling us what he knew, his life wouldn't be worth a plugged nickel. Look what happened to La Tour."

"And Scally," Longarm added.

A logger, so drunk he couldn't have hit the ground with his hat in three throws, staggered out the rear door of a small tavern and reeled drunkenly across their path in the general direction of the nearest outhouse. The two men slowed to let him pass, then continued on. The logger missed the outhouse completely and vanished in the darkness.

"Helga's back is to the wall, Marshal. She is having trouble getting financing from her bank in Seattle. She's missed her last payroll and is losing loggers. Her only hope is the coolies. And with the coolies she's bringing in here, she might make it. Unless you can cut off her supply."

"So you can take over her land and sell it to the railroad."

"Of course. I don't deny that." Duff Ryan chuckled. "That's what free enterprise is all about: seeing your chance and taking it, striking while the iron is hot. That bitch has been a thorn in my side since way back. I want her land for the railroad. If it takes that route, it will have to build a roundhouse and a switching yard in this city. Can you imagine what that will do to this town—to land values?"

"It'll put Slab City on the map, all right."

"And that woman's illegal aliens must not be allowed to stop me. It is not for myself alone that I want to stop her; it is for this town. This territory. I intend to keep her yellow devils out of Washington Territory. We have already fought one war to prove we don't need or want slave labor in this country. How many times must we make that point?"

"No more speeches, Duff," Longarm said, holding up his hand in mock defense. "No more. I think I know how you feel."

"I just want my position in this town to be made perfectly clear, Longarm."

"It is, Ryan, it is. You and Spittles are against the Yellow Peril and for Free Enterprise."

Duff Ryan chuckled. "Precisely."

By that time they were behind Ryan's general store. The man stopped and reached out to guide Longarm carefully down a short flight of steps dug out of the ground. The steps led to a solid oaken door leading into the cellar. Ryan knocked once, paused a moment, then knocked twice more. A moment later the door swung inward, and Longarm stepped into a narrow passage lit only by the dim lantern held by the fellow who had opened the door. Ryan followed Longarm into the passage, waiting for his man to close and bolt the door and then lead the way down the passage. They followed for what Longarm thought was a considerable distance, then stopped before another door.

A sharp rap on this one caused it to be pulled open swiftly, and Longarm entered with Duff Ryan. The room was small enough, with a table in the center and four rickety chairs around it, a dusty window with a shelf under it, an oil lamp sitting on the shelf. The light from this single lamp cast a dim, yellowish light over the face of the coolie sitting at the table. The man's wrinkled, prunelike face was already several shades of purple in spots. One of his eyes was closed almost completely, and a bloody smear had taken the place of his nose. Longarm had little doubt that if the fellow opened his mouth, it would reveal more than a few missing teeth.

He had been worked over pretty thoroughly—so thoroughly, Longarm reminded himself, that there was not much chance the Chinaman would not see the wisdom of telling Duff Ryan precisely what he wanted to hear.

The two men acting as the Chinaman's guards stepped back as Longarm and Duff Ryan stepped closer

144

to the table. The coolie had been slumped forward, one cheek resting wearily on an open palm, his one functioning eye staring straight ahead of him. At Longarm's entrance, he had stirred slightly, and now, as the two men stopped in front of his table, he looked up at them, stark, abject fear registering on his wrinkled countenance.

"Mu Siang," Duff Ryan said sternly, "tell me again what you told me earlier—about Helga Jensen."

"She good woman! Good woman! That all Mu Siang say!"

"Damn you! What about her foreman? What about Ton Key?"

"Ton Key! Yes . . . she bling wife for Ton Key! Good woman. She good woman!"

Ryan turned in triumph to Longarm. "You heard that, didn't you? That she-devil is now importing wives for her coolie workers! It's a wonder she can stand the competition. But there is more to it than that. This man has only recently arrived. He knows who else in Slab City besides Helga Jensen is behind—"

Ryan never finished the sentence. A gunshot shattered the silence, and the single, dirt-encrusted window shivered into jagged fragments. Longarm saw a face at the window, and then another shot exploded, disintegrating the lamp's chimney and splattering burning oil over the floor and wall. In the act of drawing his Colt, Longarm ducked away from the sudden heat.

As flames began tracing mad, flaming ropes over the floor and walls, a third shot caught the Chinaman even as he stood up in a panic and made for the door. The slug drove him sideways and sent him crumpling into a corner, his twisted form seeming to dance in the light from the flames rapidly filling the room. The heat became searing. The smoke stabbed mercilessly at Longarm's eyes. Another shot came from outside the window, and Duff Ryan let out a startled cry as the slug sang past his cheek. Longarm, in the act of backing up

145

toward the door, sent two quick, useless shots into the darkness beyond the window, then turned and followed Duff and the two men out the door.

In the darkness of the narrow passageway, the four men stumbled repeatedly against one another, falling in a sudden heap at one point. The acrid smoke was following them, stinging their eyes, stabbing into their lungs with each gasping breath. It was Duff Ryan who reached the outer door first. Longarm heard him throw the bolt. Ryan's curse came sharply, desperately.

"They've wedged it shut! I can't open it!" Ryan cried.

"Let's all give it a try," Longarm suggested, grabbing the handle.

The others tried to gain a hold on the door and pull with Longarm as he tugged on the handle. The door swung in, but something—a rope, perhaps—was holding it fast. At last he realized it was hopeless.

"Is there another way out of here?" Longarm asked, coughing.

"No!" Ryan answered.

"What's back there beside that room?"

"The place where we kept the Chinaman."

"Does it have a window?"

"No."

Longarm brushed past them and started back down the passage with the other three following behind him. The flames were leaping out of the room now, which had become a roaring inferno. His eyes closed tightly, his breath held—as if he were diving under water— Longarm ducked past the blazing room. In a moment he came to the room Duff Ryan had mentioned. He darted inside, the three following after, and slammed the door shut behind them.

He fumbled for his tin of sulfur matches and lit one. In the single, wavering flame he saw a cot, neat piles of clothes on a low table, a commode with a large pitcher of water and a washbowl along one wall. There was a small woodstove with a chimney going up through the ceiling at the corner of the room.

"Up through there!" Longarm said, as the match in his hand flickered out.

One of the men was already on his way. He ripped the stovepipe down, dragged the stove over to the corner of the room, and, standing on it, began to poke his shoulders through the narrow opening. Longarm was under him by this time, another lighted match held high. But as he watched the man through the ever-thickening coils of smoke, he saw that it was hopeless. The hole for the pipe had been cut through a beam, and the walls of the room would not give an inch. The fellow pulled his head out of the opening, swearing, and jumped down off the stove.

Longarm turned then to the pitcher. As the match in his hand went out, he reached for it. The pitcher was heavy with water. He could barely make out the cot in the dimness. He ripped off one blanket and poured the pitcher of water carefully all over the blanket. Quickly he removed his frock coat and vest, wrapped the vest in the frock coat, and gave the bundle to one of the men.

"You come out of here without that and I'll kill you," Longarm said. "And I want it in good shape, you understand?"

The fellow nodded.

Longarm lit another match and gave it to Duff Ryan. "Hold this," Longarm told him, "while I get set here." He took off his hat and placed it on Duff's head. "And you take care of that, Ryan—or I'll kill you too." Longarm smiled thinly at both men, then pointed to the other fellow. "When I say open that door, open it."

The fellow walked to the door.

Longarm turned to Duff Ryan. "I'm going out through that open window in the other room. Give me about two minutes, then get back down that hallway." Longarm patted his rear pocket where he kept his

147

knife. "If it's a rope holding that door, I'll have you out of here. If not . . . " He shrugged and turned to the bed.

First he draped the sopping wet blanket over himself, then he snatched up the mattress and held it in front of him. He couldn't see worth a damn, but he knew that once this door was opened, he'd be able to feel the heat of that room. And once past its doorway, he'd be able to cross the small room in an instant and launch himself through the window. At least that was the plan.

"Open the door!" he called.

Someone yanked the door open. A thick cloud of smoke rolled in through the open doorway. Longarm felt the heat. He lowered his head and, thrusting the mattress ahead of him, plunged across the passageway and through the wall of fire and smoke into the blazing room. He felt the soles of his feet blistering, his thighs searing. He dared not inhale, and his eyes burned in his head like coals in a potbellied stove. Slamming into a wall, he reached out and felt the shattered panes of glass still clinging to the window sash.

He flung aside the smoking mattress, ripped off the now flaming blanket, and with his arm across his face, he flung himself through the shattered window, his head and shoulders carrying the remaining glass and window frame with him. He struck the ground outside shoulder first, and rolled, aware that parts of his shirt and Levi's were smoking. Small, dark figures loomed close, then ran off as he rose in their midst, cursing. It took him a moment to get his bearings; then he darted around a corner, found the steps leading to the cellar, and descended them. He reached for his knife, but found it was not rope that held the door shut; a long, narrow beam had been slipped through the handle and across the sill.

From the other side of the door came a frantic, desperate pounding. Longarm yanked out the board and kicked in the door. An explosion of black, choking smoke struck him as Duff Ryan and his two henchmen erupted from the cellar like buckshot from the muzzle of a shotgun. Coughing and wheezing, rubbing their smarting eyes furiously, their faces black, their clothes smoking, the three men staggered with Longarm away from the building.

By this time the fire had attracted considerable attention. The back alley became alive with men carrying sloshing buckets, while the air was filled with the sound of men shouting orders. A crowd quickly gathered around Longarm and the others, and began firing questions. Duff Ryan, wheezing painfully, angrily refused to comment. His two comrades followed sullenly behind him as he brushed through the encircling ring of curious onlookers and started from the alley.

Longarm followed them. Once they reached the street, one of Ryan's men handed Longarm his coat and vest. The other gave Longarm his hat. Both of them did it with a certain amount of pride. Longarm thanked them both, gravely, courteously. Shrugging into his vest and coat, he checked out the watch and derringer with a quick pat, touched the brim of his hat to the still-besmirched and angry Duff Ryan, and then left the three men. He knew where he was going. And now he had an even better reason for going there.

When the shooting had started, he had glimpsed a face in the window—the face of Lillian M'Ling.

Chapter 9

This time Longarm did not have Charles Swinburne
Spittles to guide him, but he did not need him. Once
he reached Chinatown, the sound of the firebells in
the night behind him faded almost completely. He had
entered a fragrant, narrow world that might just as well
have been a settlement on the moon for all the attention it paid to the rest of Slab City.

Dim street lamps sent flickering orange light over
the storefronts and the faces of the men and women
hurrying past him on the narrow wooden sidewalks.
Only a few bothered to glance up at the tall, broad-
shouldered lawman in the snuff-brown Stetson. Yet
Longarm did not for a moment believe that his progress
along the street went unnoticed.

A fat Chinese merchant was stacking rough crates
of green vegetables in front of his grocery. Longarm
passed the store and was almost staggered by the
pungent smell of old fish. A very large handcart was
being pulled down the center of the narrow street by
two lean, wiry Chinese. The cart was piled high with
bamboo-fiber sacks of brown Chinese rice, raw brown
sugar, noodles, bamboo shoots, and great bunches of
dried seaweed stacked on top, reminding Longarm that

150

nearly all the food these Chinese ate came from China, except for chicken, fresh vegetables, and fish. Passing an alley, Longarm glanced in. A family was huddled in a corner of the building, the woman bent over a great kettle hung above a wood fire. She was stirring the contents of the kettle while the concoction boiled in great, slow bubbles. Another member of the family was pouring a bowl of fishheads and bloody chunks of chicken—including feet, neck, and heads—into the swelling, steaming mass of vegetables and unhulled rice.

Longarm cut up a narrow side street and soon found himself in front of a shabby building with its steps and door unpainted, its windows solidly shuttered with thick, rough planking. He recognized it as the same building he had come out of when he had left Lillian M'Ling's apartment. Unlike so many of the other buildings, the street floor wasn't given over to some shop, a rarity in this crowded section.

He went up the three steps and knocked on the door.

Nothing happened.

Longarm knocked again, harder this time. Still nothing. Descending to the street, he picked up a fist-sized rock, then mounted the stairs and smashed resoundingly on the door. This time he heard sounds of scraping and clicking coming from the other side.

He stepped back and waited. The noise from behind the door continued for at least two minutes before the door swung open—a bare four inches. Longarm saw one slanting eye and a slice of a brown face looking out of the crack at him, well above the chain that still held the door. The fellow was at least as tall as Longarm.

"Whata wan'?"

"I want to see Lillian M'Ling."

"No savvy. Maybe closs stleet."

"Damnation! You tell Lillian I want to see her!"

"No can do! No savvy you!"

151

"You tell her I'm here," Longarm said, smiling suddenly, turning his back on the door, and taking out a cheroot and a sulfur match. He struck the match with his thumbnail, lit the cigar, then leaned back against the door. He felt the door slowly pushing against his weight; then it clicked shut and the clicking and scraping commenced again behind him. Longarm puffed on the cheroot, contenting himself with the thought that a single smoke once in a while—and especially after what he had just had to contend with—did not mean that he had fallen completely off the wagon.

What he would do, he would stop buying them altogether. When he got back to Denver, that is.

Longarm sat down on the top step to wait. Chinese passed up and down the narrow street, shuffling along in their slippers or banging along in oversized shoes that Longarm doubted could ever be made to fit their feet. A few glanced curiously at him, but most paid him no attention at all as they moved past in that steady, near-trotting walk they had.

Close to half an hour passed. Longarm had gone to the dogs and was now smoking his last cheroot when he heard the familiar scraping and clicking behind the door again. A moment after, he heard the door creak open.

Longarm did not turn his head.

"Go 'way. No catch 'em M'Ling person!"

Longarm said nothing as he continued to puff on his cheroot.

"Whata wan'?"

"I want to see Lillian M'Ling," Longarm replied, without looking around.

Another pause, ended by the banging of the chain against the door frame.

"All light."

Longarm ground out the glowing tip of his cheroot on the step, put its remains in his side pocket, got up, and stepped into the building. In the dim light he

152

could make out a few pieces of cheap, battered furniture—all sitting ghostly under a pale sheen of dust. He had to wait while the burly Chinaman put four arm-thick bars across the door and padlocked them there. Longarm did not remember such elaborate precautions on his last visit. The bodyguard nodded sullenly at him and padded swiftly across the dusty room. A bull-necked fellow with rope-thick muscles trembling under his olive skin, he did not glance back as he led the marshal into a narrow passageway and then up a winding flight of stairs, down another corridor, up another flight of stairs, and then to the left through a long, empty room until he stopped before a door and knocked.

The big Chinaman's twin opened the door. Wherever Lillian M'Ling was getting these hefty bodyguards, there sure as hell seemed to be a large enough supply. Holding back the curtain that covered the door, he stepped to one side. Longarm went in and found Lillian M'Ling waiting for him. She was reclining on a sofa against the far wall, her long legs enclosed in silk pajama-like slacks of a soft green color, and tucked in under her. Her jacket was of the same color, but it was tight, so tight that Longarm had little difficulty in discerning the full, rounded heft of her breasts. She was smoking a tiny clay pipe. The air was thick with the smell of opium smoke.

The big Chinaman closed the door behind him. Lillian M'Ling uncoiled her feet and rested them on the floor as she placed the pipe down on a small table in front of the sofa. She looked at him through gleaming cat's eyes.

"You've moved around some since our first meeting," Longarm remarked.

"My palace has many suites."

"Some palace."

"It will have to do." She smiled lazily. "Sit down, Longarm."

153

His nickname seemed to have become common knowledge in Slab City, he realized as he sat in an upholstered chair beside the sofa and placed his hat on the floor beside him, for want of a better place to put it. He looked at her. "Surprised to see me? Alive, that is."

"Of course not. The great Longarm is indestructible. Is that not true, O Mighty One?" she said, her eyes alight. That stuff she was smoking was doing wonders for her disposition, Longarm thought.

"You know what I am talking about, then."

"In my present state," she said lightly, "I find I know all and see all. You ought to have a smoke with me, Longarm. It would help you to unbend. You must get tired, standing up so straight and tall all the time, ridding the world of robbers and murderers and smugglers."

"No thanks," he said. "I'm having a tough enough time with these damn cheroots. Besides, knowing and seeing everything could get a mite tedious, it seems like. Anyway, I don't seem to be doing such a good job at ridding the world of smugglers. So far, that is. But I've got a pretty good idea where I can find some murderers. I suspicion I'm sitting not two feet from one right this minute."

Lillian M'Ling's face grew pale. She looked coldly at Longarm for a long moment, then clapped her hands smartly. Through a curtained doorway beside the sofa, her servant entered the room as if he had been catapulted.

"Whiskey," she said to the little man. "Bring two glasses and get rid of this!"

The servant swept up the tiny pipe and vanished through the bamboo curtain.

"Why do you hate me, Longarm? Why do you take sides with my enemies against me? Why do you save them from a death they so richly deserve? The fire was unintentional, but once I saw those flames, I applauded. Fitting! So fitting!"

Longarm regarded her silently. The workings of this enigmatic woman's mind were becoming an increasing complex puzzle.

The servant returned with a decanter of whiskey and two glasses on a gleaming silver tray. He placed it on the table before the sofa and fled the room. Lillian poured healthy amounts into both glasses, then handed one of them to Longarm.

"That poor old Chinaman was an unfortunate accident," she continued. "It was Duff Ryan I was after! And those others with him. In the darkness and the confusion, the old Chinaman took the first bullet. But it was Duff Ryan we were after—and we would have got him, if it were not for your foolish heroics."

"Ma'am, I was just trying to save my own self, that's all. I didn't have any hankering to roast with those three."

"That old Chinaman was not what he was presented to be, I am sure. Duff Ryan had been keeping him for weeks, priming him, feeding him. What libel on me did he get that old fool to spout?"

"It wasn't you he told me about at all. It was Helga Jensen." Longarm sipped his drink carefully. "You killed that poor old duffer for no reason, Lillian. It was Helga he was pointing the finger at—he said she was fixing to bring in a woman for her foreman."

Lillian rose to her feet, placing her now empty glass down on the tray as she did so. Longarm took a belt of his own whiskey and leaned back in his chair. He smiled. "Are you going to attack me, Lillian—or sick your bully-boys on me?"

"You are really so melodramatic, Longarm," she replied, smiling suddenly, brilliantly. "I have something to show you. It is in the next room. Will you follow me, please?"

Longarm got up and followed Lillian as she led the

155

way through the bamboo curtains into a much larger room, one with a wide window that looked out over the moonlit roofs of Chinatown. A large desk sat in one corner of the room; it was littered with papers and ledgers. Over it, a small wall lamp flickered. A large bed occupied the center of the room, its green, silken spread rippling like water in the lamp's trembling light.

"Over here," she said, leading the way to her desk.

When she reached it, she sorted quickly through rolls of parchment until she found the one she was searching for, and opened it. Placing it flat on the desk and using paperweights to keep its edges down, she pointed with long fingers at the rows of Chinese characters.

"That doesn't mean much to me, Lillian. Looks like a list of some kind, though."

"These are the names of Chinese workers in Slab City. Many of them, but not all by any means, work for Helga Jensen. All of them have come to me for help."

"Help?"

"Yes. I am their broker. I bring in their women. At least, that is what I have been trying to do now for the past six months—without much success."

"You admit you are smuggling in Chinese?"

"Yes. Chinese women."

"Of course, you'd deny this in court—and you're not about to sign a confession."

She smiled. The question did not even warrant a response.

"Why are you telling me all this, Lillian? You suddenly got a bad case of the come-cleans?"

"Have you seen many Chinese women in Slab City, Longarm?"

"Some, but not many. There does seem to be a shortage, at that."

"I try to meet the needs of these men, Longarm. But it is a costly business, providing willing prostitutes for Chinamen in this savage country, and all of the men are saving their money for their return home. It is a melancholy situation."

"I see. And of course you ain't making any profit on it. None at all. You just don't like to see grown men cry."

"Be as flippant as you like, Longarm. Laugh at me, if that pleases you. But what I am telling you is the truth." Her voice trembled now with conviction, and Longarm found himself a little uncomfortable for mocking her a moment before. She read correctly the change in his expression and went on. "The best solution is to bring in women—wives—for these men. It is, in fact, the only solution."

"What's stopping you? I've tried twice now to halt a shipment, and it's pretty plain that poor Hitch Scally had no better luck."

"Tell me, Longarm. Did you see any of the Chinese who were being smuggled in?"

"Yes."

"You got pretty close to them?"

"Too damn close, as a matter of fact."

"Did you see any Chinese women among them?"

Longarm thought for a moment. Then he shook his head decisively. "No, I didn't."

"Someone, Longarm, is diverting our shipments of Chinese women to Seattle, taking our ships, and using our landing spots in Canada to ship in coolies for work on the Great Northern."

"And you think it's Duff Ryan?"

"Who else could it be?"

"Duff Ryan is dead set against Chinese laborers. You ought to know that."

"Well, it is not Helga Jensen. She has come to me for help in finding wives for her workers. And I have taken money in payment from those men to deliver their women to them. So it is not I, Longarm, who is

157

diverting those women and shipping in those coolies for the Great Northern."

"You ever heard of Cyrus MacRae?"

"Vaguely."

"He's the chief engineer for the Great Northern. He's the one who needs those coolies. But you're sure as hell barking up the wrong tree if you go after Duff Ryan."

"He is a powerful man, Longarm. He controls most of Slab City, including the bank that is trying to squeeze out Helga Jensen by refusing to give her more capital to meet her payroll next month."

"He hates Helga; he wants her land. And with her out of Slab City, he could wipe out Chinatown, send the coolies packing. He is not a nice fellow, now that you mention it. But that's no reason to send a pack of your bully-boys after him. The death of that China-man, Mu Siang, is something you will have to answer for, Lillian."

"I know that, Longarm. And I am sure you will see that I do answer for it."

"One way or another, Lillian. I am a lawman."

"But you are also a gentleman?"

"That's what I like to tell myself. It ain't always easy, but I've got a few rules I like to keep."

Lillian had moved provocatively close to Longarm. "Do any of those rules forbid you from responding to a woman, Longarm?" she asked, lifting her face to his.

The scent of her—perhaps even the faint tendrils of opium smoke that still clung to her hair and clothes—assailed his nostrils. She moved still closer, and he felt the length of her body fit against his, the warm abundance of her breasts pressing close against him. Looking into her eyes was like peering into unfathomable depths. She was holding him and pulling him into her by the sheer force of her sensuality.

With her lips inches from his, and his arms aching to enfold her, to pull her close to him, he stepped back, amazed. "Now, Lillian, there ain't any law says I have to run away from a beautiful woman, but I got a job to do."

She was stung slightly by his moving away from her, but there was an amused glint in her eyes. "I am glad you think me beautiful, Longarm. I was beginning to wonder."

"Lillian," Longarm began, feeling a mite crowded, "tell me. When's the next shipment due in? And where?"

"A shipment of coolies?"

"Women. I understand Ton Key's future bride is supposed to be with this next bunch."

"Yes. She is supposed to be."

"Tell me what you know, Lillian. When's the next shipment due, and where are they landing?"

She smiled at him. "But the ship has been delayed and my . . . sources . . . have lost track of it."

"Your sources?"

"One of the Five Families in San Francisco, Longarm. You don't really need to know any more than that. And more I will not tell you."

"Not the Ong Leong Tong, I reckon. Or would that be pushing on you a mite too hard?"

"It is *not* the Ong Leong Tong."

"Where was the ship supposed to let your women off?"

"Fisherman's Cove, on the evening of the fourteenth. There will be a full moon that night."

"And how had you planned on smuggling these little women into Slab City?"

She smiled. "With the vegetables—on handcarts."

"Very clever."

"Perhaps it would be better if you forgot what I have just told you, Longarm." She stepped closer and put her arms around his neck. Leaning her body tightly against his, she drew his face down to hers and kissed him—as she had kissed him at the door the last

159

time. Longarm tried to pull away, to continue the conversation—and then he told himself the hell with it. He would finish the conversation afterward.

Their mouths locked together passionately, she steered him gently back to her bed and sat him down on it. Still holding him with the passion of her kiss, she began swiftly to undress him. His frock coat went first, and then her fingers flew down the front of his vest. After that came his shirt and the front of his longjohns. He heard the vest clunk heavily to the floor beside the bed, and tried to reach for it, but she pushed him gently but firmly back upon the bedspread and began nibbling on his earlobe while her quick fingers unbuttoned his fly. In a moment he was naked beside her on the silken bedspread, her lips now moving hungrily down his chest, her tongue toying maddeningly with his nipples before moving on down.

"Undress me, Longarm," she whispered.

To his delight, when he unbuttoned her jacket he found nothing under it but her. In a moment, he had slipped her silken pants from her long legs and found only the incredibly smooth softness of her naked limbs beneath his probing hands.

Longarm was acutely aware that he was being seduced, by a woman of incomparable skill in these matters. She was also a ruthless, unprincipled bitch willing to do anything, including murder, to gain her ends. He realized then what the male black widow spider must feel as his female pulls him close: a sense of doom, perhaps, coupled with an urgency that simply cannot be denied.

Well now, old son, he told himself, *if you wanted a safer line of work, you ought to've been a store clerk. This sort of thing comes with the territory, I reckon. You'd best enjoy it while you can!*

She was easing her long body onto him by this time, her lips still moving hungrily over his face, his neck, her incredible fingers sending bowel-churning flame through his loins. She had managed to release her hair, and it cascaded over his face and neck in wild, intoxicating profusion—a shimmering nightscape of subtle perfume. Abruptly, she forked a thigh all the way over and astride him. She sank deliciously onto him with a wondrous ease that left him breathless, and he heard her pleased gasp as she straightened up and began to ride him like a pony, a trotting pony, her head thrown back, her marvelously firm, upthrust breasts rocking too, her hair an inky cloud coiling about her head.

Longarm tightened his buttocks and found himself driving up to meet her, thrust for thrust, as she ground her pubic bone against his. She was crying out softly now with each movement. He ran his hands up and down her spine. He could feel her bones riding under her tight, smooth skin. His interest heightened abruptly. He got a firm grip on each of her small buttocks and started pulling her down upon him, helping her on each downstroke. Her groans told him that this was precisely what she wanted as her tempo increased and Longarm found himself stretching tightly under her, rising violently now to meet her every thrust.

Gasping in the enjoyment of his first climax, he found her still anxious to increase her pleasure. She kept going, and would not let him go. Despite the wetness, she still held him with a force that delighted and dismayed him at the same time. And then she shuddered, grew rigid, and flung her head back, letting out a tiny cry. It seemed to go on for some time, and the warmth now enveloping his vitals sent Longarm rigid once more, even as she collapsed, sobbing softly, onto his chest. Groaning, her lips found his and she began to kiss him wildly, her tongue thrusting like something alive as it probed deeply into his mouth. The smell of her was intoxicating, as was the sound of her panting, the feel of her perfumed breath on his face. She was all animal now, lust unhitched from any traces, wild, unrestrained.

Aroused now beyond anything he had experienced in a long time, Longarm took charge. He rolled Lillian over so that he was atop her. Astonished and delighted at his own abandon, he plunged deep within her. The force of his thrust caused her to gasp delightedly, and her legs rose to lock firmly around his bouncing buttocks. He held off as long as he could, since he was enjoying himself so completely, then came in a powerful, involuntary rush. But he was part of her now, grafted to her flesh, and he stayed inside, moving swiftly up farther onto the bed for a better purchase. He took his time now, savoring each thrust, pleased at the sight of her tossing head, her wide eyes, the deep, guttural grunts of pleasure that broke from her mouth involuntarily. At the last, it was so slow that she began to beat upon his powerful chest with her fists—and then, suddenly, she climaxed violently. She moaned and raked her nails along his back. Longarm paid no attention to her frenzy as he continued to stroke. He was hitting bottom each time, and soon she was back with him, her heels locked securely around his back.

She was growling now, the sound coming from deep within her throat. He heard her hoarse whisper, "You bastard! You're outlasting me! I'm coming! I'm coming again!"

She was right. This time they had a long, shuddering mutual orgasm, and she went suddenly limp beneath him. Aware of how heavy he was, Longarm allowed himself to lie upon her just long enough to catch his breath, then shifted his weight to his elbows and eased off her.

"Damn you!" she hissed softly. "I'm not through with you yet!"

She reached down and felt of him.

"You see! Longarm, you are well named! You are

long, succulent! I've never before met your equal—or mine. I refuse to believe you can outlast me!"

"If this here's a contest, I'll let you win it, if it means all that much to you. But you'll have to give me a little time to catch—"

The sound behind him was not what alerted him. It was the sudden gleam in Lillian's cat's-eyes. Aware in that instant of her betrayal—and of his foolhardiness in going naked against such a woman, he flung himself off the bed and groped for his vest. But he never reached the derringer. A powerful boot caught him in the face and sent him flipping backward against the wall.

As the wall slammed into the back of his head, lights exploded deep within Longarm's skull. But he shook it off and rose to meet the nearest giant of a Chinaman, who then waited for his friend to join him. Together they came at him. Fists hammered at Longarm's chest and face until he felt his knees turning to soup. As he began to sag back against the wall, pawing at them with all the fury of a week-old kitten, they moved in close and sent punishing, vicious slashes to his midsection. Twisting away only gave them a better target—his kidneys. The pain exploded just under his ribcage. He heard himself cry out as he plunged to the floor through a roiling sea of pain. . . .

Dimly, from far above him, he heard Lillian's voice. She was angry. Her words came in a fierce hiss of fury: "Damn you! Why didn't you wait? I wasn't through with him!"

As Longarm drifted off into blessed unconsciousness, he wondered if maybe it wasn't better this way. It was a cinch that Lillian M'Ling had not been about to let him go—not until she had wrung the last ounce of his manhood from him.

Spinning off dreamily, he thought he heard Lillian's voice rising to a crescendo. He wasn't sure whether it was a scream of dismay or simply her fury at being robbed of her plaything. . . .

Longarm regained his senses lying flat on his back on a low cot. Opening his eyes, he turned his head and found himself looking up into the face of Chang Li Chang. The old man smiled, his feathery chin whiskers stirring faintly. He was sitting in a chair by Longarm's side. Glancing past Longarm to his wife, he said something to her in Chinese. Li Fan left the room in a rush of silk.

Longarm was sore all over. He felt as if, while he had been unconscious, one of Lillian M'Ling's Neanderthals had tried to tie him into a pretzel. His head throbbed, and every breath he took brought a painful response in his right side.

He smiled cautiously at Chang, and said hoarsely, "Looks like the Terror of Evildoers has fallen flat on his face."

The old man bowed his head slightly. "It is as you say, O Fallen One. The body is that of a noble giant— but the intellect that inhabits it is very weak indeed." The old man shook his head sorrowfully. "What is it your Bible says about the Strange Woman? *The lips of a strange woman drop as a honeycomb, and her mouth is smoother than oil, but her end is bitter as wormwood, sharp as a two-edged sword.*"

"Never mind the Good Book, Chang. Stick to Confucius. What would he have to say about a fellow like me?"

"He would be speechless, O Fool of Woman, I am sure. Yet he would compliment you on your manners, of that I am equally certain."

"What am I doing here, Chang?"

"You are my guest."

"Now just how did you manage that? I got the impression that Lillian M'Ling's boys were just about to dump me onto a greased chute into hell, and they

164

weren't about to worry if I got there head first or ass first. As mean and cold-blooded as rattlers with a chill, they were. So how in tarnation did a little fellow like you get up the gumption to pull me out of that rat's nest?"

Chang smiled and shrugged his frail shoulders. "Things are not always what they seem, Longarm. Sometimes, perhaps, a humble tailor can see more— and do more—than a tall, striding Monarch of the Law. It is just a thought."

"You saw me go into Lillian M'Ling's place."

"Those who serve me saw you enter, that is true."

Longarm looked long and hard at the old man. There was steel in his eyes now, and beneath the frail appearance, the wrinkled brow, and the bewhiskered chin, Longarm glimpsed a strength and a power that until that moment the man had kept scrupulously hidden. This was no coolie tailor, no comical end man in the local minstrel show. Here was a power, Longarm sensed instantly, that rivaled or even surpassed that of Lillian M'Ling or Helga Jensen. Perhaps it was a power that exceeded even that of Duff Ryan himself, since it was so well hidden.

"Which of the Five Families do you represent, Chang?"

The old man bowed slightly. "The Ong Leong."

Longarm took a deep breath. "I am honored that such a person as yourself has seen fit to extend himself in my behalf."

The old man smiled in appreciation of Longarm's gentle mockery of him. "It is nothing. I can do no less for one such as yourself—one who bears such a talisman."

"Talisman?"

At that moment Chang Li Chang's wife appeared with a tray. On it was a hot, strictly Western meal: steak and fries, with thick slabs of bread and two steaming cups of black coffee, a heaping bowl of brown sugar beside them. She placed the tray on a small table beside the bed, and as Longarm smelled the hot, buttered bread and the coffee, his stomach contracted painfully. He had evidently been unconscious for some time, and as he thought this, he put his hand up to his face. A day-old stubble was spread across his chin.

As he swung his legs down off the bed and pulled the table close to him, he looked at Chang. "How long have I been out?"

"Last night and most of today. It is already past the sun's setting." Chang got up. "Eat well and then dress yourself. I shall await you in the next room. You will find your clothes over there on the table. Your weapons are there, as well. You will forgive me for having removed the bullets."

"Reckon I might as well, since you've already done it."

Chang bowed and started from the room, Li Fan darting ahead of him through the curtains. As soon as the old man had followed her out, Longarm fell upon the tray of food like a famished cougar.

It was after Longarm had eaten and while he was climbing back into his longjohns that he felt a soft, warm hand on the small of his back. He spun about to find himself looking down into the doll-like face of Li Fan. Startled, he moved back quickly, buttoning his balbriggans up the front with a speed that reflected his panic. If there was one thing Longarm did not need at this point, it was an affair with Chang Li Chang's wife.

"Shhh . . . !" she said, in a voice that was barely above a whisper. "To me listen, please!"

Longarm put up his hand. "You just stay right there, Li Fan, and I'll listen all you want."

"Tell Ryan I see him tonight! You tell him . . . !" Her voice was urgent, and the fire in her eyes brooked no contradiction.

166

"He knows where, I reckon," Longarm replied carefully.

"Yesss . . . !" she hissed. "That man know!"

She turned and fled the room.

Longarm took a deep breath. He would tell Duff Ryan, all right. But it might be a good idea to tell him at the same time just what kind of man he was messing with. A little old Chinese tailor Chang Li Chang was not.

As Longarm resumed dressing and looked around, he could not help being impressed. The room was obviously well in back of the building where the old man had his tailor shop, and it was easily as large as the shop and the room behind it. Such living space in the Chinese quarter, Longarm realized, was almost unheard of, except for those powers who ran the show. Two of the walls were covered with heavy, dark maroon, gold-bordered curtains. Longarm had a sneaking suspicion that it was real gold in the threads from the way the borders gleamed against the dark fabric. Two hazy Chinese landscapes hung from scrolls on the third wall. There were tiny Chinese figures in the corner of one and at the very bottom of the other, and both of them contained great mountain peaks rising out of mists to dominate each of the pictures completely. Chinese characters ran up one side of each of them.

The furniture was all small, but exquisitely detailed and finished. All the surfaces were lacquered to a shiny black sheen that was almost alive in its brilliance. The chairs and sofas were covered with gleaming gray silk, and the coverlet upon which he had lain was of the same incredibly smooth gray silken material. Thick, tightly-woven rugs covered the floor in a rich, careless profusion.

For some reason, Longarm mused, *as he buttoned up his vest, this rich and powerful old Tong leader has made himself responsible for your well-being. Maybe you better figure out why, before you start to take it for granted.*

Longarm was reaching for his Stetson when he paused and patted his chest. Frowning, he reached in past the buttons on his shirt. The medallion was gone. It was a valuable piece of jewelry, one that would instantly catch the eye of a thief; but more importantly, it was a gift he had prized.

He slapped his hat on, ducked low, and strode through the curtain into the other room. Chang Li Chang had been waiting patiently for him, and the little man came promptly to his feet and bowed as Longarm crossed the room to meet him.

"Your recovery is complete, I am gratified to see," the old fox said, smiling. "Once again you resemble the Knight of the Road who championed this insignificant and thoroughly unworthy creature."

"And his wife."

"Yes." The old man's eyes grew cold in spite of the role he was playing. "You are right, of course. And his wife."

"You mentioned a talisman a little while ago."

Chang sat down and waved his slight hand at an armchair close to his. Longarm sat down in it and waited.

"I have it now, Longarm."

"I'd like it back."

"We are, of course, talking of the medallion you wore on your chest."

"That's what I figured."

"Where did you get such a powerful talisman, if I may be so bold as to ask?"

Longarm told him of the fire in Denver and his rescue of the young Chinaman. When he had finished, Chang Li Chang nodded sagely.

"The young man whose life you saved rewarded you handsomely—with your own life, as a matter of fact. It was one of my men—employed unwittingly by Lillian M'Ling—who saw the medallion and contacted me. I had told him about it: that if he was to see a man wearing it in this humble city, he was to consider that man under my protection. Since it is the symbol of his Tong, he did not hesitate for an instant when he saw what his companion in the service of this M'Ling woman was up to. I now have the talisman, Longarm. The debt is paid. What it is worth, in monetary terms, is waiting for you in this."

Chang produced a fair-sized leather pouch from under his jacket and handed it to Longarm. Longarm took it. The heft of it astonished him. He looked questioningly at Chang.

"Two hundred dollars—in freshly minted gold coins."

"Take your gold, Chang. I want the medallion."

Chang shook his head. "It is on its way back to California, to the Ong Leong family, and the young princeling who was so foolish as to give it to a Caucasian."

"Princeling?"

"In terms of wealth, yes. He is now the heir to what will soon be the most powerful family in the Pearl River Delta." The old man smiled contentedly. "Soon he will be sailing in under the peak of Lintin, past the Dragon's Eye and into the Tiger's Mouth, past the forts and through the fleets of junks . . ." Chang closed his eyes and Longarm could tell he was seeing it all in his mind's eye. " . . . on into the Sea of Lions. From there he will be able to see the rice fields covering the flats on the eastern shore, the islands, the Pagoda of Nine Stories. . . ."

Chang opened his eyes and peered with sudden intensity at Longarm. "This young man—this princeling you saved—will return to his village in great pomp. There will be a banquet, firecrackers, and even a three-day-long theatrical performance at the temple. A beautiful concubine will warm his young body. And

169

then he will organize his clans and lead them against the Hakka and their Manchu hirelings, drive them from our ancestral holdings! Yes, he will do that," Chang finished more calmly, peacefully. "He has much luck, or he would never have found the Disperser of Crowds in that pestilential City in the Mountains."

By which, Longarm realized, Chang meant Denver. He handed the sack of gold coins back to Chang and stood up. "I'm glad I was able to help that young fellow. But I don't want any money for it—or for that medallion he gave me. Can you understand that, Chang?"

The old man rose to his feet also, and tucking the sack of coins in under his jacket, he bowed his head slightly. "Chang Li Chang is not without honor himself. He understands perfectly."

"We part as equals, then. Is that it, Chang?"

"Precisely."

"And the next time our paths cross—?"

"We will let the events decide themselves, shall we, Terror of Evildoers?"

"No holds barred."

The old man bowed again. "I tremble at the thought of such a confrontation. But so it must be, I'm afraid."

"And you're the one behind all this smuggling."

"I am a humble tailor, Longarm. I know nothing of what you speak. Now, go in peace, as you Christians are so fond of saying, and with the blessing of my ancestors as well."

"Thank you, Chang," Longarm said.

As he spoke, a not very tall but very tough-looking Chinaman appeared in the curtained doorway—Longarm's escort.

He followed the man out of Chang's apartment, down a series of hallways, and eventually to the street. He came out of a building that was at least two storefronts down from Chang's tailor shop. He heard the door being locked securely behind him, and felt just a bit like a little boy who has been spanked for messing his pants and is now sent out to play all by himself.

And then he remembered the message he had for Duff Ryan from Chang Li Chang's hot little wife, and hurried off. Duff Ryan was in trouble if he didn't keep his pants buttoned. The look in Chang Li Chang's eyes back there had told Longarm that the old duffer knew all about his young wife's shenanigans.

Chapter 10

Longarm was unable to find Duff Ryan at the Skidroad Palace, and only when he questioned the desk clerk at Ryan's hotel did the marshal learn that Ryan had left town earlier that day. The clerk did not know where he was headed, however, and Longarm was about to let it ride when he spied Charles Swinburne Spittles on his way down the stairs, apparently dressed for an evening on the town.

Longarm hailed the reporter, who pulled up smartly and turned toward the lawman, a cold smile on his face. Longarm walked over to him.

"You wouldn't happen to know where your boss has gone, would you, Spittles?"

"To Top Gap, I believe. Why?"

"Had a kind of urgent message for him, that's all."

"He left on the evening stage. He's going to see Cyrus MacRae, I believe, on some business concerning the Great Northern. Why not send him a telegram, if it is that urgent? If you address it to MacRae, he's sure to get it sometime tomorrow."

"Never mind, Spittles. This ain't exactly the sort of message that reads so well in a telegram."

Spittles frowned, obviously unwilling to make the

effort to understand this boorish deputy marshal. "Well, that's all I know. He left on the afternoon stage."

"Thanks."

The man nodded curtly and hurried out of the hotel. He left behind a faint odor of cologne. The editor who was so noisily afraid of the Yellow Peril, and who printed every libel on their race he could dig up, was on his way to Chinatown for a night's diversion. Longarm turned back to the stairs and headed for his room. If he was to get to Chilliwack and alert Inspector Brock Wilde in time to meet that next shipload, he had better make tracks.

This time they were going to be there and waiting well before the Ong Leong could set up another of their ambushes.

It was a saddle-weary, damp Longarm who slacked his long frame into a chair beside Brock Wilde's desk late the next afternoon. Wilde insisted on a drink before he would let Longarm begin.

"My own special stock, Marshal," Wilde told him, as he handed Longarm a generous tumblerful of Scotch.

Longarm took the tumbler and drank deeply. He felt better at once. He was already grateful that he was no longer sitting on something that rocked continuously under him. He crossed his long legs in front of him, leaned back, and told Wilde what he had discovered and why he was there. Wilde listened to Longarm's story with great interest, his sandy eyebrows rising devilishly at the more ribald details. When Longarm finished, he smiled broadly.

"Let me get Scott in here; I want him to hear this. Fisherman's Cove, you say?"

"I don't want Scott in here just yet, Inspector."

Wilde frowned. "And why not?"

"I don't know for sure. All I do know is that every

time I stick my head out when that man's around, there's somebody standing close by with an axe in his hand, ready to chop it off. I think it would be best if we kept this information between the two of us, for now."

"And that remarkable Eurasian woman, Marshal. She knows, as well. What do you think became of her?"

"I've been pondering on that. She told me what she did only because she had no idea I was going to walk out of Chinatown alive. I've got to say, she surprised me. And the way it looks to me, Chang surprised her not too long afterwards."

"Then Chang has her?"

"That's my guess," Longarm affirmed.

"So she'll tell him what she has already told you."

"Chang already knew about the shipment. But there's a good chance she's mean enough not to tell Chang she told me. She'd like it to be a surprise to Chang's men."

"If, that is, Chang's men have intercepted this Eurasian's latest shipment."

"She suspicioned he had. Her 'sources' told her that the ship was being held off the coast near Seattle."

"Then the ship will be delayed."

"Maybe, but we can't be sure of that. And the landing will most likely be at Fisherman's Cove."

Wilde stood up. "Which means the sooner we get to the coast and set up our welcoming committee, the better."

"Three days should be plenty of time."

"What about Scott?"

"Tell him I've got word it's Pirates' Cove—and not the fourteenth. Say it's later, maybe the sixteenth."

"And when he finds out differently?"

"He will, of course, when we get to Fisherman's Cove. So we watch what he does then."

Wilde took a deep breath. The inspector obviously

174

liked Scott McPherson and disliked having to distrust the man, but he saw the wisdom in Longarm's precaution. "All right, then. So be it. I am sure that Scott will exhibit no untoward behavior. He is a stout and loyal servant of the Queen—and a bloody good fighter to boot. You'll see."

"Has he recovered yet from our last brush with the Ong Leong?"

"Yes, completely. He was sick at heart that he had left you behind with those barbarians, but I assured him you'd be all right." He smiled. "Do you want to tell me what happened?"

"Later, Inspector, later. Right now I'd like a bath."

He got to his feet. Wilde slapped him on the shoulder and escorted him to the door. "Use my quarters and rest up. We'll be moving out before sundown."

It was late afternoon of the next day when Constable McPherson rode up beside Longarm and Wilde. He seemed somewhat agitated, his dark bushy eyebrows knitted angrily. Wilde glanced swiftly at Longarm before addressing the constable.

"Yes, Scott? What is it?"

"Inspector, I just spoke to that damn scout. He says you told him we're going to Fisherman's Cove."

Wilde glanced quickly at Longarm. The two men had agreed that as soon as they got close enough to their destination and Scott began asking questions, they would admit to the man their real plans. Looking back at Scott, Wilde said, "Just a precaution, Scott. We felt the best plan this time would be to tell no one of our true destination—except for the scout, of course— until we got there. It is Fisherman's Cove, Scott, and we're expecting a ship to put in there on the fourteenth."

"Not the sixteenth?"

"That's right."

"Do you know what ship it is, Inspector?"

175

"No, I don't."

Scott was thoughtful a moment as he rode alongside the Inspector and Longarm. Then he nodded quickly to his superior. "Good idea, sir."

As Scott galloped ahead to rejoin the scout, Wilde looked at Longarm. "He took it well, I'd say. Nothing suspicious in the way he reacted. An intelligent and resourceful man, Marshal. I'm sure your suspicions are groundless."

Longarm did not reply. Maybe Wilde was on target about Scott, but as his mother used to say, they'd best wait until the pie was out of the oven before they started eating it.

This time Wilde had brought twenty-five of his mounted police. Counting Wilde, Scott, the scout, and Longarm, there were in all twenty-nine men making camp above the cove. Most of the day had been spent sending small patrols up and down the coast and inland as far as a couple of miles in some cases, looking for any sign of Chang's men. They still had a day to go before the fourteenth, and they had already selected the spots where they would lie low and wait for the ship—and Chang's men—to make their appearance.

"We got here first, I'd say," Wilde remarked. He had lit his pipe and was sitting on a log before the evening campfire. "This time the surprise will be ours."

Beside him, smoking a cheroot, Longarm nodded. "Looks that way."

"It surely does," said Scott.

The constable had been pacing steadily beyond the campfire's light, his hands clasped behind his back. It seemed to Longarm that the fellow was completely well by this time. There appeared to be nothing at all wrong with his shoulder. Of course the man could simply be fighting back the pain, apprehensive that his wound might keep him out of action if he allowed its effects to show. If Wilde's estimation of the fellow was correct, then this was precisely what Scott was doing.

"I think I'll turn in," said Scott. "Goodnight, Inspector, Marshal."

The two men watched Scott disappear into the darkness toward his bedroll. Wilde looked at Longarm.

"What now, Marshal?"

"We watch him. You take the first watch. Wake me at midnight. I'll take it from there."

Wilde nodded and the two men went to their bedrolls. As Longarm settled into his soogan, he went over the possibilities in his mind. If Scott was in Chang's employ, he would need to warn Chang, or whoever was directing the operation for him, that a trap had been set. If Scott had known of this shipment, he would have been quite willing to go on an expedition with Wilde to Pirates' Cove, since they would have caught nothing there. Now, however, Scott knew different. The fellow was probably in a fever at that moment, trying to figure out how he could sneak away to warn his confederates.

Longarm smiled to himself. Talk about jumping to conclusions. Poor Scott was probably sound asleep at the moment, with not a single errant thought in his head, as innocent as a babe.

Maybe.

The métis scout was shaking Longarm gently. At once Longarm was awake, his right hand closing automatically about his Colt's butt. The handsome, impassive face of the scout bent close.

"Constable Scott," the fellow said, his accent thick, "he ees gone now. I geeve him good start, sure. You want to follow, eh?" The man's gleaming white teeth flashed in his swarthy face.

"I'll be with you pronto," Longarm said, throwing back the soogan's flap and reaching for his stovepipes.

As soon as he was dressed, Longarm moved over

to the inspector. The fellow had propped himself up on his saddle to give himself a better view of Scott's bedroll. Then he had promptly fallen asleep. The man's suspicions concerning Scott had not been of sufficient intensity to keep him awake after the day's long ride. Longarm had expected this and had alerted the scout.

"Inspector," Longarm called softly.

The man awoke immediately, blinking his eyes in surprise.

"Scott's gone," Longarm told him. "I'm taking two men and the scout. I'd like to see where he ends up. We might be gone awhile."

Without waiting for Wilde's chagrin at his lapse to show, Longarm stood up and left the man. The scout was waiting for him outside the campsite with two Mounties they had both decided on earlier. Longarm looked at the métis and nodded.

"Let's go," he said.

They mounted up and moved off in the light of the nearly full moon, the scout in the lead. The trail led north into the roughest, most thickly timbered country along the coast. Wilde's patrols had done their best to scour this area for Chang's men, but the country had been entirely too rough for anything but a superficial look-see.

The métis was remarkable. Only twice did he have to dismount to study the ground—and each time only for an instant. They kept on through the thick wood, the horses not making good time due to the many rotting deadfalls, vines, and thick underbrush. And the wetness was everywhere, clinging to every branch, every pine cone, every fern. The trunks of the trees glistened damply in the dim moonlight. The four of them were soon soaked to the skin about the shoulders and along the outer thighs.

The advantage of this dampness, Longarm realized

with some resignation, was that they made almost no sound at all as they followed Scott.

The valley opened up before them suddenly. The scout reined in and dismounted, a single wave of his arm causing Longarm and the two Mounties to peel off their horses rapidly. As Longarm approached, the métis turned and smiled at him.

"In the valley—a small settlement I see. You see that smoke, eh?" The métis pointed. "And there. It is a roof, I think. Corral farther on."

The man's eyes were good, and with his help, Longarm was able to pick out the buildings in the dim, pre-dawn light. Two large log shacks, a barn, and a corral. The smoke was coiling out of a chimney on the largest of the two log buildings.

"Look there," the métis whispered. He was pointing to a horse in the corral. It was Constable Scott's chestnut, obviously, the quality of the horseflesh visible even from this distance.

"He's there, all right," Longarm said.

"What you want now?" the métis asked, his eyes and teeth gleaming in his dark face. He had probably habored a grudge against Scott for some time, judging from the enjoyment he was getting out of all this.

"Leave our horses here and move in," said Longarm.

The métis nodded briskly. The four of them quickly led their horses well back into the woodland and tied them securely; then, with the métis in the lead, they proceeded into thick brushland that extended down the slope of the ridge behind the two log buildings. The damp ground, spongy and inches deep in pine needles, enabled them to move through the tangle of woodland and down the slope with scarcely a sound.

Longarm and the métis carried Winchesters in addition to handguns; the two Mounties were lugging their Snider-Enfield carbines, their long-barreled Deane

179

& Adams revolvers tucked away in their flapped holsters. The métis reached the log building first. Peering through a rear window, he motioned to Longarm to come quickly.

Longarm joined him at the window and saw Scott McPherson and another man, standing with their backs to the window. Sitting on a fur-covered sofa, his face clearly visible to Longarm, was Cyrus MacRae. Scott was having his Royal Canadian ass chewed. The voice of the other man with his back to Longarm came sharply through the closed window. Duff Ryan was also lacing into the constable.

"How can you be sure you were not followed? Worse, your usefulness is at an end. How can you possibly explain this absence, sneaking away in the dead of night? You fool!"

"But I had to tell you! Otherwise you'd walk into a trap!"

"We had no intention of doing that. What do you take us for? We saw them coming. Our lookouts brought us the news yesterday when a few of your patrols searched north of the cove. We simply decided to lay low and let the damn Mounties have this batch. They're a mean, ungovernable lot of coolies to begin with!"

"So you see, Scott," Cyrus MacRae said from the sofa, "your trip here was not needed. It was a pure waste."

"I'll go back," Scott said hopefully. "I'll say I thought I heard something and went to investigate."

Duff Ryan glanced at MacRae. "You think he could get away with that?"

"I doubt it."

"It would be worth a try," Scott insisted.

"You'd be a fool to try it," said MacRae.

"But he might get away with it," said Ryan. "And he would still be of some use to us."

180

"I'll get away with it," Scott assured them. "But my cut. Where is it?"

Ryan answered, "At my bank. A savings account in your name. All quite proper."

"The full amount?"

"What we agreed on, yes."

"All right. I'll return to the cove."

"Then you better get a move on," said MacRae. "And have a good story ready."

Longarm turned from the window. Catching the métis's eye, he indicated with a quick nod of his head they should all move back into the brush.

Once in the cover of the brush, Longarm told them, "Move out. Fast. We can pick up Scott later."

The métis frowned. "You not wan' to take them beeg fish now, eh? They behind all this smuggling, you bet!"

"Right now," Longarm explained as he led them back up the slope, "the only evidence we've got on them is that they like hanging around in log buildings in this here timber—that and what we just overheard, which wasn't all that much. Duff Ryan is too powerful a man to get convicted on that kind of evidence. I'd like him back in Slab City, where I can maybe rile him some and just let him play out that rope a little more. The important thing is to stop this shipment of coolies —and to get the man who has been telegraphing every move the inspector has been making. Scott will have quite a story to tell us, I'm thinking, and those two back there will find themselves operating in the dark from here on."

The métis shrugged.

A moment later they broke out of the dense underbrush and moved back through the timber to their horses. With the métis in the lead, they rode back the way they had come. When they broke out of the timber, it was full daylight. They spread out in a broad fan, dismounted to rest their horses—and waited. The métis and the Mounties were under orders to take Scott without a fuss, if possible. He was more valuable to them alive than dead.

It was Longarm who spotted Scott first. The Mountie was urging his horse across the difficult ground with grim impatience, his quirt blistering the magnificent chestnut's flanks. Mounting up swiftly, Longarm rode to intercept him. A moment before Scott caught sight of Longarm, the métis scout broke out of the timber just beyond him, a pleased smile on his dark face.

Scott pulled up at sight of the scout, and was about to issue him an order of some kind, when he saw Longarm moving out of the timber on the other side of him. He glanced swiftly from one to the other. The man's face hardened as he realized what was up. His hand dropped to his holster.

Both Longarm and the métis lifted their rifles casually. Longarm reined in less than twenty feet from Scott, rested his rifle in the crook of his right arm, and sighted along the barrel.

"Leave that cannon in your holster, Constable. No sense in acting foolish. I'm sure you've got a reasonable explanation for being out here this early."

Scott relaxed and forced a smile. Longarm lowered his rifle, dropped it back into its boot, and rode closer. The métis rode alongside Scott and halted, his head tipped to one side as he regarded the Mountie through cool, appraising eyes.

"You're damn right I've got an explanation," Scott told Longarm. "I thought I heard something last night and I rode out to investigate. This timber here is pretty thick. We never did get a chance to scout it very thoroughly yesterday."

"Ain't that the truth."

"So what ees it you find, eh, Scott?" the métis asked, his swarthy face intent as he looked at the Mountie.

Longarm reached across the horse's neck and lifted

out Scott's carbine. "He found a small valley," Longarm explained, "with two large log buildings, a barn, and a corral. Inside one of the buildings, he spoke with Duff Ryan and the chief engineer of the Great Northern."

Scott made a sudden move for his revolver, his face drawn and white with desperation, but the métis grabbed Scott's right wrist, and while he held it immobile, he lifted Scott's revolver from its holster and stuck the firearm in his belt.

"Damn you!" said Scott, through clenched teeth.

"I don't reckon we need any more conversation, Constable," Longarm said. "Save it for Inspector Wilde."

The expected full moon had been out earlier in the night, an enormous silver dollar illuminating the cove and the shoreline with a clean, blue light. But clouds had moved in off the Pacific, and soon a light, miserable drizzle was falling.

The ship had arrived late and moved in as close as it was going to. Now it stood offshore, a dim hulk in the rainy dawn, its bow and aft lights flickering sporadically through the rain. From across the waters, the sound of shouts and curses—and once, a shot—came clearly to Longarm and Inspector Wilde as they waited.

According to what Scott had admitted to them before the métis escorted him back to Chilliwack, this particular shipment of coolies had probably been trouble from the start. Longarm remembered Duff's calling them an ungovernable lot, and Scott's explanation of the operation made it pretty clear why. Duff Ryan's henchmen boarded Lillian M'Ling's ships as soon as they anchored off Seattle, the captains and first officers having already been paid off. Ryan's men offloaded the Chinese women and sold them to a Tong for its cathouses along the coast. In return, the Tong supplied

Duff Ryan with coolies shanghaied from the mines or anywhere else they could be found. Longarm had no doubt which Tong Scott was referring to: the Ong Leong.

This particular batch of shanghaied Orientals, it seemed, had decided not to go quietly, either when they were first taken or now, when they realized they were to be sold into still another bondage. But they would have no choice, unless Longarm and Wilde gave them one.

The creak of oarlocks came clearly across the water. But as yet, nothing could be seen through the rainy mists that hung over the surface of the cove.

"My men are deployed, Marshal," the inspector told him softly. "Once all the coolies are ashore, you will move in close and hail whoever seems to be in charge. That will be our signal to reveal ourselves. Perhaps we can manage this without firing a shot."

Longarm nodded. The inspector hurried away through the rain. Longarm peered out across the water. Small, dim shapes were creeping closer across the rain-dimpled water, the sound of the oars growing louder with each passing second. Longarm was crouched behind a fallen log well above the beach, on a low bluff that overlooked the entire cove. Four miserably wet, tight-lipped Mounties were with him.

The first rowboat nudged well up onto the sand. A fellow sprang from the bow and steadied the boat. The coolies piled out, splashing through the knee-deep water up onto the shore. Armed men left the boat with them, and they were not gentle as they herded the coolies into a solid mass along the beach. The boats kept coming. Each boatload had its contingent of armed men. Longarm found it hard to believe that Duff Ryan would allow this shipment to land and be taken without making any effort to foil the Mounties. Yet that was obviously his intention. He and the inspector had deployed a small force well back in the timber, however, in case MacRae and Ryan should try anything mischievous.

There were sporadic outbursts of violence on shore, as irate Chinese tried to break loose. One Chinaman was shot as he raced down the sand toward a clump of pine. Another was cut down when he tried to wrest a gun from one of the guards. The men in charge of the shipment were cursing audibly at the resentful Chinese, and some could be heard angrily demanding the appearance of those who were supposed to meet them to take this heathen delivery.

A sailor left the huddled, chattering Chinese and started up the sandy incline toward the bluff. He was obviously looking for those he had expected would be waiting for the coolies. The drizzling rain made it difficult for the fellow to see very much, and he slipped more than once as he pulled himself up the sandy bank to the lip of the ridge. Longarm cautioned the Mounties with him to lay low.

With a last, angry scramble, the tall sailor reached the crest and stood before Longarm, his shoulders bent under the rain, while he peered into the gloom past the log where Longarm crouched. The man appeared hesitant. He obviously did not know whether to continue this fruitless quest or turn and go back down to the beach.

Longarm solved his dilemma for him. He stood suddenly. "That the lot of 'em?" he asked the sailor. "What's the matter with the buggers? They don't seem like a very nice bunch."

Startled, the sailor recovered his composure quickly. He seemed relieved. "Oh, there you be, is it? Whyn't you get here sooner? You're damn right them heathen are trouble. But they's your responsibility, so get your men. I want to get out of this here cove!"

"You the captain?"

"First mate. What's it to you?"

By that time, Longarm was standing beside the man,

the muzzle of his Colt suddenly thrusting against the man's side. When he started to protest, Longarm pushed the muzzle in deeper. "I'm not alone," Longarm confided softly. "Now if you want me to pull this trigger, I will. It won't make any difference to me, but it might make a hell of a lot of difference to you."

"Don't pull the trigger, damn you. What do you want?"

"I want you to stand here until all the coolies are landed. Let your men see us. They'll think I'm one of the people you expected. As soon as all the coolies are landed, you call up your crew. Tell them you want to see them."

"Up here?"

The deputy nodded. "That's right."

"What are you going to do?"

"If you do as I say, we won't shoot and nobody'll get hurt. Otherwise, I can only promise some bloody excitement. But this here cove in the middle of this wet wilderness is a hell of a place to die, wouldn't you say?"

The man swore softly, but relaxed after that and turned his gaze down upon the beach, Longarm standing casually beside him. Longarm was pleased with Inspector Wilde's good sense in not making a sudden break for the beach when Longarm exposed himself. If Longarm had left the ridge and hailed one of the sailors, he'd have moved swiftly to back the marshal's play. But Wilde had seen Longarm's intention when he had approached the first mate—and had kept his Mounties in check. There was still a good chance they could accomplish this mission without firing a shot, as Wilde had hoped.

The two men had already decided what they were going to do with the shipload of shanghaied Chinese. They were going to send the lot of them back to China in the ship, since Wilde really had no place to put them. There would be nearly a hundred of them, and they would create an impossible strain on Chilliwack's larder and living quarters. Furthermore, the coolies would find enough wealth on the ship to satisfy their fondest dreams. Indeed, the ship itself would become their booty. It would be a perfect solution, leaving Wilde free to swoop down on that valley to which Scott had led Longarm on his way back to Chilliwack.

The rowboats kept hitting the beach, the unruly coolies piling out, their high-pitched, outraged voices cutting through the constant patter of the rain. Obviously this chill, rainy morning was, for most of them, the last straw. The sound of truncheons or marlinspikes coming down hard on skulls and soft flesh came to Longarm clearly—and the larger the crowd of coolies grew, the more disturbed and unmanageable it became.

The sailors complained bitterly to the first mate as he stood beside Longarm. But the mate kept his head and simply shrugged down at them or told them to hurry it up. At last, all the coolies were on the beach. Longarm nudged the first mate with the muzzle of his Colt.

"All right, you lubbers!" the man cried through the rain. "Over here! All of you!"

The sailors trudged through the muddy sand toward the ridge, looking intently up at the mate through the dim, rain-shrouded light. Longarm counted swiftly. There were eleven seamen in all. Most of them appeared to have weapons. He could see the gleaming butts of revolvers hanging out over their belts. They appeared to be a tough, hard-bitten crew, as mean as centipedes with chilblains.

"Okay, Inspector," Longarm cried. "Make your move!"

As Longarm called out, he pulled the first mate back from the lip of the ridge. The Mounties behind him grabbed the mate. Longarm went down on one knee, his revolver trained on the sailors as the Mounties dashed out onto the beach. The seamen tried to break back to their boats. One of them, Longarm saw, had his gun out. It gleamed dully in the rain. Longarm aimed quickly and fired. The sailor's arm went slack, and his sixgun fell heavily from his hand.

This stopped the lot of them. As the Mounties encircled them with leveled carbines, they raised their hands aloft. Longarm rose to his feet, grabbed the first mate, and, pushing him ahead of him, slid and stumbled his way down the sandy embankment to the beach.

A very pleased Inspector Wilde greeted Longarm. "Magnificent!" he cried. "Only one shot fired, and we got every one of them."

"There's still the captain and those of the crew remaining on board."

"What now, Marshal?"

"Bring the captain and the rest of them ashore."

"And how do you plan to do that?"

Longarm shrugged. "Row out after them."

Longarm and the first mate, with four Mounties wearing stocking caps and sailor's jackets, rowed out to the ship. The first mate was first up the ladder, with Longarm right behind him, the muzzle of his revolver boring a hole in the man's back.

"That you, Beasley?" a tall fellow in a captain's cap asked, hurrying forward from the bow. "What's keeping you?"

"I'd like to have a word with you, Captain sir, if I may," said the first mate.

"What is it, damn you? What is it? This whole operation has taken entirely too—"

He did not finish what he was saying because he saw the revolver gleaming in Longarm's hand. He started to turn and cry out, but by that time the four Mounties had joined Longarm on deck, their rifles trained on him. The captain halted, his shoulders sagging.

"You're on my ship," he said, without much conviction. "Get off my ship at once."

"The rest of your crew," Longarm said. "Call them."

"I warn you, sir! This is my ship. You can't do—"

"I said *call* them."

"All hands!" the captain cried. "All hands!"

Four more sailors scrambled topside from below decks. At sight of the Mounties, a tall seaman went for a weapon tucked into his belt. One of the Mounties dropped him with a rifle stock to the head. At once, the rest of the sailors quieted. After the Mounties relieved the sailors of their weapons, the unconscious sailor was dumped unceremoniously into the rowboat. The crowded boat sank almost to the gunwales, but the sailors rowed with a frantic care back to the beach.

The problem then was to find a coolie who understood English well enough to be able to comprehend what Longarm was proposing. At last, one of the coolies, obviously nervous at being singled out in this fashion, approached Longarm, a Mountie escorting him.

"You speak English?" Longarm asked the little Chinaman.

The Chinaman nodded uncertainly. "Yes, please. What you wan'?"

"I want you to tell your countrymen that we are giving them the ship."

"Ship?"

"Yes. We are giving it to you." Longarm pointed to the ship and then back to the Chinaman. "You! Take ship back to China! Home! To China! You tell them!"

It took a moment for Longarm's meaning to penetrate. When it finally did, the fellow lit up like a storm lantern in a coal mine. As soon as the Chinaman settled down, Longarm explained to him that the captain and the first mate would serve under the coolies, a couple of the more necessary sailors going along as well. The Chinese would be given all the arms they needed to keep the captain and his few crew members in line. They would have to provision the ship, but Longarm suggested they find small fishing villages along the coast above Seattle that might sell them what they needed. Longarm had no doubt that there would be enough money on board for the purchasing of supplies.

Leaving the happy Chinaman to tell all this to the rest of the coolies, Longarm approached the captain, who was keeping himself aloof from the rest of his men by standing off to one side with his first mate. Inspector Wilde, enjoying this turnabout immensely, joined Longarm.

"Captain," Longarm said, "I've got some news for you."

"I have news for *you*! I am Captain Peter Jarvis. This is my first mate, Beasley. We are United States citizens, and I demand to be taken to the proper authorities!" The captain looked drenched and about as sociable as an ulcerated tooth, but he was clinging stubbornly to what was left of his authority.

"Captain Jarvis," Longarm said quietly, "I am Deputy U.S. Marshal Long. You can go back with me and stand trial for smuggling illegal aliens—or worse, for smuggling in shanghaied coolies after selling Chinese women in exchange for them—or take these coolies back to their homeland."

"Take them back? To China? You must be out of your mind, Marshal!"

"Do you want to go back with me and face those charges? How long would you have your captain's papers after that, Jarvis?"

The man paled. As the rivulets of rain streamed down his face, it appeared to Longarm that the man was falling apart, literally. He looked about distractedly—first at his crew, huddled under the guns of the Mounties, then at the mass of coolies watching

190

from the beach. He looked back at Longarm, the defiance in his eyes completely gone now.

Longarm took off his hat and swung it to rid the brim of the collected moisture, then slapped it back on. "I'm tired of standing here in the rain, Captain. What's your decision?"

The man took a deep breath. "I'll go back with the coolies. That . . . deal goes for my crew as well, doesn't it?"

"Just for your first mate and two other sailors. We figure you'll need them to teach the coolies how to man your ship."

"Two seamen, along with the first mate and me—to take that vessel all the way back to China! You must be mad!"

"Choose the two you need the most and make it quick, Captain. You'll be surprised at how fast these coolies will catch on."

"I'll . . . I'll need four seamen, at least."

"All right. Four, then."

"This is insane, Marshal! What's to prevent those heathen from murdering us as soon as they become able to handle the ship? You'll have to give us back our weapons."

Longarm was getting too wet to continue this palaver. As far as he was concerned, he was giving the captain a break he hardly deserved. He turned to Wilde. "Tell this horse's hind end to get on board as soon as he's figured out which four of his crew he wants. If he still wants to palaver, I'll let his first mate take the coolies back."

Without looking back at the irate captain, Longarm trudged across the beach toward the excited huddle of coolies to make sure they had succeeded in electing themselves a head man, as he had suggested. He found they had chosen the interpreter, and by midmorning, as the rain let up and a belated sun burnt the mists off the cove's surface, the captain and his small crew, with the armed coolies in charge, were back on board.

Longarm, standing beside Inspector Wilde, watched as the clipper ship—it was called the *Sea Wind*—pulled up anchor and eased itself around into the wind. Soon it was leaning eagerly before the freshening breeze, a white spray breaking at its bows. Longarm could see the Chinese nimbly clambering up the rigging while others raced over the decks on various chores. They *were* learning fast, and no wonder. Their journey to the Land of the Golden Hills had been a nightmare from the very beginning. They had been bought and sold, hauled about like the carcasses of slaughtered buffalo, cursed at, and reviled—even by their own countrymen.

But now, after all that, they were setting sail for the open Pacific, and China. They were going home!

Chapter 11

Three days later, Charles Swinburne Spittles looked up as Longarm pushed through the low gate and stopped in front of his cluttered desk. Longarm was still damp from his long ride and just a mite gamey. Spittles could not prevent himself from sniffing unhappily at Longarm's sudden unannounced appearance. After all, he seemed to be saying, I have a paper to get out. I don't want to waste my time with the likes of you.

Longarm grinned at the slick-faced dude. "You got your front page all set up yet, Spittles? I've got some news for you."

Spittles leaned back in his chair, a weary frown on his face. "The front page is ready, Longarm. But I am a newspaperman. What have you got for me? Another stagecoach robbery you foiled?"

"Mind if I sit down?" Longarm said, pulling a chair over to Spittles's desk, yanking off his hat, and sitting down.

"Would it matter if I did?"

"Your boss is a crook, Spittles. He is the man behind the smuggling—him and Chang Li Chang, the head of the local Ong Leong Tong."

Spittles leaned suddenly forward in his chair, the

smirk no longer on his face. "You must be insane, Longarm. Ryan would have nothing to do with smuggling in Chinese coolies! And Chang Li Chang is a local tailor, a complete nonentity."

"Are you really interested in publishing the truth in this rag, or would you prefer to spend your talent as a newspaperman spreading Duff Ryan's lies?"

Spittles paled. The man had intelligence, something Longarm had never doubted, and now it showed— though reluctantly. "All right, Longarm. What do you have? But I warn you, it had better be documented. I'll publish no slander on Duff Ryan."

Longarm was not too far into his account of the past few days before Spittles reached for his pad and a pencil and began taking notes. Before long, Spittles called past Longarm to the men working in the shop to hold everything. At last, when Longarm had finished, Spittles got to his feet.

"You say Ryan's bank can provide the proof for this story. How?"

"Come with me, and I'll show you."

They left the newspaper office and walked down the street to Duff Ryan's bank, the Slab City Trust, and entered. With Spittles just behind him, Longarm approached one of the tellers.

"I'm Scott McPherson," Longarm told the man. "I'd like to know what's in my savings account by now. I keep forgetting."

The teller was wearing a green eyeshade. He nudged it a bit higher on his forehead. "You say you're Scott McPherson?"

"You heard me."

"Excuse me."

The teller hurried back through a door. A moment later he returned with a short, pompous fellow in shirtsleeves and green sleeve garters. An unhappy frown was on his face. "I'm sorry, Mr. McPherson. I have strict orders from Mr. Ryan to verify your identity—and also to contact Mr. Ryan when you arrive."

"You have my account?"

"Well, yes. But I must first see your identification, and before I can release the funds, I must have Mr. Ryan's personal approval."

"Where is Mr. Ryan?"

"I don't know. He has been out of town now for some days. I believe he is in Top Gap on business."

"Railroad business? The Great Northern?"

"Why, yes. I believe so."

"You figure I should just wait for him, then. Is that it?"

"Why, yes, Mr. McPherson. That would be best." The bank manager took out a handkerchief and mopped his brow. "Those are my instructions."

"Well, hell, I just want to see how much I've got in there; I don't want any of it." Longarm smiled. "I'd only spend it foolishly on the fleshpots of Chinatown."

The fellow frowned unhappily. "You say you just want to know the total of your account? You don't wish to withdraw it?"

"Why, sure. I just like to see how all that interest is helping out."

The bank manager turned to the teller. "Find the total for Mr. McPherson, Andy." The manager looked back at Longarm. "Will that be all, then?"

"Just one thing." Longarm took out four of the silver dollars he had taken from that persistent assassin who had tried to kill him after Scott's ambush had failed. He placed the cartwheels on the counter and shoved them toward the bank manager. "You recognize these, do you?"

"Of course. Those are newly minted silver dollars, direct from the mint in San Francisco. This bank prides itself on providing its customers with this fine issue."

"I noticed they were fresh—real fresh and sharp,

like they hadn't hardly been used. Would you say they came from here direct?"

"Of course. We distribute them to our favored customers. But that is not to say that they do not soon find their way into the business life of our city."

"When did you start using these silver dollars?"

"When?"

"Yes. When did you start passing out these silver dollars in Slab City?"

"Last week, I believe. On Monday."

Longarm calculated swiftly. That made it four full days *after* he had relieved the hired killer of his silver dollars. Longarm smiled at the bank manager and pulled the coins back. "Did you have these here new silver dollars in the bank before that?"

"Yes, of course. We had to process this new issue and get rid of the old coins. As many as we could, that is."

"Old Duff was in charge of that new issue then, was he?"

The bank manager frowned at Longarm's unseemly way of referring to his employer. But he was not quick enough to keep his mouth shut. "Yes, he was in charge of them, Mr. McPherson."

The teller approached at this moment and passed a slip of paper through the window to Longarm. It was the amount of money that Duff Ryan had placed in Scott McPherson's account in payment for his services. Longarm glanced at the figure scribbled on the piece of paper and then handed it to Spittles.

"Thank you," Longarm told the bank manager. "Guess I'll go wait for old Duff."

Back in the newspaper office, Spittles tossed the small piece of paper down before him onto his desk, then sat wearily down himself.

"Five thousand dollars," Spittles said. "That's a lot of money for a constable of the Northwest Mounted

196

Police to have saved—in a Slab City bank or anywhere else. A very great amount, I must admit." He looked unhappily across the desk at Longarm, who had slacked into a chair. "And that business with the silver dollars. You told me you got them from the man who tried to kill you. And you told me *when* you got them. It was before the coins were in circulation. Duff Ryan himself had paid that man to kill you."

"Yes. And not long after that, I saved Duff Ryan's life."

"That fire, you mean. The one that gutted his store."

"Uh-huh."

"And you say Duff Ryan and MacRae are in this together, with that Tong leader?"

"Yes. Ryan has been supplying MacRae with coolies for his railroad. In return, Ryan's been demanding the pick of the litter when it comes to buying land for the northern spur of the Great Northern. The only thorn in his side has been Helga Jensen, who owns that land. I suspicion he is doing everything he can to wipe her out and force her to sell that land to him." Longarm smiled. "That's why his bank is refusing to extend her loan. Small wonder that she hates Duff Ryan, ain't it?"

"I get the picture, Longarm. I guess you were right. I'll have to get busy and set up a new front page. The first three columns anyway." Spittles shook his head. "It'll mean my job, you know."

"How could you stay loyal, Spittles, to a man who never really believed as you do?" Longarm got up.

"Believed as I do?"

"That the Yellow Peril is the only real threat this Washington Territory faces."

Longarm slapped his hat back on, took out a cheroot, and left the newspaper. He needed a bath. After that, he was going to see if he could find Helga Jensen. He had some apologizing to do. Among other things.

It was after his bath at the barber shop and a good feed in the hotel dining room that Longarm entered the lobby of the hotel and started up the stairs. A couple of towering loggers were lounging nervously in the lobby, so when Longarm saw the matchstick he had left in the doorway a few hours before lying on the hallway carpet in front of his door, he was not at all surprised.

He knocked on his own door, politely but firmly. Then he said, "I know you're in there, Helga. Do you want me to shoot my way in?"

At once the door was pulled open. Helga stepped back to let him in. As Longarm took off his hat and walked in past her, he remarked, "What's the matter, Helga? You've got all your clothes on."

He thought she was going to hit him. Instead, she slammed the door shut and placed herself squarely in front of him, her arms akimbo.

"This time is my men outside, ya? You try something funny, you get broken head!"

Longarm backed off with a laugh and sat down on the edge of his bed. Fully clothed once more, she was dressed similarly to the way she had been dressed when she had first planted herself in front of him. She was wearing a bright red stocking cap, a red plaid cotton shirt, open at the neck, and denim pants with the legs tucked into her high-laced boots. Her denim jacket she had taken off and thrown on the bed. As before, her thrusting breasts, narrow hips, and long, tapering thighs seemed only accentuated by her masculine garb.

Longarm thought with a slight pang of all that he had missed as a result of that earlier interruption. "I won't be trying anything funny, Helga. As a matter of fact, I'm glad to see you."

"No honey-sweet talk to Helga! You listen to me!

You tell that octopus! I fight! He not take Helga's land without fight."

"I'm on your side, Helga," Longarm said softly. "Why not listen to me for a minute. Pretty soon the paper will be out with the whole story."

"Story? What you tell Helga now?"

"First, Helga, let me get something straight. Those two men who broke in on us. Did you recognize them?"

"They were not my men like you think!"

"I know that, Helga. But did you recognize them?"

"No, but I describe them to my men. And later they see them." She smiled suddenly at Longarm. "You hurt them real bad."

"Where did your men see them?"

She snorted angrily. "Working for that railroad."

"For Cyrus MacRae?"

"You mean that man who build the Great Northern? Yes, for him."

"Sit down, Helga, I have something to tell you. I think you'll agree it's good news."

She hesitated only a moment, then sat cautiously down beside him on the bed. Her nearness was distracting, but there was no time for that now. Maybe later. He sensed her softening toward him, as if she understood his thoughts. But she too kept her composure.

"I need good news, Longarm," she said with sudden, slightly exaggerated melancholy.

"No Chinese women have been getting through. Is that it?"

"That is true. Ton Key is Helga's foreman. He need woman, Chinese woman from the Delta. Helga promise him. Lillian M'Ling promise him. It is bad now. My coolies stay if Ton Key tell them to stay—even without payroll. But now Ton Key is so unhappy with Helga." She shrugged. "And he not want Helga. Woman his size, he want."

"That so?" Longarm asked, smiling.

"Ya! Chinaman crazy, I think."

"About some things, maybe. Listen now, Helga. When I get finished, I'd like your help. I think I'm going to need it."

"Helga listen."

And she did, intently, only stopping him occasionally to get a few of the details straight. When Longarm had finished, she was pacing like a blonde bear in front of him. "That all?" she asked.

"That's it."

"You know where is Lillian M'Ling?"

"No, I don't."

"She has disappeared. You find her and we both help you." She smiled grimly. "I see it now, real clear. It is we two women against those men—Chang and Duff Ryan. Two snakes—one Chinese, one white man. They work together all this time." She nodded sagely. "I think sometimes Ryan scream too much about coolies. You know Shakespeare, Longarm?"

"Not much, Helga."

"Smart writer. You should read him, maybe. He say sometimes he think guilty person does protest too much. Many times I think that about Duff Ryan."

"And Spittles?"

"No! That man is a fool, I think. He believes that stuff about Yellow Peril."

"Well, when tonight's edition of the paper hits the street, there's going to be some scurrying for cover. I need your help, Helga. You and your loggers, as many as you can spare."

"Why?"

"I'm going into Chinatown to pick up Chang."

"You arrest Chang Li Chang?"

"Yes. We've got Scott McPherson's testimony that he is behind the smuggling into Top Gap of most of the Great Northern's coolie labor. Duff Ryan won't be hard to find. He's a real visible fixture in this territory. But Chang might melt away without a trace if we don't latch onto him pronto. Will you help me?"

"Sure, Helga help! Like you say, this is good news!"

"All right. Get your men together; I'll meet them at your mill in an hour. Is that enough time for you?"

"Plenty time!"

She halted at the door as she pulled it open, and looked back at Longarm. "Hey, maybe you can get together with Helga when this over. This time no crazy men to stop us! Ya! I like that for sure."

And then she was gone.

Constable Tim Curry was asleep with his mouth open. His feet were propped up on his desk, his arms folded across his chest. Again Longarm marveled at the man's lack of heft. He looked like he'd have to stand twice to make a shadow. But this was all the official law—besides Longarm himself—that Slab City had, so Longarm shrugged and prodded the fellow awake.

He came awake slowly, like a snake in the morning. He focused his eyes at last on the tall lawman, cleared his throat, and pulled his long legs down off the top of his desk. It was a shame, Longarm realized, to have to wake Tim Curry. He was obviously a man who needed his sleep.

"Pull yourself together, Curry," Longarm told the town constable. "I've got work for you."

The man blinked at Longarm, still trying to focus his watery blue eyes. "What do you mean, Deputy? There's no trouble. It's not even dark yet."

"There will be."

Curry shook his head and sat up straight. He was finally awake. "Now just who do you think you are, coming in here like this and telling me what to do!"

"This is still a United States Territory, Curry. You'll do as I say. I represent the federal government, is that clear?"

Longarm saw the man's long chin begin to tremble

with suppressed indignation. But no further protest came out. Swallowing hard, he squared what little shoulders he had. "All right, then. What do you want?"

"I'm deputizing you and a few loggers. We're going to hunt up a Tong leader."

"A what?"

"Never mind. Just come with me. And stick close beside me so you won't get lost."

"Just hold it right there," Curry blustered, as he unfolded himself and got to his feet. "I don't have to stand for that—"

But Longarm was already on his way out the door. He heard the constable shuffling hurriedly across the floor after him.

Longarm went first to the Skidroad Palace, where he found his two old sidekicks, Gus Mullen and Stokey, at a corner table fighting over what remained of a quart bottle of whiskey. They were both well along, but still a match for any adventures that might offer themselves. The constable pulled up unhappily beside Longarm when Longarm stopped at their table.

Gus Mullen smiled in anticipation when he saw Longarm, his clear blue eyes alight despite the whiskey.

Stokey rubbed his round fireplug of a nose and squinted unhappily up at the marshal through black button eyes. "Oh, Jesus!" he cried. "Here comes trouble! No more, Longarm! Have pity on two besotted drunks and leave us be!"

"Heard you got out of that mess up there all right," said Gus Mullen. "What you got for us this time? More sailors?"

"This time," replied Longarm, "we're going to do some local housecleaning."

"Is *that* coming along?" Gus asked, looking at Tim Curry.

"Just to make everything nice and legal," Longarm said.

"His tail is already between his legs," observed Stokey, who was already getting used to the idea of some action, since it was local. "You sure we can trust him?"

"He's going to deputize you," Longarm told him, "and a few of Helga Jensen's loggers."

Gus Mullen smiled. "How about a drink first, Longarm? This promises to be a lovely evening after all. Join us."

"Don't mind if I do."

Longarm sat down at the table with the two men and waved over a waitress. Constable Tim Curry took a chair across from Longarm very reluctantly. "These two stumblebums," Curry said, "will be of no use whatsoever. I'm surprised they're still on their feet. It's almost seven. Another hour and they'll be under the table."

"We'll just ignore that, Curry," said Gus, looking at the town constable with amused contempt, "seeing as how Longarm brought you in here himself."

"We figure," Stokey put in, "that you're under his protection, sort of."

"But we might lose our heads in a few minutes and break this bottle over your head," Gus said amiably, "if you continue to abuse our hospitality. I do hope you understand our position."

Curry started to reply, but held himself back with a great show of forbearance.

Longarm ordered their drinks and then told the two men what he had in mind. Curry listened with growing interest—and fear, especially when Longarm pointed out that Chang Li Chang could probably count on quite a few hatchet men, well-armed and dangerous, to protect him. Gus and Stokey, however, seemed raring to go.

Finished with his drink, Longarm consulted his

203

watch. He had told Helga to gather her men at the mill in an hour, and the hour was almost up. He was about to get up when he saw an irate Duff Ryan storm into the saloon.

Ryan's big fist clutched a copy of the *Slab City Citizen,* and it was this he was brandishing as he stood swaying before the still-swinging batwings and swept the crowded saloon with his angry, gleaming eyes. He looked rumpled and unwashed, his high-crowned white Stetson askew, his cordovan boots muddy. He had obviously not been in town long and had just picked up this fresh copy of Spittles's handiwork. It had taken Spittles this long to rewrite and set up the front page; Longarm guessed the paper could not have been out on the street for more than a few minutes, since he had seen no sign of it on his way over to the saloon.

At any rate, late or not, it was on the streets finally, which meant it was time for Longarm to get moving. The rats would soon be abandoning the ship. Longarm got to his feet. The moment he did, Duff Ryan caught sight of him and stormed across the saloon toward him.

"Here now! What's this!" Ryan cried, thrusting the paper into Longarm's face. "What's the meaning of this? What are you and that pen pusher up to? These allegations of yours are pure slander! I'll have your badge for this day's business!"

"Well, you'll sure as hell try, I imagine. If you'll just read a little further, you'll see we've got Scott. He's made a full statement, all signed and sealed, with all the proper witnesses on hand. And we've burned down those log buildings, Duff—and taken the horses. There ain't anything left."

Duff Ryan's handsome face went slack, his complexion suddenly the color of a white linen tablecloth.

"That's right, Duff," Longarm said coldly. "Like you figured it, we trailed Scott all the way to that little valley. Only I didn't want to take you in up there. I wanted jurisdiction over you—for the murders of Hitch Scally and Rolf La Tour. Glad you made it back to Slab City all right."

"The murder of Scally! You can't mean that, Longarm! Smuggling, yes; I admit to that. But murder? No!" Ryan began to back up, his face hardening in resolve.

"What are you going to do, Duff?" Longarm asked mildly. "Shoot it out? With all four of us?"

"I'm no fool," the man rasped. "That's just what you want! But I have lawyers. Good lawyers, the best money can buy. You can't pin this on me, Longarm." He looked down once more at the newspaper crumpled in his hand. "But that sniveling pen pusher! I'll make him pay for this!"

He turned abruptly and stormed out of his saloon, as everyone in the crowded place watched in stunned silence.

As soon as he was out of the door, someone cried, "Anyone got a copy of that paper?"

No one in the place had. In less than a minute, it seemed, the patrons of Duff Ryan's Skidroad Palace had stampeded from the place in search of a copy of the *Slab City Citizen*.

Longarm was passing the Redwood Hotel on the way to Helga's sawmill when the desk clerk dashed out, waving a telegram at Longarm. Longarm stopped and took the message from the fellow. Ripping open the envelope, he noted that the telegram had been sent a full day ago. In the rapidly fading light, he read:

TO DEPUTY LONG SLAB CITY STOP MC-PHERSON KILLED GUARD STOP ESCAPED TO COAST STOP SCOUT WATCHED HIM BOARD CHINA BELLE STOP CHINA BELLE

SAILING SOUTH ALONG COAST TO PUGET
SOUND STOP SIGNED WILDE

Crumpling the telegram, Longarm tossed it away.
"Bad news, Longarm?" asked Mullen.
"Don't know yet. But there's nothing we can do
about it, so let's keep moving. It'll be dark soon."

Helga was waiting in front of her mill with a crowd of
loggers. There must have been at least twenty, and all
of them were armed, Longarm noted with satisfaction.
As he stopped in front of them, he looked over at
Helga. She too was armed, and seemed even more
formidable than usual.
"I don't want you sticking your neck out, Helga.
You better wait this one out."
"Ya! You make Helga do that. You try, I betcha!
Ya!"
The loggers laughed at that response, and Longarm
shrugged. Helga would probably be worth two loggers,
at that. Longarm turned his attention then to the loggers, and told them to raise their right hands. It didn't
take him long to swear the men in—with Helga's voice
louder than all the rest.
Longarm warned them not to fire on any Chinese
unless they were fired on first and impressed on them
the need for discretion. He did not want this to turn
into any wild looting operation—an indiscriminate
venting of spleen against the Chinese—similar to what
he had witnessed in Denver. They were going to surround the block containing Chang Li Chang's tailor
shop, and then Longarm would enter the building and
bring out Chang. It was that simple—and that dangerous.
By the time Longarm had finished, it was completely
dark. Longarm—with Gus Mullen, Stokey, the unhappy constable, and Helga at his side—led the silent,
well-disciplined gang of loggers down the narrow street

toward Chang's tailor shop. At their approach, the Chinese inhabitants of the quarter immediately left the streets, so that as Longarm and the loggers advanced, they appeared to be sweeping the streets clean of humanity.

Chinatown was ominously silent as Longarm brought his posse to a halt. On a prearranged signal from him, some loggers raced ahead to a side street, while others darted down a narrow alley that led behind the building. Pausing to give the loggers time to completely surround the block, Longarm approached the doorway from which he had emerged when he had left Chang's opulent apartment. It was a few doorways down from Chang's tailor shop. Toward that he directed Stokey and Helga, not a little nervous, by this time, at Helga's insistence on taking part in this operation.

Holding back until he heard Stokey smash open Chang's tailor shop, Longarm approached the door. Remembering how well Lillian M'Ling's door had been barricaded, he turned to the two loggers he had kept with him. They were the biggest and toughest of the lot. At a nod from Longarm, they lowered their powerful shoulders and charged the door. The first assault caused one of the hinges to bend. The second smashed both hinges and the door sagged inward crookedly, chains and padlocks hanging. A final assault slammed the door flat onto the floor of the hallway, which suddenly loomed emptily before them.

Out of that long, dark hole two shots flared. Longarm ducked to one side of the doorway, but not before a slug whispered past his right cheekbone. Behind him, Constable Curry flung himself to the ground, groaning in terror. Longarm paid no attention to him and snapped two quick shots into the hallway. Gus Mullen did likewise, with the loggers also chipping in. The fusillade was fierce and, after a few minutes, there was no answering fire from the hallway.

Poking his head around the doorjamb, Longarm

207

thought he saw a couple of huddled bodies well back on the hallway floor. From around a corner a dim light filtered, coming from one of the many smoking lanterns hung from nails on the walls of the passageways. Longarm knew at once where to go from here and, waving the rest in after him, he ran into the building. He recognized one of the downed men as the fellow who had led him from Chang's apartment. The other fellow was just as big—and just as dead.

Stepping over the bodies, he peered around the corner. The hallway was empty. Longarm went first, and soon the others were strung out behind him as he followed the winding route that led at last up a narrow, winding flight of wooden stairs to Chang's apartment. The door was barred solidly from the other side. Again Longarm turned to his two big battering rams. This time they were in such cramped space that it was difficult for them to gain much momentum. But at last they splintered the door and tore it from its hinges.

Longarm expected firing from within the apartment. There was none. He waited a decent interval, flattened like the rest of the men against the wall on either side of the door, then darted into the apartment with his Colt drawn. The place was undisturbed and apparently empty. He was in the largest room of the suite. The room where they had nursed him was off to his right, and he shoved his way through the curtains.

The room was exactly as he remembered it. The walls were still covered with the maroon-and-gold curtains; the delicate Chinese landscapes still hung in place; the lacquered furniture, exquisitely inlaid, still gleamed in the lamps' soft light. The only difference was the bed on which Longarm had awakened. Lillian M'Ling was lying on it now, a jade-handled dagger buried in her chest.

Chapter 12

"Jesus," said Mullen, standing beside Longarm. He spoke softly, almost reverently.

Longarm did not know whether the reason for Mullen's reverence was the presence of violent death or the fact that Lillian M'Ling was stark naked, her smooth olive skin still glowing softly in the dim light. A thin, gleaming red sash of blood began at the blade and snaked under her left breast and down her slim waist, to puddle darkly under her buttocks on the silk bedspread.

To Longarm's eyes she was still beautiful. To his nose, however, the stench of death filled the room.

As the loggers and Curry crowded into the room beside Longarm, there was a soft but sudden thud and a compression of the atmosphere. At once the air seemed to scorch Longarm's lungs. They all turned and pushed back through the rooms to find the landing outside the apartment a mass of seething flames. Black, choking coils of smoke were already reaching into the apartment.

There was no chance of making it out that way.

Longarm led the way back into Lillian M'Ling's death chamber. "Pull down these wall curtains!" he directed. "Slice them up. Make a rope out of them."

The loggers worked furiously, yanking down the curtains and ripping them rapidly into long strips with their knives. As they worked, the flames moved into the apartment, providing a pounding, scorching accompaniment to their grimly serious labor. The doors had been removed. The only barrier between the rooms was the curtains. It was not enough now to keep back the smoke and heat. The smoke coiled thickly in the room. The men began wiping their eyes.

At last a long enough rope had been fashioned. Longarm broke through the window, cleaned out the broken glass lining the frame with the barrel of his Colt, and flung the rope out the window. Someone tied the other end of it to the foot of the bed. Longarm looked down. The rope was not long enough. Pulling it back up, he strode over to the bed and yanked the silk bedspread out from under the dead woman. She rolled stiffly over, like an overlarge doll, and toppled to the floor. Longarm tossed the bedspread to the men.

"Use that," he shouted, "and hurry!"

Longarm was the first to drop to the alley floor. He did not have time to get his bearings before he was fired upon from a doorway across the alley. He returned the fire and kept firing as the rest slid down the knotted fabric to the ground. Dark figures dashed ahead of them down the narrow passage, and the loggers took after them. Reaching the street, Longarm found it empty. Whoever they had been shooting at had vanished.

The street was deserted. It was weird. Behind them, the flaming building was sending smoke billowing into the night. Sparks were dancing skyward. The crimson light was transforming the dismal shops and buildings of Chinatown into fresh, bright structures glowing in the darkness.

But there was not a soul on the streets. Not a single Chinaman.

Stokey staggered toward them, coming from the other direction. He had been wounded. As Mullen ran to him and helped him to come closer, Stokey called out to Longarm, "They got her! They've taken her! They've taken Helga!"

The lawman hurried to Stokey's side.

"Chang?" he asked.

"Yes. Chang and Duff Ryan."

"How did they get out?"

"A passage under the buildings to the river. They took a boat to the other side. There was a carriage waiting for the old man, and horses."

"Which way did they go?"

"West, along the old logger's road. I tried to follow them, but they saw me and shot me up some. I didn't think I'd make it back. I had to swim the damn river to get back here. Where the hell have you been, anyway?"

"We had a little fire to contend with."

"Well, damn it, Longarm, this is it. After this business, I'm not going to that saloon to drink anymore."

As he said this last, he slumped unconscious into Mullen's arms. Longarm looked at the stricken Mullen. "Take care of him, Gus. I've got a hunch Duff Ryan has been up to more mischief."

Selecting four of the loggers and a reluctant, wild-eyed Curry, he hurried from Chinatown to the main part of town, heading for the newspaper office. Behind him, the growing conflagration lit the sky—with not a single white man rushing to help put out the fire. The fire would spread, Longarm knew, and when dawn broke again over Slab City, another Western Chinatown would have been turned to smoldering ash. Only this time it would be one of their own who had set the torch.

The moment Longarm entered the building housing

the *Slab City Citizen,* he prepared himself for what he knew he would find. At first he saw only the overturned chairs, the shattered gate, the type fonts strewn over the floor. And then he saw Spittles. The man was lying on his back on the floor beside his desk. As Longarm hurried closer, he saw that Duff Ryan, in what must have been an ungovernable fury, had pounded at least a fistful of type into the editor's mouth and, from the look of things, had stomped the type in with his boot. Then he had apparently finished the job with two bullets into the man's chest. Spittles's formerly immaculate white shirt was a bloody mess. Curry and the loggers crowded close behind Longarm, looking down at the beaten editor with sick expressions on their faces.

Longarm was about to move away when he saw Spittles turn his head slightly toward him. At once Longarm went down on one knee beside him. The editor took hold of Longarm's shirt front and pulled him closer. His voice was a broken, rasping whine. Longarm could hardly make out a word. He leaned his head still closer.

"Ryan . . . escape . . . tried to stop him . . . Chang with him. . . .!"

A bloody froth bubbled out through Spittles's torn lips. Longarm shook the editor gently and picked a few pieces of type out of the fellow's torn face. "Anything else?" he asked.

The man nodded feebly. Again Longarm leaned his ear as close as he could to Spittles's mouth.

"Heard Chang . . . *China Belle* . . . Indian Point . . . "

Spittles gasped. Longarm pulled back and saw that the newspaperman's eyes were open wide, but were as still and lifeless as glass beads. He was dead.

Longarm sighed wearily and rose to his feet.

He had expected Duff Ryan to get angry. In fact, he had counted heavily on the man doing something foolish once that issue of the *Slab City Citizen* hit the streets. But he had not counted on this—a wild, undisciplined rage that led to murder. It was now impossible for Duff Ryan's power and immense wealth to protect him—or to help him beat the charges of smuggling and of complicity in the killing of Hitch Scally and Rolf La Tour. Scott's statement was damaging, all right, but it would have little real value in a U.S. courtroom with Ryan's high-powered lawyers on hand to discredit the word of a renegade Canadian Mountie.

But no longer. Everyone in that saloon had heard Ryan's threat as he stormed out. There was no way the man could escape the noose for this deed. Longarm just did not care for the price, however: the life of a very courageous newspaper editor. Not that he had liked Spittles much, but Spittles's instincts as a reporter had triumphed in the end over his willingness to peddle Duff Ryan's lies. He had even, it seemed, tried to prevent Duff Ryan from escaping.

Longarm turned to the hushed loggers. "Any of you know where Indian Point is?"

The loggers all shook their heads, but Tim Curry cleared his throat. "I was brought up near there," he said. "It's on the Sound."

"You know how to get there?"

"Sure."

"Well, now. I knew you would come in handy, Constable. I just knew it. You're going to take us there—and fast."

"We'll need horses."

"We'll get them. Is there a good trail to the coast?"

"The only halfway decent trail is the one that follows the Skagit. But it's a long way around."

The marshal shook his head. "I want a faster route."

Curry nodded wearily, as if he could already imagine the grueling trip ahead of him. "I know a way. But it goes through very thick timber."

"How much faster is it?"

"A day, maybe."

"That'll be it, then." Longarm glanced down once more at Spittles, then looked up at the constable and the loggers. "Take care of Spittles while I go see to the horses. I'll meet you at the livery in half an hour."

As Tim Curry and the loggers turned their unhappy attention to the corpse on the floor, Longarm hurried from the newspaper office.

As Tim Curry led the party through the thick, incredibly lush wilderness, Longarm began to realize that the frail town constable, for all his whining and seeming faintheartedness, was holding up his end surprisingly well. This experience might very well make a man of him, Longarm mused. The fellow appeared to be gaining assurance and a certain amount of grit with each passing hour.

It was daylight now, which made the going only a little faster. The ground was a duff-covered tangle of vines and deadfall, of berry bushes and thick, close-to-the-ground evergreens that were easily as tough as the chaparral he had ridden through in Texas. And all of it was wet. To brush against a tree limb was to dislodge a shower of heavy, soaking drops.

Late that same day they reached the coast. By nightfall they were camped above the promontory Tim Curry identified as Indian Point. The town where he had grown up was a few miles farther up the coast, well out of sight.

They slept with watches changing every two hours. At midnight Longarm was awakened. A ship's lights were visible on the Sound. As the large sailing vessel grew closer, Longarm became certain it was the *China Belle*. This was evidently a stop the ship made regularly before returning to China as its captain kept in contact with Chang and Ryan; only this time it brought Scott McPherson, who was most likely anxious to advise Chang and his Occidental partner of the havoc wrought on the Canadian arm of their operation. He had no way of knowing yet what damage had been done to their operation below the Canadian border.

Longarm waited until the ship had dropped anchor before building the fire and lighting the torches. As soon as the torches were lit, a couple of the loggers took them and began signaling the ship with them. Longarm let the two men decide on their own signals, since he had no idea what the usual method was. He was counting on the captain's curiosity upon seeing the torches. Surely he would send a boat ashore to investigate. With Scott McPherson on board, he was expecting the unusual now. And he was expecting trouble, as well. The fact that he had kept his ship in these waters this long before returning to China testified to that.

Gus Mullen and Tim Curry were standing beside Longarm, watching with him for any sign that the ship's watch had reported their signals. Abruptly a lantern flashed three times from the ship's bow.

"Put out those torches!" Longarm called. "They've seen our signal!"

The loggers ran down to the water and extinguished the torches, then tossed them away. Curry and Mullen joined with the rest of the loggers in heaping sand on the fire. It was Longarm's intention to make it impossible for them to continue signaling to the ship. In this way there was little chance they would give themselves away. All they could hope for now was that the captain would send a boat ashore to investigate—a boatload of armed men, of course, ready for trouble.

If all Longarm had wanted was to apprehend Chang and Ryan, he could simply have waited here and captured them when they showed up, leaving the *China Belle* to sit offshore, unaware of what was happening. But the deputy had his heart set on taking the *China Belle* too. Not only was Scott McPherson on board, but Longarm had a few scores to settle with a black-

215

bearded first mate and that Chinese captain who spoke like an English lord.

Longarm's plan was to take the ship and then wait for Chang and his party to climb on board. In this way the surprise would be so complete that there would be little likelihood of Helga's being cut down in any exchange of fire: something that would be more likely if there were a gun battle on shore.

First, however, they had to take the ship. For that enterprise, Longarm had ten loggers in addition to himself, Gus, and Curry. Surprise would be their sole advantage.

"Here comes a boat," said Mullen softly.

At once everyone melted into the darkness, guns drawn. There were enough embers still burning to attract the landing party. From a nearby clump of bushes—each leaf and branch a cold, dripping nuisance—Longarm watched the boat nudge up onto the sand. Eight men jumped out and splashed through the shallow water toward the shore. All of them were armed—some with rifles, others with handguns. A few unsheathed knife blades glinted in the moonlight.

One of their number saw the glow of the campfire's embers and led the rest up the slope to it. As the men gathered uncertainly about the orange coals, their voices querulous as they tried to figure out what was going on, Longarm stepped out of hiding and brought the butt of his Colt down on the head of the nearest sailor. As the man uttered a soft cry and sank to the ground, the rest of Longarm's party closed about their quarry just as silently. There were no shots fired as one after another of the sailors fell beneath the solid, battering blows of Longarm's burly loggers.

Quickly the unconscious men were stripped of their sea jackets and caps, then trussed securely and dragged away into the brush. Leaving Curry and four loggers to guard them, Longarm and Mullen, together with the remaining loggers, donned the sailors' hats and jackets and rowed back out to the ship.

As they drew within the ship's shadow, a voice called down to them from the deck: "Ahoy! That you, Jeff? You're back soon enough! What's up?"

With his head down, Longarm managed an inarticulate response. The boat struck the side of the ship. Longarm reached out for the rope ladder, hauled himself out of the boat, and began to climb the ship's side. Before he reached the ship's rail, he took out his Colt. He found himself looking into an astonished face as he hauled himself over the rail and landed lightly on the deck.

"Hey, now—!" the sailor managed before the barrel of Longarm's Colt caught him on the side of the head.

As Mullen and the rest of the loggers clambered over the side to join Longarm, two sailors appeared, coming from the aft deck. They suspected nothing and, in the darkness, must have assumed that Longarm and the men with him were the party they had come here to pick up. But as they drew closer, they became suspicious.

And then they saw the crumpled figure of the sailor at Longarm's feet. At once they raised an outcry, and turned to run back up the deck. Two quick shots brought them down as sailors began to pour out of the hatches from below decks, guns blazing. Slugs whistled through the air, but few men were hit in the darkness and the confusion. Before long it was a hand-to-hand melee, with Longarm finding himself trying to contend with two sailors, one behind him, another in front.

He managed to get off one shot that hit nothing at all, and then he found himself on his back, with a heavy, sweaty body on top of him. His Colt clattered away on the deck as he managed to roll over and take a swipe at his assailant, but the blow did not land as another body struck him from the side and bore him back with crushing force against a bulkhead. This one

217

had a knife. As he drew it back to plunge it into Long-arm's gut, the federal man took a step forward, grabbed the fellow's wrist, and twisted it sharply. The sailor cried out in agony as Longarm felt the bones snap. The knife fell to the deck. Snatching it up, Longarm whirled, and his first assailant impaled himself on the blade as he rushed the deputy with a raised marlin-spike. The fellow's cry pierced the night, but it was barely heard above the shouting and slamming, the occasional shots and the cries of wounded men. Drop-ping the bloody blade and looking quickly around the deck for his Colt, he snatched it up and glanced around to see that most of the loggers were on their feet, the deck about them slick with blood and littered with the smaller, somewhat mangled bodies of the sailors that had gone against them.

Suddenly there was a stillness broken only by the panting of the loggers as they regained their breaths. Longarm saw Mullen hurrying across the deck toward him, stepping deftly over the sprawled bodies, a look of sheer delight on his face. A free-for-all of this quality was just the spice his life needed. Mullen pulled up in front of Longarm.

"They're gathering farther up the deck, with some Chinamen with swords. Looks like they're going to charge. Want us to close with 'em?"

"No," Longarm told him, remembering the light-ning efficiency of those thin blades. "We'll stand our ground here. Have the men spread across the deck so those bastards can't surprise us from the rear."

Mullen nodded and hurried over to the loggers. Soon they were spread evenly across the deck from one rail to the other, guns drawn, waiting. Longarm moved closer to the line of men, then held up just behind them, peering up the deck. In the glow from a mast lantern he could see the captain and his black-bearded first mate. Behind those two, lost in the shadows, were at least a dozen seamen; the two sword-wielding Chinese were crouching just behind the captain.

"Hold it right there, Captain!" Longarm cried. "There's no need to continue this bloodbath!"

"Who are you, anyway?" the captain called back. "What's the meaning of this?"

"I'm Deputy U.S. Marshal Long, Captain. We met earlier, if you remember."

"Yes, I remember. It was a foolish consistency that caused me to free you. It is perhaps the last time I will listen to the dictates of my ancestors. I am Captain Waldo Sung. And I warn you, this is my ship! I will not surrender it!"

"I give you my word, Captain Sung. That will not be necessary—and that's the word of an officer and a gentleman. You may keep command of the *China Belle*. It is not you or this ship that I am after. Come forward and we can discuss this like gentlemen."

This was a bare-faced lie, but Longarm was not above a lie or two to advance his cause, especially when the alternative was foolish bloodshed. He heard the captain and his first mate discussing Longarm's proposal.

"Drop your weapons and come forward, Captain," Longarm urged after a short interval. "Just let us have Scott McPherson and Chang and his party when they get here. You will be allowed to sail back to your home port. Wash your hands of these men and you will have your ship in exchange. I think that's fair enough."

"All right," the captain called. "But I expect you to honor that promise, Marshal."

"You have my word," Longarm repeated.

Captain Sung and his first mate stepped out of the darkness behind the mast and walked down the deck toward them, with about six sailors following behind. The two sword-wielding Chinese were nowhere in sight. Longarm stepped through his line of men and waited for the captain to reach him.

219

"Where's Scott McPherson?" the lawman asked, as the captain stopped before him.

One of the mast lanterns shone fully in the captain's face, revealing the insolent Oriental lines, the slitted eyes smoldering now with suppressed fury. The captain was having difficulty controlling himself. The first mate was carrying a long knife, and the captain still had a revolver in his hand.

"McPherson's below," Captain Sung said, his meticulous British accent still a surprise to Longarm, coming as it did from a man who was so indisputably Oriental. "You'll have to go down after him yourself, I am afraid."

"Captain Sung, I told you to drop your weapons."

As he spoke, Longarm kept his eyes on those of the captain. He saw the powerful Oriental's eyes grow suddenly cold a split second before the man began to bring up his revolver. At that same instant, from out of the darkness on either side of the captain, the two Chinese sailors darted for him, their thin blades held high.

Longarm's Colt flashed yellow fire, sending a slug into the man coming at him from his right. The Chinaman dropped his blade and slid past Longarm, screaming and clutching at his stomach. Dropping to one knee, Longarm turned, just managing to get off another quick shot at the second Chinaman. This slug caught the man high in the chest, but his momentum carried him over Longarm's left shoulder. Meanwhile, from behind Longarm, Mullen was returning the captain's fire, catching him twice in the upper torso and slamming him violently back against his first mate. Shots came from the other sailors, but they were returned by a volley from Longarm's men, and two of the sailors were flung backward along the bloody deck.

"Drop those weapons!" Longarm called.

Knives and revolvers thudded to the planking. As Longarm got slowly to his feet, he noticed that his left

220

shoulder was tingling and something warm was slowly enclosing the back of his hand. He looked down at it and saw that his knuckles were covered with blood. Holstering his Colt, he felt of his left shoulder with his right hand. A thin slice had been cut in his frock coat, all the way through to the flesh. Only now was he beginning to feel the sharp protest of nerve ends where the sword's blade had sliced into his shoulder. Flexing his arm, he assured himself that there had been no muscle damage.

"You all right, Longarm?" Mullen asked.

"Pretty much. How's the captain?"

"Dead."

"How many of our men are hurt?"

"That first skirmish took two of them; this last one wounded another. But that's all."

"Clean off the decks, fast. No telling when our guests will get here, and we've got to make everything look shipshape. I'm going down after McPherson."

"Sure you don't want me to go with you? That looks like a nasty wound."

"Just clean all this up, Mullen. I'll handle McPherson all by myself."

At the head of the companionway, Longarm reloaded his .44, patted the derringer in his vest pocket, then called down to McPherson, "I'm coming down, Scott! No need to get nervous. I just want to talk some!"

"You armed?" Scott's voice seemed to be coming from directly under the companionway's stairs. He had been crouched there all during the battle, Longarm surmised.

"Yes."

"Throw down your Colt!"

"Sure, Scott."

Longarm tossed the revolver down the companionway. He heard it strike the bottom tread and spin off down the passage. Longarm heard Scott then, his feet

221

pattering as he raced after the weapon. After a moment Scott came to a halt. He was picking up the revolver, Longarm realized.

"Come on down, then," Scott called.

The passage between decks was lit by two lamps, and as Longarm reached the bottom of the companionway, Scott stepped out of a cabin, holding Longarm's own Colt on him.

"That was a foolish thing to do, Marshal," Scott told him. "That damn captain wouldn't let me have a weapon once I was on board. He held me prisoner." Scott waggled the revolver menacingly. "You're going to do as I say now, and let me get off this ship."

"Get off?"

"I can swim. You just escort me topside and I'll jump over. And there'll be an end to it. You'll not see or hear from me again."

"I don't want to do that, Scott."

"You'll have to—or I'll shoot. I have nothing to lose, Marshal! Nothing!"

"All right, Scott. I'll let you off. But how about satisfying my curiosity first?"

Scott licked his lips nervously. "What do you mean? I gave you and Wilde my statement earlier. I told you all I knew about the smuggling. It's all there."

"Is it?"

"Hell, you know it is."

"That first band of hooded men who ambushed the inspector and me while you were nursing your wound: those men were loggers, weren't they?"

"Yes."

"Were they Helga's men?"

"No. MacRae's. They were the loggers he was using to clear the right-of-way for the Great Northern. They were always MacRae's men, in Ryan's pay. He was very generous, I might add. That was why he made such a stink about bringing in coolies, and about Mac-

Rae's use of coolies on the railroad. He was just covering his tracks—and later he could run on the issue."

"Run on the issue?"

"Sure. He wants to be governor when this territory becomes a state. Getting the railroad through Slab City would put it—and him—on the map for sure. It would give him enough clout to start agitating for full statehood. His stand on coolie labor figured to give him the loggers' vote for certain. He's got real big political ambitions, that man."

"Not anymore, he hasn't. Who sent those two Siwash after me? Ryan?"

"That's right. He told them not to come back unless they fixed you. When they saw those silver cartwheels, their mouths must have watered, I'll bet. They could get drunk for a year on all that wealth. But of course he never had to pay them. You took care of that. You turned out to be a pretty hard man to kill, Longarm."

"One more thing, Scott. It was Ryan who had Scally and La Tour murdered, wasn't it?"

"Hell, you knew that."

"I just wanted to be sure. Why did he kill them?"

"Scally and La Tour had caught on to his tie-in with Chang. Lillian M'Ling had wised them both up."

"And Li Fan?"

"Yeah. I guess she wised Scally up some, too."

"So when Scally and La Tour came to you with this information—told you what they knew—you went right to Ryan with the good news."

"That's right. But I didn't think Ryan would kill them."

"What did you think he would do, you son of a bitch? Each time you told Ryan, you signed their death warrants."

Scott straightened his small, stocky body a little, holding the Colt a bit steadier. "All right, damn you! I answered your questions—questions you were too dumb to ask before. Now turn around and lead the way up onto the deck."

Longarm appeared to hesitate. He did not want to seem too eager. Then he nodded. "Follow me, Scott. And just don't let that cannon go off by mistake."

As he turned and started up the companionway, Mullen's head appeared in the opening above him. "You all right, Longarm?"

"I'm fine. You just stand back and keep the men out of the way. Scott's going for a swim."

"A *what*?"

"Just get back, Mullen," Longarm said, his voice carrying a sudden edge to it.

As Mullen nodded quickly and ducked out of sight, Longarm lifted his derringer from his vest pocket. Palming it smoothly, the motion of his arm hidden by his body as he moved up the companionway, he waited until he was close to the head of the stairs before glancing back at Scott. The man was keeping the Colt trained on Longarm as he followed close behind him, but his gaze was momentarily diverted to his footing on the narrow stairs. Longarm sat down suddenly on the top step and, bringing his derringer around, fired point-blank at Scott.

The .44 slug caught Scott in his left eye. A misshapen hole appeared where his eye had been a moment before. The man appeared to hang upright, staring out of his remaining eye at Longarm, a crazed look on his face, his thick black eyebrows raised almost comically. Animated by pure malice, he still seemed capable of firing on Longarm. The Colt in his hand steadied. Longarm emptied the other barrel, catching Scott in the mouth with his remaining bullet. Scott folded back suddenly, appearing to launch himself backward. As he struck the stairs and bounced to the lower deck, the Colt in his hand detonated. The round chipped out a piece of the wood framing over Longarm's head.

Mullen came running. "Jesus, Longarm! What happened?"

"Like I said, Scott's going for a swim. Drag him up and dump him. We've got to clean this ship up and get ready for our passengers. They should be coming by soon."

Chapter 13

With Mullen and Curry at his side, Longarm stood at the ship's railing, watching the two boats drawing closer to the ship through the predawn mists. Chang and his party had appeared on the beach less than an hour before, signaling with torches in no less original a manner than Longarm and his band had employed not long before. The sailors that had rowed ashore after them were accompanied by well-armed loggers dressed in sailor's garb, whom Longarm had warned to keep their faces averted; despite the darkness, there was always the chance that a sharp-eyed member of Chang's party—including Helga herself—might recognize one of Helga's loggers and give the whole masquerade away.

When the boats were within hailing distance, Longarm left Mullen and Curry with the first mate, whose instructions were to hail the boats as usual. As Longarm had learned from this worthy, this rendezvous with the *China Belle* had become a regular thing, since this was when Chang or a trusted henchman brought MacRae's payments for the coolies and when plans for future shipments were discussed. Longarm had had much to digest during these past hours, and he preferred now to wait for Chang and Duff Ryan in the captain's cabin where the light was better and he could watch his guests more closely.

He had that odd feeling that came over him every now and then—an itch on the back of the scalp that told him things were going just a mite *too* smoothly.

Longarm was sitting behind the captain's impressive mahogany desk when the cabin door opened. An inscrutable Chang Li Chang entered first, with Li Fan on his heels. Behind them came a distraught Duff Ryan. The big man seemed curiously shrunken; his broad shoulders now appeared narrow, his stride uncertain.

"What's the meaning of this, Longarm?" he demanded. But his tone had none of the authority it had once wielded.

"I'll just leave that to your imagination, old son."

"Now, see here—!"

Longarm ignored Ryan and looked past him at Mullen as Gus stepped into the cabin after the three and pulled the door shut. "Where's Helga? On deck?"

"She was not with them, Longarm," Mullen replied.

Longarm looked quickly at Chang. "What have you done with her?"

"All in good time, Master of Surprises." Chang bowed, his feathery chin whiskers stirring slightly. "And where, by the way, is Captain Sung? A most excellent seaman, late of the British Royal Navy."

"If there are any sharks in these waters, Chang, he's fed them well—along with a few of his crew. And that's where you'll likely end up unless you tell me what you have done with Helga."

"Will the Prince of Law-Enforcers allow an unworthy old dust-catcher such as myself to sit in his august presence?"

"If it'll help this Ancient Dealer in Human Flesh

to collect his addled thoughts, go right ahead. But I warn you, my patience is wearing mighty damn thin."

Longarm took only meager pleasure in seeing how Chang—however slightly—reacted to his words; he was too anxious about Helga. But he knew he would have to go a little slowly with the old reprobate if he wanted any help from Chang in finding her. That uneasy feeling that things were going a little too smoothly had been on target, all right.

Li Fan moved to her venerable husband's side as Duff Ryan stepped closer to the desk. "Listen, Longarm," the man said, "we can make a deal. Do you have any idea how much money we brought on board this ship? Enough to make us all wealthy for the rest of our days! We can deal, Longarm!"

"Shut up!" snapped Chang.

The old man's voice carried such surprising authority that it stunned Ryan into quick silence. Chang sat in a chair beside Longarm's desk, Li Fan in concerned attendance upon him.

Chang looked at Longarm. "I have left Helga Jensen in a very precarious position, Longarm. The woman was most troublesome and it occurred to me from the first that her person—used intelligently—might serve me well in this uncertain time. I see this addled old man was not far wrong."

"You want to deal?"

"Her life for my own. That is, I tell you where you may find her and you allow me to sail back to the Pearl River Delta. Agreed?"

"I don't like that."

"You want to dicker like a fishmonger! How ungenerous of the Champion of the Lowly. I warn you, with each passing hour, her condition grows more perilous."

"Sounds corny, Chang."

There was a barely perceptible shrug of the old man's narrow shoulders. "Life itself is melodramatic.

But you do not have to believe this Ancient Dealer in Human Flesh if it pleases you not to."

"All right. I'll deal. But I want Duff Ryan. He's not a part of this exchange."

"Why do you want my friend?"

"He had Hitch Scally murdered. To find the man responsible for that killing is one of the reasons I'm on this case."

"That's a lie, Longarm!" Ryan cried.

"I killed him," Chang said serenely, "before Ryan could bring it about."

The lawman's eyebrows rose in surprise.

"You? Why?"

"He took my wife."

Li Fan gasped and backed quickly away from Chang, her tiny porcelain hand covering her mouth, her eyes wide in sudden fear. Chang turned and looked at her, his ancient face suddenly appearing to Longarm as old as Time itself. There was a sad wisdom in his eyes—and an ageless pain as well—as he began to speak to his wife.

"Did not the sweet comforter of my venerable bed not realize how transparent her infidelities were? It is as easy to hide betrayal from an old husband as it is to hide fire under straw. There is no way the flushed face, the fiery glances can be kept hidden. I saw all this in your face and in your eyes often, Li Fan—but never when you gazed upon this ancient ruin." Chang Li Chang closed his eyes and seemed to sink into himself. When he opened his eyes again, a bitter fire burned within them. "Now that you know I am aware of how you have shamed me, I must punish you, Li Fan. Your ancestors and mine demand it."

Before Longarm could make a move from behind the desk, Chang's right hand left his other sleeve and flung a small, pearl-handled knife through the air. It buried itself up to its hilt in Li Fan's chest between her two small, exquisite breasts. She crumpled without

229

a sound. Mullen and Ryan both sprang forward to see to her, but Chang Li Chang looked serenely back at Longarm, who was now standing beside his desk, staring down at the old man.

"You see, Terror of the Lawless, I am the one who killed your man Scally, not Duff Ryan. I had good reason."

"Why do you want Duff Ryan?" Longarm asked.

Chang smiled. Ryan looked up at Chang from the dead Li Fan, his eyes burning with hatred. "I am sure you know already," Chang replied.

"Because Duff Ryan also stole your wife."

"Yes." Chang looked over at Duff, smiling thinly. "I have plans for you also, Duff Ryan," he said softly, a malignant gleam in his old, tired eyes.

With a choking cry of rage, Duff Ryan left Li Fan's side and flung himself upon Chang, his powerful hands closing convulsively about the old Chinaman's ropelike neck. Longarm and Mullen had all they could do to pull the enraged man off his frail victim. When at last they had peeled his fingers from around Chang's neck, Longarm saw that the Chinaman's face had gone deathly white, while his cheeks had sunken in so far that his wrinkled visage resembled the ancient face of an Egyptian mummy recently exhumed from its dusty tomb. For a moment, Longarm thought the shock of Ryan's attack might have put an end to Chang's nefarious career, that his old heart must have given out at last under the strain.

But slowly, miraculously, color returned to Chang's face. His eyes opened, a small, fierce light still glowing within them. Chang looked at Duff Ryan and smiled. "Your unhappiness, my old friend, is my joy. It warms this old heart to see such grief etched on your face. Can you imagine how long I have waited for this moment?"

"You yellow fiend!" Ryan cried. "You're . . . un-Christian!"

"Yes, so I am, Ryan."

Chang smiled almost benignly upon the man who had taken the love of his wife. This was too much for Ryan and he began struggling frantically to free himself so that he could hurl himself once more upon his tormentor. But Mullen grabbed his right arm and twisted it painfully up behind his back. With a sudden gasp, Ryan ceased struggling and sagged forward in resignation.

"Take him up to the deck," Longarm told Mullen.

As Mullen led the now almost docile Ryan out through the cabin door, he looked back at the tiny figure crumpled on the floor. "I'll send someone down for her," he told Longarm.

Longarm nodded.

As Mullen closed the cabin door, Chang said, "Leave the body of my beautiful but most unfaithful wife where it is, Marshal. Let that be my responsibility, once we get under way."

"Where's Helga?"

"My passage from these hostile waters in exchange?"

"Agreed."

"With Captain Sung no longer in command, that will be difficult."

"The first mate can manage."

Chang nodded. "It will have to be so."

"I am not happy at letting you slip out of my net, Chang."

"Yes. I killed one of your number. It is a point of honor, is it not?"

"It is. Now tell me about Helga."

Chang got wearily to his feet. "Let us go on deck, then. As soon as I see you and your men ready to disembark, I shall tell you of Helga's whereabouts. I warn you, you do not have much time."

"If she's not alive, Chang . . . "

The old man held up a frail hand. "Does the Champion of the Weak question the word of an old man—

231

one who saved him from the claws of that Eurasian scorpion?"

"You didn't need to kill her, did you?"

"Her treachery was without direction. It knew no limits and had no scruples. She it was who told me of incoming shipments of Chinese women. She gained as much from me as she did from the poor coolies who paid her for the passage of their wives."

Chang turned then, and led the way out of the cabin.

On deck, Longarm found that the sun was now well above the horizon. Chang's powerful bodyguards, four of them in all, were standing sullenly along the far railing, with two of Longarm's loggers keeping an eye on them. Duff Ryan was standing beside Mullen near Curry and the rest of the loggers, who were clustered just above the rope ladder. Mullen had given them the word that they were soon to disembark. From the look on the loggers' faces as they caught sight of Chang, Longarm could tell that Mullen had also informed them that Chang had Helga hidden away somewhere, that she was still in danger.

"All right, Chang. Where's Helga?"

"Just a moment. I must speak to my men. It is imperative."

Longarm frowned. "Damn you, old man. Hurry it up."

Chang turned to the four bodyguards and beckoned them closer. As they hurried obediently toward him, he shouted to them in their language, something that sounded to Longarm very much like a command.

At once the four bull-like Chinese altered their direction and, before they could be stopped, ripped Duff Ryan from the rail. They fell upon him like savage beasts who had just pulled down a wounded animal. Ryan's cries were almost immediately silenced, and even before Longarm could reach the swarming gang of angry bodyguards, Duff Ryan was lifted high over their heads. What Longarm saw then sickened him.

Ryan's head had been nearly torn from his shoulders. It hung slackly, his bloated, purple face staring wildly around at them all as the bodyguards carried the broken, oddly hinged torso to the railing and flung it out over the side.

Rushing to the railing, Longarm saw Ryan's body strike the water like a piece of dead meat. It sank almost immediately.

Longarm turned angrily to Chang. "Damn you, Chang! I wanted him!"

The old man shrugged. "I simply told these men that Ryan had placed his foul hands upon my person—that he had tried to murder me. They lost control."

"No more stalling, Chang. Helga—where is she?"

"In a cabin."

"Where, damn you!"

"Does she not have an old camp along the Skagit—one she has since abandoned?"

One of the loggers stepped forward. "I know the place, Longarm. We finished cutting there last spring. It's abandoned now."

Chang smiled. "She is there—in a somewhat precarious position, I might add. As I said before, speed is of the essence if you wish to save her."

Longarm looked at the logger. "Can you give me directions?"

"Sure. It's north of here, inland."

Longarm looked back at Chang. "It hurts like hell for me to let you go like this, Chang. If there was any way I could hang on to your wily scalp and still save Helga . . . "

Chang bowed. "I am sure the Terror of Evildoers wishes nothing better than to incarcerate this old reprobate for his crimes. But my action in snuffing out the life of that foolish federal lawman, Scally, was the just response of a betrayed husband. Surely you will allow this feeble old man that much."

Longarm was tired of fencing with Chang. "Goodbye, Chang. Now stand back while we load the landing boats and go ashore. Send two of your bully-boys, if you want, to row the empty boats back to the ship."

Chang nodded and spoke to his bodyguards. Two of them stepped forward. The loggers swarmed down the rope ladder first, with Chang's two bodyguards following, each one stepping into a different boat. Then Curry and Mullen followed. Longarm lifted a foot over the rail and turned back to look at Chang.

The old man was watching him, his face blank. He did not wave, nor did Longarm as he ducked his head and began his rapid climb down the ladder.

Longarm reined in his Morgan and looked back down the long slope at the surface of the cove. The sun was high overhead, its light gleaming off the placid mirror of the water. The *China Belle* was just putting about—and having not a little difficulty due to the ship's lack of a full complement.

But this was not what Longarm was watching. Another ship had entered the cove while they were still rowing ashore from the *China Belle*. It had not been close enough for Longarm to see much, and he had been too busy saddling the Morgan and getting instructions from the logger as to the exact whereabouts of Helga's abandoned camp to pay it too much attention. It was closer now—much closer—and as he watched, it suddenly came to him where he had seen the ship before.

It was the *Sea Wind*!

Longarm remembered that he had suggested to the coolies now commanding the ship that they might be able to buy provisions from fishing villages along the coast. So they had sailed down the coast, perhaps to the coastal village where Curry had been brought up, and now here they were, sailing into Indian Point, bearing down upon the *China Belle*.

Squinting through the bright sunlight, Longarm

found he could see the coolies swarming like ants over the rigging. All of them were armed, the barrels of their revolvers and the blades of their knives and swords gleaming brilliantly in the morning light. They were preparing to close with the *China Belle!*

Longarm laughed. Of course those coolies knew the *China Belle.* Was there a Chinaman on the West Coast who did not know of its evil reputation, and that of its captain? And Chang! How delighted those coolies would be to discover Chang Li Chang on board— Chang and the treasure Duff Ryan had mentioned.

The two ships were so close now that Longarm could see no water between them. Grappling hooks snaked out from the shrouds of the *Sea Wind.* Faint shouts and the rattle of gunfire carried across the water. The coolies, their queues flying out behind them, leapt across the narrow gap that separated the two ships and were soon in command of the decks of the *China Belle.*

It was not long before the assault was over, the fighting done. Old Chang had not escaped, after all.

As Longarm spurred his horse inland, he was pleased—very pleased—to contemplate the revelry on that captured ship this night, as well as that which would come later, among the villages of the Pearl River Delta, as husbands and sons returned laden with the booty they had taken from the fabulous Land of the Golden Hills.

Chapter 14

Longarm was afraid he might have missed Helga's camp until he came across the tracks of a buggy. He surmised that it was the one Chang had used on his trip this far from Slab City. The tracks led inland from the northern bank of the Skagit. Longarm followed them as far as the soft forest duff would allow, kept going, and broke at last into the abandoned camp. Chang's buggy was sitting where it had been left in front of what must once have been the camp's livery.

Dismounting, Longarm tied up to the buggy and stepped into the livery stable. The smell of old, moldy hay and well-rotted horse manure assailed his nostrils.

"Helga!" he called.

There was no answer.

He left the stable and looked around at the camp. The cookhouse was still in good shape, as was the bunkhouse, with only a few windows broken. He tried the bunkhouse without luck, and trudged across the camp to the cookhouse. Entering through the kitchen door, he kicked a dusty, rusted kettle out of his way and looked quickly about. There was not a sound in the place.

"Helga!" he called, this time with very little hope in his voice.

There was no response to his call—not that he had expected any—and he turned to walk back out of the building. Then he paused, his head tipping just a little to one side. *What was that?* he wondered. It *could* have been a response, but surely a very faint one.

He turned and called out again, louder this time. The response was almost immediate, but low and barely audible, coming from the mess hall adjoining the kitchen. Quickly, Longarm walked through the kitchen into the hall. The first thing he saw was a pile of benches and tables in the center of the hall, a kind of rough pyramid reaching up to—

Helga Jensen—completely naked—was hanging by her wrists, which had been tied with a strip of rawhide to a rafter. Her long golden mane reached almost to her buttocks. Only her toes touched the top of the rickety structure of piled furniture. Longarm saw at once how this torture was intended to work: as long as Helga stood on her tiptoes, her weight would not be quite entirely supported by her wrists, but if she attempted to relax her legs, her body would be stretched painfully. As her strength gave out from pain and lack of food, water, and rest, she would lapse into unconsciousness and eventually suffocate through inability to draw air into her constricted ribcage. After another few hours of this cruel traction, she would have been dead.

Longarm took out his pocket knife, opened the blade, and holding it between his teeth, clambered carefully up the makeshift scaffold until he stood balancing gingerly beside her at the top. Since he was considerably taller than Helga, he could easily reach the rawhide thongs to cut them. As he did so, Helga turned her head to look up at him. She tried to say something to him, but could only manage a faint croak. He shook his head to discourage her from trying to say

237

anything and reached out with his knife, vehemently cursing Chang's diabolically inventive mind. He sliced swiftly through the rawhide bonds, catching Helga against him as she swung loose.

"Oh, God," Helga said, her voice barely audible. "Thank you, Longarm."

He helped her gently down, then carried her out of the kitchen and across the camp to the buggy. Inside it he found warm cushions and a blanket. She lay back on the seat and covered her self with the blanket.

"Your clothes," he said. "Where are they?"

"The bastards!" she spat hoarsely. "They ripped them off me—and that wasn't all, Longarm! Ya! That wasn't all!"

"I'll tell you what, Helga. Lean back and rest. I'll hitch the Morgan to this buggy and take you back to Slab City. How does that sound?"

"It sound fine, Longarm. Ya! Very fine!"

They arrived in Slab City just past midnight. Helga was asleep on the seat beside him. Pulling up in front of the hotel, he wrapped Helga securely in the blanket, then lifted her out of the buggy and carried her into the hotel and up the stairs to his room. She stirred only fitfully as he placed her on his bed. Downstairs in the lobby, Longarm told the desk clerk he wanted a doctor to come to his room, fast. Longarm's tone communicated his sense of urgency to the clerk, who went quickly for a doctor.

Longarm stepped outside the hotel to wait for the clerk's return. As he stood on the porch, he became aware of the sharp, unpleasant odor of burnt, charred wood. It hung heavily in the air and seemed to blanket the entire town.

Then he saw Curry and Gus Mullen crossing the street on their way from the Skidroad Palace—which, despite Duff Ryan's absence, seemed to be doing just fine. Longarm was not surprised to see them. He had

238

expected them and the loggers to arrive before he did. He hailed them and hurried over to see him.

"How's Helga?" Mullen asked. "Them loggers are sure anxious."

"The doctor's on the way. But it looks like she'll be all right."

"Fine."

"How is Stokey?"

"Drunk as a lord," Mullen said, grinning. "With two of the best house girls playing up to him, the lucky bastard."

Longarm indicated the air about him with a wave of his hand. "What happened? Smells like half the town burned down. That fire in Chinatown get out of hand?"

"That it did," Curry replied. "Seems like most of the shopowners and businessmen of Slab City thought it would only be Chinatown that got burnt out. So they didn't try to fight the fire none when it started down there. They decided to just let it burn. So it did. They saved Helga's mill, but a lot of Main Street got gutted good and proper."

"The newspaper office. Is it still standing?" Longarm asked.

Mullen nodded. "Just barely."

"Do me a favor. Get all the copies you can of that last paper Spittles put out and bring them to me at the hotel here."

Mullen grinned. "You like to read all that much?"

"I think maybe the stockholders of the Great Northern might be interested in reading what Spittles had to say in that issue about their chief engineer and Duff Ryan."

"Sure," said Mullen. "We'll go over there now."

"And thank those loggers for me. As soon as I learn for sure how Helga's feeling, I'll let them know."

As the two men hurried through the night in the direction of the *Slab City Citizen*, Longarm saw the clerk hurrying across the street toward him with a local sawbones. He went to meet the doctor, thanked the clerk, and escorted the doctor up to his room.

The doctor was gone, the news about Helga good. She was sitting up in his bed now, naked from the waist up, her long, gorgeous hair flowing like golden threads across her full breasts, Longarm was having difficulty keeping his eyes off them as she talked.

" . . . and so Helga is much ashamed, Longarm. I send in those two loggers to teach you something. But you teach *them*. Besides, by the time they come in here, I not want them to teach you one single thing."

Longarm laughed. "I had you all wrong too, Helga. Ryan and Chang were in cahoots, supplying the coolies for MacRae. And Lillian M'Ling was working both sides of the street, putting you squarely in the middle."

"That Chang! A horrible old man! Ya! He did not laugh, but Helga see in his eyes how he enjoy seeing Helga like that. You bet!"

"Those coolies have already taken care of Chang. They didn't seem to be in any mood to be gentle with anyone connected with the *China Belle*. I reckon that ship must be pretty well known by every coolie along the coast, and those shanghaied coolies will not go easy on anyone they found on the *China Belle*. I can just see old Chang trying to explain that chest of treasure he was taking back to China with him."

"So now I can have my land and make big deals with the Great Northern to supply all the railroad ties and telegraph poles they need! Hey?"

"That's right. And Ryan won't soon be calling in any loans, either. Trouble is, I have lost myself one damn fine tailor."

"And is still no woman for Ton Key. Those Chinamen, they are like all the rest of us. They need someone to make love."

"I'm sure a few Chinese women will make it through, Helga. It'll take more than this to stop the Ong Leong

Tong from smuggling Chinese into this country. You'll see."

"You mean love find way."

"I guess that's what I mean, all right. Just as long as it can be made profitable, that is."

Helga patted the bed beside her. "Hey, Longarm, the doctor, he says I am big and strong now, like a horse. So I am all right for you again—and this time, like I say, we finish what we start. How you like that?"

"I was beginning to wonder if you had forgotten."

A moment later Longarm blew out the lamp, placed his Colt under his pillow—purely out of force of habit —turned back the covers, and got in beside Helga. As he found himself coiled in her warmth and answering her moans with his own, he told himself that if a couple of big loggers or hatchet men interrupted them this time, he would just have to kill them.

There was no way he and Helga were going to be separated this night.

SPECIAL PREVIEW

Here are the opening scenes
from

LONGARM AND THE MOLLY MAGUIRES

tenth novel in the bold new
LONGARM series from Jove/HBJ

Chapter 1

Longarm quit his job on a Friday afternoon with a roundup Saturday coming on. He'd threatened more than once to leave the U.S. Justice Department to its own pettifogging devices, but this time he meant it. There were things you could ask a fellow to do, and there were things no man who had to look in the mirror while shaving could even be asked to *study* on, and this time they'd really handed him the sheep shears.

Marshal Billy Vail stared blankly down at the U.S. deputy's badge on his green desk blotter for maybe two heartbeats before he took the cigar out of his mouth, sighed, and said, "Hell, I'll assign another deputy to cover the job in Carboniferous if you're *that* serious about it!"

But Longarm was in the doorway and moving out quickly. Vail shouted at his broad back as it receded, "Come back here, you damn fool! You're a third of the way to your government pension!"

The office door slammed in Vail's pink face, but not before he'd heard where Longarm had suggested that he stuff the pension *and* the badge.

Cursing wearily, Vail got up to chase after Longarm. He moved at almost a trot, for while the tall deputy had left walking, Longarm's lanky legs were known to eat up ground faster than most men could manage at a trot. By the time Vail was out in the marble corridors of the Denver Federal Building, the tall, dark figure of Longarm had made it to the stairs. Vail caught up at the bottom of the stairwell and grabbed one of Longarm's tweed-clad elbows. The big man stopped, but growled, "Let go of my arm, Billy. We ain't friends anymore and I tend to take it personally when men I ain't talking to clutch at my only decent coat."

But Billy Vail had faced Comanche in his day, so he hung on long enough to insist, "I said you didn't have to take the Carboniferous assignment! I'll send one of the other deputies! You've got no reason to be pissed off at me now."

Longarm stared down at the smaller, older lawman as if he'd just noticed a horse turd in his soup. Then he said, "When I joined the Justice Department it was run by gentlemen. I joined up to be a peace officer, and they told me I was hired to enforce the laws of these United States."

"I know that. And you've enforced the hell out of them. I've sometimes had to cover for your, uh, primitive notions of justice, but between the two of us, we've civilized the shit out of these parts."

Longarm cut in to say, "I ain't finished. You've sent me to arrest owlhoots and you've sent me to fight Mexicans and Mormons. You've sent me on a lot of jobs I didn't care for and I've had to shoot some folks I wasn't all that sure were in the wrong. But that Carboniferous job ain't got shit to do with any law passed by Congress."

"Look, I said I'd send another deputy!"

Longarm scowled blackly and demanded, "What in tarnation does that mean? Any man you send would

245

have to be a shit-eating hound, and I don't ride with jaspers like that on either side of the law!"

"Longarm, you never let me finish. You got your balls in an uproar and started throwing badges at me before I got to the bottom line!"

But Longarm shook his erstwhile superior off and strode on, muttering half to himself, "There ain't another word I need to hear. Any man who'd hire a government gun out to union busters should be tarred and feathered. But since you likely have more friends than me in high places, I'll just say adios."

Longarm stepped outside and strode down the stone steps, not looking back as Vail shouted some damn fool thing about President Hayes and a veto. Longarm wasn't feeling too neighborly about the president either, right now. The son of a bitch had been elected on a reform ticket and it had looked for a while as if Washington really had been trying to mend its ways. But that mess in Carboniferous was raw—as raw as anything old U. S. Grant's political hacks had tried to pull in the gunsmoke-scented seventies.

Someone tore past on a painted pony, firing an S&W .38.

Longarm saw that the drunken drover was aiming at the street lamps along California Street, so he didn't take it personally. Head cocked to one side and scowling, Longarm headed for his rooming house on the far side of Cherry Creek. He wasn't sure what he aimed to do once he got there, but the price of beef was up, and what the hell. He was a little over the hill to start as a new hand, but he still had lots of friends from the old days. He'd heard that the ramrod of the Lazy Seven had been shot a week ago and they might need a segundo.

He turned down 14th Street, figuring to stop for a drink near the Larimer Street Bridge before going home to pack his possibles. As he got closer to Cherry Creek, the streets of Denver were more crowded and noisy than usual. Some of the boys were celebrating Saturday night a mite early.

After a spell of dry summers, the drought had broken to green the range in time for the spring calving, and the price of beef was at an all-time high, with business starting to boom again in the East.

So the boys were bringing in the herds. Big herds, with lots of riders cussing the cows along a vast spider-web of trails centered on the Denver railroad yards. The Burlington Line was having a rate war with the U.P. that summer, so many a cow that might have headed for Cheyenne had been herded south across the Platte. Southern herds from as far away as the Arkansas Divide were bawling their way into the Burlington yards as the trail bosses fought for access to the loading pens, and meanwhile, every cuss with a scrub critter that could still walk was herding it in from the small spreads all around. It figured to be an interesting Saturday night, and some hands had been paid off already.

Longarm stepped around a buckboard someone had parked on the sandstone sidewalk and almost jumped as a bullet spanged off the pavement near the heel of his right boot. He ignored the grinning drunk who'd tried to make him dance, and would have moved on peaceably, but the young hand interested in chore-ography blocked his way and demanded owlishly, "Wha's the matter with you, townie? Didn't you hear my invitation to the walsh?"

Longarm muttered, "Aw, shit," and backhanded the drunk into the street. The kid landed spread-eagled on his back and blinked a couple of times before he passed out cold. Longarm kept walking. He hadn't meant to hit him that hard, but damn it, a fellow had no call to shoot at a man's feet when he was in a testy mood.

Somewhere a window cascaded to the paving, and two idiots were having a pony race down the sidewalk. So Longarm cut across the street to get out of the way, and decided to pass on that Larimer Street saloon. He was still sore as hell, but he didn't really want to kill anybody he didn't know, and the boys were getting a mite out of hand. Larimer Street was no place for a peaceable man, this side of Monday.

Longarm turned a corner and headed south, but the street was filled from wall to wall with bawling calico cows. It was against the city ordinances to trail cows through the business district, but the Denver P.D., in its infinite wisdom, had taken note of the Texas hats worn by the dozen-odd dusty trail herders and had decided to overlook the matter just this once.

Longarm stepped into a doorway and slapped a steer who seemed interested in joining him across the muzzle with his hat. As the herd moved on, he dusted his pants with the same battered hat and resumed his journey, watching where he walked, for cows have digestive troubles in unusual surroundings.

He got to the banks of the winding little Cherry Creek that had given birth to Denver back in the Gold Rush of the sixties. There wasn't enough gold in Cherry Creek to think about these days. Wasn't enough water to think about, either. Cherry Creek crawled through town maybe two hundred feet wide and two inches deep. The bottom was sandy and much of it was dry. So, though he was nowhere near a bridge, Longarm knew he could cross dryshod by jumping from one sandbank to another like 'Liza crossing the ice in that fool play.

As he moved down the bank to make his way across the creek, he noticed a man in faded denims squatting on a sandbank downstream. The man was panning sand in a battered tin pie plate, but Longarm didn't stop to tell him he was an idiot. If he didn't know by now that the last gold had given out years ago, he would soon enough. The cuss looked sort of hungry and desperate as he mucked sand and water like the greenhorn he probably was. Next to a hopeless drunk,

Longarm couldn't think of anyone who wasted as much of his life as the half-mad prospectors he stumbled over in the most unlikely places.

He climbed the far bank and cut through an alley between the ramshackle frame houses on the wrong side of Cherry Creek. He was almost home when he spied another wild bunch headed his way along a cinder path. He swore and found a dooryard to stand aside in, as he wondered what the boys were after this far from the main drag. Some of the Mexican gals in his neighborhood were said to be no better than they were supposed to be, but he'd heard they only took care of local trade.

One of the crowd yelled out, "There's a telegraph pole! We can string the son of a bitch up right here!"

Longarm saw that the gang of about fifty had a smaller, bewildered figure in tow, and he recognized the captive as his Chinese laundryman, Ho Quah! He sighed and headed toward the mob, reaching for his wallet even as he remembered he no longer carried a badge.

A large part of Denver's Chinatown had been burned to the ground not very long ago, and on that occasion, Longarm had had to rescue another Chinaman from just such a mob as this one. He shuddered slightly at the thought of the chain of events that had followed that occurrence; he harbored no craving for a repetition of *that* business. On the other hand, it appeared that this rabble was about to deprive him of one of the few luxuries of his austere life—a clean shirt now and then. That tended to rile him a mite.

One of the lynch mob's ringleaders spotted Longarm about this time, and there was something about the way the tall man in tobacco-brown tweed was walking that made him mutter, "Oh, oh!"

Then he considered the odds and called out, "How do, stranger. Us old boys is fixing to string this god-

249

damn heathen up. You have anything to say about this, one way or t'other?"

Longarm unbuttoned his frock coat, allowing it to swing clear of the double-action .44 in its waxed cross-draw holster before he nodded and replied, "Yep. If you boys hang Ho Quah, who in thunder's going to do my laundry?"

Another white man shouted, "He just killed a white woman, mister. We caught him in the alley behind her house just now!"

"Two alleys over? Yard full of laundry poles and such?"

"That's right on the money! The old lady's house-nigger ran out screaming that her mistress had been killed. So us boys fanned out to catch the rascal who done it and—"

"You damn fool!" Longarm cut in, "Ho Quah's laundry yard is in that alley. Of course you caught him. He was likely hanging up some of my shirts. How about it, Ho Quah? You got my shirts ironed right with no starch this time?"

The laundryman didn't answer. Longarm noticed the wet streak down one trouser leg and surmised that poor Ho Quah wasn't able to speak right now.

Longarm asked, "Who's the lady who was killed? I know most of the folks around here."

But before anyone could answer, the ringleader who'd first spoken snapped, "Enough of this bullshit. I say we got the Chinaman and I say we hang him directly!"

The crowd roared its approval. So Longarm drew his revolver and said, "Let him go. I don't aim to talk about it anymore, either."

There was a hush. Then someone farther back in the crowd guffawed and said, "Shit, let's string 'em *both* up."

The ringleader licked his lips, and then he grinned and said, "You see how it is, mister. The boys are dead

250

set on justice and we got you outgunned forty-seven to one."

A new voice to Longarm's right called out, "You're wrong. It's forty-seven to *two*, and I'm feeling mean as hell."

Longarm glanced to his side to see Billy Vail crouched behind a backyard woodpile, aiming his old single-action thumb-buster through a picket fence. The gun wasn't pointed at Longarm, so he nodded and said, "Ho Quah, why don't you mosey over there to Marshal Vail while me and the boys sort this whole thing out?"

The Chinese hesitated. Then he suddenly wrenched free of the two men holding him and ran forward. As one of the men in the crowd started to draw on his back, Longarm fired into the cinders between the man's toes, as he said in a conversational tone, "Next one's going to geld you, and if you don't mend your ways after that, I might have to *hurt* you."

The ringleader raised a hand and called out, "Simmer down, boys. Didn't you hear the man say they was law?" He turned to Longarm and added, in a blustering tone, "If you boys is law, we'll likely have to let you have the fool Chinaman. All we was aiming for was simple justice."

Longarm nodded and said, "I can see you are peaceable, law-abiding gents, so why don't we just call it a day? I hear they've got a lady who does a scandalous dance in pink tights at the Drover's Rest, and the beer is still three cents a stein at the Silver Dollar."

There was a murmur of consultation from the crowd. Some moron shouted, "Shit, I say we take him!" but the leaders, who were in Longarm's line of fire, doubtless felt more reasonable. One of the latter yelled, "Hell, we turned the rascal over to the law and it's almost sundown. Let's go see if that lady in pink tights has some saucy friends!"

Longarm edged back as the mob marched past, some muttering darkly as others merely cussed him in restored humor. As they straggled out of sight down the lane, he turned and strolled over to where Marshal Vail and the laundryman were hunkered down near the woodpile. Vail came out to meet him with a grin as both men holstered their weaponry. Longarm said, "Billy Vail, you are still a son of a bitch, but I thank you anyhow."

Vail said, "You can pay me back by having a drink with me and listening to the end of my tale."

Longarm nodded, but said, "First let's clear up this mess about some murdered lady." He smiled at Ho Quah and added, "Tell us what happened over at your place, old son."

But the laundryman could only stammer back at them in a high sing-song. Billy Vail suggested, "He's had his English as well as the piss scared out of him."

Longarm took the Oriental gently by the elbow and turned him toward home, explaining to Vail, "He told me once that he'd survived the Chinese riots out on the West Coast. I suspicion he saw some ugly happenings."

Vail fell in on the other side of Ho Quah to brace him by the other arm as he observed, "He's scared skinny, sure enough. I've never seen a man more scared, even a Chinaman. You'd think he'd have more sand in his craw after a few years among white folks."

Longarm shrugged and said, "Some Chinese fought back when the Frisco mob came to burn them out. The ones who survived were the ones who ran like hell. It's like that Professor Darwin says. They call it evolution."

"Damn it, Longarm. That fool evolution is a notion of the devil. The old time religion was good enough for my daddy and it's good enough for me!"

Before they could argue the point, a pair of blue-uniformed men with drawn guns came around the corner of a shed, and one of the Denver patrolmen, recognizing Longarm, said, "Oh, praise the Lord. Some kids back yonder just told us Ho Quah had been grabbed by some cowboys!"

Longarm nodded and said, "We un-grabbed him. Who got murdered over by his laundry?"

"The widow Clancy. You know her, Longarm?"

"Old lady with a busted nose and a drinking problem? Knew her to tip my hat to on the street. Any idea how she was killed, or why?"

The policeman said, "She was stabbed six times by person or persons unknown. As to why, her house-nigger says the old lady drew a pension from the Burlington Railroad and had just cashed her check at Mama Palaver's saloon. A couple of our detectives are over at her house right now, trying to put the rest together. From the way her house got tore up, it looks like she surprised a prowler who'd likely heard she had cash to hand."

Longarm looked over at Marshal Vail as he observed, "This sounds like a case for the local courts, doesn't it, Billy?"

Vail nodded and answered, "Hell, killing old ladies ain't a federal crime."

Longarm said, "There you go, then. If I was you boys, I'd mosey over to Cherry Creek and pick up a jasper in faded denims. You'll likely find him still going through the motions of panning for gold. But I'd hurry, as he'll light out as soon as it gets dark."

The two patrolmen looked surprised, but they knew Longarm, so they started running like hell for Cherry Creek.

As Longarm led the still-bewildered Ho Quah homeward, Marshal Vail said, "I noticed the prospector as I trailed you across. Got water in one of my boots, too. What makes you think he murdered that old woman?"

Longarm was still mad at Vail, but he was sort of pleased with himself and, what the hell, Ho Quah had forgotten his English, so he said, "The gang who grabbed this poor fellow would have noticed any strangers near enough to matter. It sounds like they started looking while the killing was still fresh. The killer hadn't had time to get clear of the neighborhood."

"Damn it, I can read sign as well as most lawmen, but you're playing a wilder card than they were. I don't see a thing connecting that fool gold panner to this side of the creek."

"I always said you were addled, Billy Vail. When was the last time you've seen even a schoolboy trying to pan gold from a played-out sandbar? And even allowing for stupidity beyond the call of duty, when was the last time you saw *anyone* pan for color with a sharp-angled tin plate?"

"Hell, I knew when I saw him that he didn't know what he was doing, Longarm. But being dumb doesn't make a man a murderer."

Longarm shrugged and said, "Maybe. We'll see what he has to say when they pick him up and shake him down. He was out of place, the only man in the neighborhood who wasn't acting right. He doesn't belong to the natural scenery in these parts, even though he's busting a gut trying to account for being part of it."

They turned into an alley as Vail mused, "Hmm, a drifting thief with no visible means might figure the old prospector makes a tolerable cover. Come to think of it, he was dressed like a hobo, and a mite young for the part. Had no pack or digging tools, either."

Before Longarm could answer, Ho Quah broke away and ran toward his own backyard gate. Then he turned, came part of the way back with tears in his eyes, and blurted something in Chinese at the men who'd rescued him. Longarm nodded and said, "You just go on along home, old son. We'll talk on it when you get a mite calmer. But if you starch my collars *this* time, I'll likely string you up myself!"

Ho Quah nodded and ran into his laundry, probably to change his pants.

Vail said, "About that favor you owe me . . . "

Longarm nodded and said, "I will buy you one drink at Mama Palaver's and have one drink on you. After that, you'd better git, for you are still a son of a bitch and after three drinks I get mean."

Mama Palaver kept an orderly house and served bottled-in-bond Maryland rye at a fair price. She was in a tacky neighborhood on the wrong side of Cherry Creek because she was a lady of color. She was a big, fat, friendly woman who slept alone and tolerated no serious vices in her little neighborhood establishment, but City Hall refused to grant ex-slaves a tavern-keeper's license in the more respectable parts of their fair city.

Billy Vail tried to steer Longarm to a booth in the back, but the tall former deputy insisted on standing against the bar. He knew Vail could talk the horns off a buffalo in a comfortably seated position.

Mama Palaver slid a grin and two shotglasses their way as Billy Vail explained, "The reason Justice is interested in that strike down at the Carboniferous mines is—"

"Strikebreaking," Longarm cut in flatly, adding, "You may not have noticed, but I was born and brought up as a member of the working class. That's what those prissy Eastern moguls call us: the working class."

"Longarm, I was hardly weaned on a silver spoon myself, but damn it, you and me are lawmen, and the laws down in Carboniferous have been busted all to hell."

"I know. Those poor immigrant coal miners likely never heard it was against the law of the land to ask for a living wage. Do you know what they pay those poor bastards for scratching a ton of coal out of a mountain?"

"That ain't our problem, Longarm. Washington reports that the Molly Maguires have moved into the Colorado coalfields. You know who the Molly Maguires are, don't you?"

Longarm drained his glass and held up two fingers to Mama Palaver before he nodded and said, "Sure. A union terrorist outfit who raised some hell in the Pennsylvania fields a few years back. So what? In the first place, a private detective named Fink had their leaders rounded up and hung. In the second place, the Molly Maguires weren't the only folks throwing bullets and dynamite at folks. Union-busting is a dirty business, Billy, and I see no reason for Uncle Sam to stick his nose in it. Can't those mine owners afford the Pinkertons these days? God knows they ought to have a few nickels saved by now. They sure ain't paid their workers enough to mention."

Vail sighed and said, "The Pinks say they ain't interested in the strike at Carboniferous. The owners have a smaller outfit called Enforcement Incorporated guarding the mineheads and machinery, but—"

"Jesus Christ, Billy! E.I. ain't a detective agency— it's a hired execution outfit! If I did go down there with a badge, it would be my pure constitutional duty to arrest the owners and their hired killers, not the poor striking miners!"

Vail picked up his second drink and snapped, "God damn it, Longarm, we've established your anarchist tendencies. If you'd *listen* to me, for Christ's sakes, you'd know I don't give a damn *who* wins the goddamn strike!"

Longarm muttered darkly, "The owners will win. They always do. But I'll be double-damned if I'll help."

"Longarm, the governor of Colorado has asked the federal government for aid, with good reason."

"Hell yes, he's got good reason. One of the owners of the Carboniferous mines is a state senator. The whole thing stinks to high heaven, Billy."

256